I0574223

IF TWO
OF THEM
ARE DEAD

IF TWO OF THEM ARE DEAD

A LEAH CONTARINI MYSTERY

LIBI SIPORIN

First published by Level Best Books 2023

Copyright © 2023 by Libi Siporin

All rights reserved. No part of this publication may be reproduced, stored or transmitted in any form or by any means, electronic, mechanical, photocopying, recording, scanning, or otherwise without written permission from the publisher. It is illegal to copy this book, post it to a website, or distribute it by any other means without permission.

This novel is entirely a work of fiction. The names, characters and incidents portrayed in it are the work of the author's imagination. Any resemblance to actual persons, living or dead, events or localities is entirely coincidental.

Libi Siporin asserts the moral right to be identified as the author of this work.

Author Photo Credit: Steve Siporin

First edition

ISBN: 978-1-68512-350-5

Cover art by : Gidon Siporin (IMAGE) and Level Best Designs

This book was professionally typeset on Reedsy.
Find out more at reedsy.com

To Steve, Dov z'l, Lev, and Gidon / My North, South, East, West

Praise for the Leah Contarini Mysteries

"Author Siporin's novel works on a couple of different levels, first, as a murder mystery—and a very good one at that—and second, as a paean to the Tuscan region, its customs, culture and its colorful residents, all of which are richly drawn by the author. A far cry from the usual *noir*-ish streets of New York or Los Angeles, *Bitter Maremma* is a highly entertaining read, one that I most certainly recommend."—Gregory Stout, Winner of Best First PI Novel from 2022 Shamus Awards; author of *Lost Little Girl*, *Gideon's Ghost*, and *Connor's War*

"Reckless and impulsive, Leah is a travel writer and is married to steady and long-suffering Nick, a folklorist working on a book he hopes will bring him tenure. They are in Italy doing research on the Befanata, a folk custom celebrating Epiphany still being practiced by locals of a small town in Tuscany.

"From the poetic descriptions of place and time, to the carefully drawn characters, to the rapidly-paced plotting, *Bitter Maremma* is a great read."—Steve Sharp, Professor of Political Science

"I am glad to report that I was quite stunned to learn the identity of the murderer. The descriptions of the landscape were mesmerizing to me. Murder is a fairly wild action (as in wild animal) so the murders taking place in the great outdoors were scary and reminiscent of mythology—almost with a dancing quality. Your array of local characters was great! My favorite was the cop."—Laura Fisher, M.D.

Chapter One

The body lay in the half-shadow of a twisted mountain oak that jutted over the trail from above. Backlit by sunlight, the branches of the tree drooped over the pathway and swayed gently in the morning breeze, creating a dance of golden speckles across the dead man's torso and his waxen, but still handsome, face. As if surprised, he stared upward through the limbs of the tree, which parted and closed in the breeze. Overhead, in a cerulean sky, the bloated cumulus clouds lumbered over the fields and ravines below.

The man had been dragged up and along the trail. If some hiker, out on that honeyed fall day for an hour of peace, were to come upon him and gently turn him over, he would see that the back of the man's jacket and trousers were shredded from the brutal way his killer had lugged him through the ditch, jerked him rudely over the tops of the rocks and boulders, and wrangled him to the spot where he now lay on level ground.

In life he had been a clean, dignified man, and to anyone who had known him, this death would seem an ignominious end. After the initial shock of discovering him dead, one who cared for him would be angered at the injustice, the desecration, and would mourn not only the man himself, but also the loss of history, learning, and compassionate generosity he had embodied in life. Some would have known his sudden, fierce anger and passions as well, but except for a few, they would have forgiven him.

He lived through World War II and came home to his small Tuscan town of Scansansiano to run a small, modestly prosperous business. He served on the city council, sent a regular anonymous (but people knew) contribution to the town library, supported the museum with time and a hefty yearly sum, and gave anonymous (but people knew) gifts of food and money to the poor of the town.

Ants scuttled through the dapples of sunlight, circled the blood at the back of the man's head, and crawled up his neck into his hair. They explored his ears, eyes, nose, and mouth, which gaped open, as if he were about to speak. His hands, in life fluid with gestures, lay inert at his sides, the hair on the back of them ruffled in the breeze.

The ants continued their exploration.

An early morning chill gave way to a mellifluous fall heat, and the man's body began to swell. A fly buzzed lazily around his head and lit in his hair above the collar line where the blow had shattered his skull. The fly settled, then moved from ragged edge of bone to bit of brain, rose in the erratic rustle of breezes, and settled again to its meal.

The first odor of decay wafted from the body and was carried by tender currents of air through the trees and along the ground, toward the sensitive snouts of a sounder of wild boar, animals that took their place in the history of the man and the loves, hates, and greed of the living.

Chapter Two

From the window of the train, Leah Contarini watched the thick marshlands and broad, neat fields of lower Tuscany flick past. Across the fields, toward the sea, the trunks of a long line of umbrella pines rose dark and straight. Their conical cones created a deep shadow over the earth below them. Beyond the pine, the Tyrrhenian Sea sparkled in the mid-afternoon sun.

Leah leaned back against the headrest and let the soft and sonorous cadence of the local Tuscan dialect envelope her. It had been a rough flight from New York. By the time she had collected her luggage from baggage claim at the Fiumicino airport, boarded the train into Rome, and transferred to the northbound, she was disheveled and sweaty. Added to these discomforts, her mouth tasted metallic, like rusty nails. She searched her mind for the positive. She had found the only empty seat by a window, and soon she would see her friends.

Three years earlier, Leah and her husband, Nick, had left Scansansiano with the plan of returning the following year. The plan seemed perfect. Their daughter, Sara, and her husband, Jonathan, offered to work remotely from Nick and Leah's small Montana ranch outside Kalispell, if their bosses agreed. The bosses had, and Sara and Jonathan were happy to feed the horses, chickens, dogs, and cats and keep the neighbors supplied with eggs. Leah's freelance work was thriving, giving her extra income and ensuring she would have the freedom to travel, and Nick could switch teaching semesters at the university, so he too would be free and have income.

Nick read over Leah's list of advantages to the trip again and again, each time countering each advantage with a negative counterpart on one of his many lists.

"Just to keep a good balance," he laughed.

After weeks of discussion and Nick's countless lists, while the two of them were at coffee before morning chores, Nick blurted, "Okay! It's a deal. But no more getting chased by a murderer, no more dead bodies, and no more of you getting shot!"

Leah scoffed. "Don't be ridiculous! Even one murder in such a small town would be a record for a hundred years. Besides, what control do *I* have over murders or murderers or dead bodies?"

"Or over yourself!" Nick quipped.

Both of them laughed. Leah's "squirrel" quality, as Nick called it, which led her into one dangerous situation after another, was infamous in the family.

"It's settled then." Nick stood, exhaled deeply, and allowed his cautious nature to give way by doing a little dance.

Much later, Leah remembered something from *The Hobbit*: "It does not due to leave a live dragon out of your calculations."

For Nick, Leah, Sara, and Jonathan, the dragon was cancer.

Now a widow, Leah was returning to Scansansiano alone, anxious to see their friends. She wondered if she could bear the memories and overcome the remnants of fear she still carried from having been shot.

The train clicked along the tracks. Leah raised her hand to her shoulder. The jolt of the bullet that nearly killed her while she hiked one of the narrow Etruscan trails below town had left its mark. The wide knot of the scar still pained her when she was overtired. In what had become a habitual gesture, she slowly massaged her shoulder and watched the countryside flicker by like a movie.

The sudden cancer that had taken Nick's life was a sucker punch to them both. Together they mustered their strength and changed their lives to accord with his illness. Nick had been stoic to the end, but Leah, with a much more volatile character, ran the gamut of responses. She felt angry, had a sense of guilt that somehow she had done something to cause the cancer, and struggled with a searing loneliness and unremitting insomnia. To keep herself smiling, she took walks through the fields and rode horseback along the river when Nick was sleeping.

It had been a long road. After Nick was gone, Leah distracted herself with gardening, workouts at the gym, and long walks with her daughter, each of them extending comfort to the other. At first, friends came often, but time between visits lengthened and soon tapered off. Leah walked the forested trails in the nearby mountains, or sat by the river that bordered their land.

The months passed and turned into two years. Leah stayed in touch with her friends in Scansansiano. She thought of the plans she and Nick had made. She dreamed she was on the trails in Tuscany. The three of them, Leah, Sara, and Jonathan, got through the worst, kept going.

Unaware of the strength she was gaining as she won over each difficult day, Leah climbed out of immediate grief. Then, one day, spreading hay in the feeding trough, she resolved to return to Scansansiano, unflinchingly determined to walk the trails alone, in fear or not.

Her spirit revived, she anticipated time with Italian friends and took pleasure in knowing she could be an experienced, valuable support to her Scansansianese friends, Elia and Anna, in their sadness as Anna walked the path of the cancer that now riddled her body.

Out the window of the train, the countryside flickered by. Leah rubbed the scar again. As she often did when she touched the scar, she thought of Secondo and smiled. Some people called him the town fool. Those who did could not have imagined he would be the one to save her as she lay bleeding on the shadowy trail, watching the trees sway above her in the moments before she passed out.

In the seat across from Leah, a middle-aged woman with gaudy red hair and a large mole on her cheek whispered loudly about *la Signora Americana*. She glanced at Leah and turned to smile knowingly at the woman sitting next to her. In imitation of Leah, the redhead rubbed her own shoulder and laughed.

Leah studied the woman's pale face, her large, dark eyes laden with sparkling lavender eye-shadow, the knobby mole perched on her jawline, and her thin, brilliant red hair, colored from a bottle. Leah put the woman's insults down to poor manners and gazed out the window at the sea, which tossed relentlessly, gently, on a long stretch of shore.

In the next instant, a field dotted with sheep flashed by. Leah closed her eyes and smiled to herself. Her marriage to Nick had been a comet, a passionate, tangled ball of love. They fought, made love, grieved for friends lost, and delighted in their work as writer and teacher. It had been an extended, tumultuous affair. They tumbled from joy to distress, and at times, a deep sense of peace, with Sara the music at the center. Sara, the one that kept them dancing, now a married woman.

Scansansiano. Leah gave a little shake of her head. The murder in Scansansiano and the attempt on her life were a memory. There was a new project. Melanie, a staff editor at one of the magazines for which Leah worked, discovered Leah was again on her way to Tuscany; she had called and offered Leah the assignment to write a piece on the local Tuscan cuisine. Feeling lucky that the offer was open-ended, Leah agreed to think about it.

She remembered with a smile how Nick admonished her when they talked about coming back: "No more murders - and not too much work."

Leah closed her eyes. It wouldn't be much work. Melanie offered her the freedom to set her own deadline, and Leah reasoned that having a project would center her. She would write part of the day, eat out often for research—she smiled to think of the restaurant Casalinga—and she would have plenty of time to defeat old fears by walking the trails, especially the one where she'd been shot.

"Hair of the dog," she muttered to herself. She would have time to spend with friends, to catch up on all the news not written in emails or letters.

Chapter Three

Off the train, Leah transferred to a local bus that would take her from the shore inland into the hills. After an hour's ride, the driver pulled to a stop in front of Scansansiano's lower-town bar. He grasped the metal handle at his side, and with a loud, hydraulic whoosh, the door jerked open.

Leah jumped down into the cool twilight air and wrangled her rolling bag from the belly of the bus. Energized by anticipation, she curved around the back of the bus and scuttled up the street toward the piazza, the wheels of her suitcase clattering behind her over the cobblestones. A few store owners, men and women Leah recognized, were standing in front of their stores to take in the cool evening air. Surprised to see her, they waved and shouted hello, but they looked strangely grim. Leah waved back, too excited to stop and ask them why they were gloomy. She rushed on up the hill, intent on getting to Anna and Elia's.

Rosamaria's call was faint, but Leah heard it and turned. Rosamaria, the young woman who ran the fruit and vegetable store, had stepped into the street and was waving at Leah to come. Her face dark with concern, she hugged Leah with an uncharacteristically warm display of emotion.

"I'm sorry, Signora. Anna took a turn for the worse yesterday evening. Late this morning…," she lowered her eyes. "Their burial people are on the way from the Jewish Community in Rome."

The suitcase fell from Leah's hand and dropped to the ground with a loud bang. She covered her face, pressing her fingers against her eyes as if she could quell the tears. Her voice came in ragged jolts.

"I'm glad you were the one to tell me, Rosamaria. I'll go on to Elia."

Aware of how sweaty and rumpled she was, Leah kissed the young woman on both cheeks, bent to take her suitcase, and hurried away toward Anna and Elia's house, her tears dropping to the cobblestone.

Rosamaria caught the eye of the wine dealer, who had been watching the two women from across the narrow street. He shook his head slowly back and forth and hunched his shoulders.

Chapter Four

L eah found Elia standing in the doorway waiting for her. They embraced, touching cheeks side to side in the traditional way.

Elia stood back, grasped Leah's thin shoulders, and gave her a sad, warm smile. "The baker called," he reached to wipe away a tear from Leah's cheek, "Leah, don't feel badly that you missed seeing her. She knew you were coming, and before she went into the coma, she told me how much she loved you and to tell you it was ok. She preferred you not see the last moments."

"Like Nick," Leah murmured. Nick had sent her from the room on a fabricated errand to the nurse's station so she would not hear his death rattle, his last sigh.

Elia nodded, "And like Nick, the end came fast. Until last evening, she felt well. We joked and laughed, and we reminisced about both you and Nick and the times we'd had together."

"If I had only come one day..."

Elia laid his hand on her arm, "Shadows are formed all along the wishes of the sun, Leah. Anna had no pain at the end, and that's even more than we could have asked, no? You understand that too well."

Leah began to cry again, tears coursing down her cheeks. She pulled a tissue from her coat pocket and nodded in assent. "What now? What can I do?"

"People from the Jewish Burial Society will be here soon to prepare the body. There's a ritual called *tahara*. Anna hoped you would be there. It's an unusual request, but she had her reasons." He patted her shoulder, "It will

9

help you feel not so bad that you missed seeing her."

"But is it..."

"Appropriate? It's unusual, yes, but she wanted it, and I've made it appropriate."

Leah gave a wan smile. Elia. The former resistance fighter.

"Go on to the apartment, get cleaned up, and rest if you can. It will be about two hours before the people from Rome get here."

Chapter Five

Leah had rented the same apartment in which she and Nick spent the months of their first visit. The owner, a young Scansansianese named Maria, was a friend. Aware of Anna's death, she made a special effort to make the apartment comfortable for Leah. On the kitchen table she stacked fresh towels, soaps, and shampoo. The refrigerator was stocked with fruits, vegetables, bread, and pasta, and Leah saw there were vases of flowers in the living room and bedroom. Noting Maria's kind attention to detail, Leah showered and lay down to rest.

Two hours later, she woke with a start and hurried to get dressed.

Anna's body lay in the small, first-floor bedroom she had shared with Elia. Two women in long skirts, their heads covered with scarves, stood by the bed. A third woman sat in the far corner, quietly reading prayers in Hebrew.

A black cloth fell in deep folds over the wide mirror attached to the oak dresser that sat next to the window. The cloth partially covered Anna's ivory brush and comb, which were arranged in a neat row next to her bottle of scent. Beside the brush and comb lay a pair of silver fingernail scissors shaped in the form of a swam. Imbued with her presence, Anna's comb and brush and her small bottle of scent reminded Leah of her daughter Sara as a child. Running into the house, Sara would stop just inside the door to kick off her small tennis shoes, toe to heel, without untying them. The shoes sat awry, beautiful in the way their tumbled aspect retained Sara's spirit in the form and fiber of the canvas.

Leah averted her eyes from Anna's body, but soon turned to regard her friend. She gazed at Anna's pallid, gentle face, which, still in death, reflected both the kindness that had distinguished her character and a sad longing. Anna's longing had been the desire for children, but she wondered now if there were other reasons for Anna's sadness. What untold stories had she taken with her into the dark? Leah remembered reading that a person is what he hides. The saying did not seem to hold true with Anna, but Leah understood that to deny a person their secrets was to deny them a part of their humanity.

Whatever her secrets had been, Anna, and Elia too, with no children in which to funnel their love, had directed their energies and caring natures into a warmhearted thoughtfulness for friends and people of the town.

Everyone had secrets. So let the secrets stay secrets, Leah thought, remembering the lines from Shakespeare, "When she shall die, take her out and cut her in little stars, and she will make the face of heaven so fine that all the world will be in love with night and pay no worship to the garish sun."

Leah picked up Anna's brush. Many times on late fall afternoons during the grape harvest, she and Anna took long walks in the countryside. Holding the brush in hand, Leah recalled how on those walks her friend's hair, thick and healthy, glittered like a crow's wing in the late afternoon sun.

The *tahara* was long, intricately detailed, and progressed gently, but quickly. The women, skilled at their task, cleansed and bathed Anna's body. Leah watched, thinking that this softer going was almost the way a child is welcomed into the world after hard labor.

In the dim light of the room, the dark shadows of the women moved along the wall, working in concert, like twins of the women themselves. The sight of Anna, once vital, opinionated, gentle, and ready to laugh, but now compliant in the women's hands, thrust Leah into a dusky, liminal world of tenderness and care. Beautiful, pure under the women's gentle attendance, it seemed to Leah as if Anna could feel the love they were giving her as they washed her body and finally wrapped her in a linen shroud.

Perhaps, Leah thought, Anna had asked Elia to request her presence at the *tahara* simply to include her, just as Anna had included her on many Jewish holidays, helping Leah feel a part of Jewish life. Or perhaps Anna had wanted to soothe Leah in the only way she could.

The women turned and nodded to Leah. They were finished. Leah slipped out quietly and hurried along the street toward the apartment, sadness welling to tears in her eyes.

The following morning, she returned early to sit with Elia's before the funeral.

Chapter Six

"I want to see her!"

The shout, followed by muted voices in response, came from the street. Leah motioned to Elia that she would look. She moved quietly down the hallway, opened the door of Elia's apartment, and stepped out onto the landing.

At the base of the stairs, a husky, frumpish woman in a faded print dress and oversized, threadbare brown coat batted her purse at a group of four anxious men. The men, slight of build, with neatly-trimmed black beards, all wearing yarmulkes and dressed in finely-tailored black suits, dodged back and forth with their arms raised in self-defense, trying to shield their heads and shoulders from the woman's blows.

The woman's dark eyes sparkled with anger, and her face flushed deep red in the effort of drubbing the rabbis with her heavy purse. Unable to stop her, and not wanting to touch her, the rabbis stood their ground, shoulder to shoulder, arms folded, forming a wall she could not pass. They bobbed from side to side as she flailed back and forth like a windmill gone awry. Leah watched, paralyzed by the insanity of what was happening in front of her. The woman's harshly bleached hair ruffled in the wind. The hair and her anguished eyes signaled a woman desperate to recapture the woman she had seen in the mirror when she was young, or perhaps wild to gather the fragments of the woman she had been before life struck her with an inveterate wound.

Leah's heart was split between outrage for the desecration of Anna's memory and compassion for the living woman flailing in pain in front of her.

Swiping his hands through the air, a neighbor man attempted, without success, to grab the woman's arms. She ducked and thrust forward, plowing into the rabbis, but she was unable to break through the half circle they had formed around her.

One of the rabbis pleaded. "Signora, please! This is inappropriate. There's a death!"

Leah stared at the outrageous travesty. If she had been an outside observer, she would have been able to set aside the desperate agony of the woman and laugh at the absurdity of the situation. But she could not laugh. The woman was struggling in the grasp of some profound pain. Who was she? What could a stranger want to see in a house of the dead?

The shutters on the second floor of the house across the street banged open. A woman stuck her head through the opening.

"Irreverent woman! It's a funeral!! Let them bury her in peace!"

The crazed woman froze, purse raised midair, and looked up. The rabbis' eyes followed her gaze. For a few seconds they all stood still, like a movie stuck on one frame.

Abruptly, the film started again. The arc of the woman's purse descended, its clasp glistening in the bright sunlight. She clipped one of the men on the side of the head, sending his yarmulke twirling through the air to land softly as a leaf on the street.

"Stay back!" she screamed. I'll kill you! I'll kill you all!"

A sudden wave of dizziness swept over Leah. She leaned against the wall of the house, cupping her forehead in the palm of her hand and squeezing hard on her temples. Her head ached. Jet lag, grief, and now this ludicrous squabble caught up with her.

Along the street, other neighbors opened their windows and shouted. A small crowd gathered around the rabbis, laughing, shaking their heads.

"Go home, Grazia," yelled a man who approached carrying a bag of groceries. "It's no use! They're Jews. There's no open casket. You couldn't see her even if you could get in."

The rabbis turned to people who had gathered and admonished them to be silent. In this instant of distraction, Grazia saw her chance. She bolted forward. With a powerful jerk of her body, she lurched up the steps, shoved Leah aside, and clawed at the door handle.

Thrown off balance, Leah teetered on the edge of the narrow landing. She grasped at the woman's arm to right herself and to keep the woman from entering the house and the broad front room where Elia sat with the casket in his last moments of peace before the procession to the cemetery.

Leah's arms trembled from the effort to keep hold. Thick, sinewy, strong as a man, the woman twisted her forearm back and forth under Leah's grip.

"Let me go! Let me go!"

"Signora," Leah pleaded, "Anna's in the casket, and the casket's sealed. Please. Jews don't have an open casket. It's too late, don't you see? It's too late."

As she said the words, Leah wondered if she were talking to herself as well as to this disturbed woman.

Understanding she was defeated, the woman stared Leah in the face and dropped her arms. Her eyes dimmed, and she grunted heavily, as if she'd been struck. With a sigh of relief, Leah loosened her hold. The instant the pressure was released, the woman wrenched her arm away and glared at Leah, caterwauling like a cat that's lost its young.

Leaning into Leah's face, she screamed, "Why do you get to enter when I'm the one who sweated blood over her all these years! You don't belong here!" She screamed again, jabbing her chest with her fingers, "You don't belong here!"

She gave Leah a weak push, swung around, and pitched down the steps, where she broke through the circle of men, jabbing left and right until she was free. The rabbis, the neighbors, and Leah watched as she stalked up the cobblestone street, howling with the pain of a wounded animal.

Leah's forehead beaded with sweat. She dropped to the steps, cradled her head in her hands, and covered her ears to mute the sound of the woman's misery.

The rabbis stepped past her into Elia's apartment. Just as Leah stood to follow them in, she remembered something her mother had often repeated:

CHAPTER SIX

Troubles come in threes. Nick's death and Anna's death made two.

Chapter Seven

Shoulder to shoulder, Leah and Elia followed slowly behind the hearse. It wove in solemn procession from the house, along the narrow street for a few houses, and ascended gently upward to the piazza. Leah glanced down an alleyway off to her right. The passage ended on a small porch with a view of the wooded hillside across the river.

The torn black ribbon on Elia's chest pocket flapped in the wind like the wing of a crow and startled her. She turned her attention back to the hearse.

The procession stopped. One of the rabbis read Psalm 91, and they moved forward once again. At a rough spot on the street, Elia stumbled. Leah slipped her arm through his, pulling him against her, pacing her steps to his. The mid-day September sun beat relentlessly against Elia's dark, heavy suit, and sweat ran in thick rivulets down his forehead and cheeks.

Leah glanced over her shoulder. Dozens of figures dressed in black had joined the procession. This dark thread of friends and acquaintances twisted across the expanse of the piazza and descended under the archway, where the daily flow of foot and car traffic passed in and out of town. From the archway, the road curved and dropped to the right, passing in front of the baker's small shop, just before the hairpin switchback above the cemetery.

Inside the broad gates of the burial grounds, members of the cortege fanned out in small groups and stepped carefully, weaving their way through the headstones, down the broad terraces of sparse grass. The high terraces were the larger, Christian section of the cemetery, so Anna's grave lay at the bottom tier of the hillside among dozens of other Jews' graves, marked by ancient tilted and weathered headstones. Jews had lived in Scansansiano for centuries, next to their Christian neighbors in life and in death, and mostly in peace.

Elia stood at the edge of the opened earth staring at his wife's simple wooden casket. How small the box seemed to him. Anna had been a small woman; still, how could she possibly fit into the confined, limited space of this tapered little box. In life, her spirited humor and good-will had made her seem tall, much larger than this paltry shelter where she now lay.

The head rabbi, with his three friends and the six Jews of the town, remnants of the Holocaust, began to recite the prayers.

Leah patted Elia gently on the back with the flat of her hand. Overhead, the tips of the cypress swayed in the sultry breeze rising from the river valley below. Christian friends of Elia, men accustomed to working the fields in open-necked shirts, ran their fingers under their collars and pulled handkerchiefs from their pockets to wipe the sweat from their brows.

It was Christian farmers and townspeople who formed the majority of the sad group that surrounded Elia. The Jewish population of the town had been decimated by assimilation, emigration to larger cities, and finally by the fires of the Holocaust. The townspeople did not understand the Hebrew prayers, but trusted that their physical presence would express the kindness and the concern they felt for Elia, a generous, good-spirited man, who had extended credit and lowered prices in the lean years and encouraged other store owners to do the same.

The wives of the farmers stood in their black mourning clothes beside their husbands. The points of their high-heeled dress shoes sank slowly through the sparse grass into the dirt, and with sweat running down their faces, they leaned first on one foot and then the other to keep balance.

In the dwindling Jewish community, the High Holy Days had just finished. It would soon be Sukkot, commemorating the Exodus from Egypt and the makeshift huts built on the long trek to Mount Nebo. Doubly sorry Elia had to suffer this grief at the New Year, just as the Day of Atonement had ended and the joyous time of remembering the Exodus was beginning, Elia's friends bowed their heads to their chests.

Tears spilled from Elia's eyes onto his vest and tie. Leah patted his back again. At her touch, he drew a sharp breath, pulled a clean handkerchief from his breast pocket, and wiped his eyes and nose. Susceptible in grief to Leah's touch, he thought of her and Nick's friendship. It was a gift. The younger couple were like the children he and Anna had been unable to have.

Leah looked out over the river valley, thick with leafy trees that had been washed to an intense green from the recent rains. Her gaze followed the course of the narrow roadway that crossed the bridge below the cemetery and wound upward along the side of the valley, toward the church on the far crest of the hill. The wild landscape surrounding the town was as much a part of the community as were the people.

She turned back to look at the people who stood scattered among the gravestones. Some of them were friends she hadn't yet been able to greet, and some were strangers. Leah scanned the faces, nodding to the ones she knew.

At the back of the black-clad group stood a handsome, strongly built man, obviously uncomfortable in his dark suit. He had come in alone after all the others. He was crying without restraint. He seemed familiar to Leah, but she could not remember his name or a situation when she may have met him. From the looks of his broad shoulders, deeply tanned face, and powerful, thick-fingered hands, she knew he farmed.

In front of him, Lieutenant Cavour, a handsome carabiniere of average height and strong build, stood stiff-shouldered, his feet slightly apart and firmly planted. Following the habit of his profession, he glanced around the group, observing every detail.

A look of tenderness passed over Leah's face as she watched the Lieutenant. Theirs had been a confusing friendship initiated by the murder Leah had witnessed. What Leah called her "help" with the case, the Lieutenant, as the policeman in charge of the investigation, called "irresponsible interloping." He pleaded with her to stop walking alone on the trails, to stop tempting fate with her determined independence. But she was resolutely independent. They fought, chastised each other. Looking at him now, Leah experienced a twinge of guilt and, strangely, a profound sense of joy. She looked forward to speaking to him again, to laughing together as they had often done.

A few steps from the Lieutenant, Secondo was wiggling restlessly beside a tall, lean man whose dress indicated he was an American. He wore casual tan slacks, an expensive navy-colored t-shirt, and what looked like loafers. Leah squinted; she had never seen him before, and she wondered what he was doing with Secondo.

Many took Secondo to be the town idiot. He was innocent as a child in some ways and suffered from a controlled mental illness. Leah knew that he was also an astute, courageous man. Secondo's part-man, part-child character and Leah's ever-present memory of how he saved her life when she lay bleeding out on the trail made Leah protective of him. When she saw the strange American put his arm around Secondo's shoulder and whisper something to him, she flinched under a sharp stab of jealousy.

Signora Vianello, one of Leah's closest friends, stood to the right, just above Secondo and the American. Although it was a warm fall day with only a slight breeze, the Signora wore the brown-mink fur coat that distinguished her and for which she suffered much abuse. The younger generation and the few Tuscans who would not forget that the Signora was Venetian, joked about her coat behind her back. "The Signora," as everyone called her, was well aware of the jokes. They bothered her not at all.

Although no one knew how, the Signora knew the details of the village people's lives: the meeting places of young lovers, the nooks where the young went to smoke dope, the houses where marriages were faltering. Unless it was necessary for a common good, she kept her own counsel, and though she heard all the gossip, she never gossiped herself. The whole town knew she knew their secrets, and she knew they knew. A few words about her coat were unimportant.

Leah respected the Signora's refusal to gossip, but was also hoping, with slim expectations, to ply her with a glass or two of prosecco for information about the woman who had battled the rabbis trying to force her way in to see Anna's body. Leah thought the Signora might at least get the name she had been unable to remember. The Signora would test her to decide if what Leah wanted was important, but she might help, and she might also know the identity of the stranger standing with Secondo.

The young Senegalese, Idrissa Benga, stood far back, away from the group. Elia had written Leah that for months he and the boy had been at loggerheads. Idrissa persisted in selling his knock-off purses in front of Elia's shop, and Elia said it drove shoppers away. Still, Idrissa had come to pay his respects. Dressed in a deep-brown dashiki and dark pants, he was sweating heavily, and his beautiful blue-black skin shone in the sun. He could have been resting under the shady trees in the piazza, yet despite the enmity between him and Elia, he was here.

Sergio Landi, who sold electrical supplies in a little shop above the historic center, stood close to the grave across from her and Elia on the small incline of sparse grass. He stared down into the mouth of the grave, unmoving, sweat pouring off his forehead.

Sergio had dressed for show, just as he did in his daily walks about town. He was wearing a shiny-black Italian-cut shirt made of silk. His pants were glossy cotton in black, and his pointed shoes were polished to patent-leather brightness. His hair, smoothed straight back from his face with heavy oil, emitted a sweet, fetid odor and reflected the same vanity as his clothes. It was as if he had tried for sprezzatura, but had failed miserably to pull off that art of studied nonchalance.

Next to Sergio stood his dumpy younger brother, Gino, or Polish, as some called him. His face was almost identical to Sergio's, but for his thick jowls. He shifted from one foot to the other in a little dance of impatience, stopping to blot his forehead and chin with a soiled handkerchief before taking up the slow shuffle again.

Unlike Sergio, Gino was slovenly, dressed in dirty, torn jeans and a partly unbuttoned, half-tucked plaid shirt. His belly protruded from the shirt and hung over his belt. Gino's sparse hair glistened in the sun. When a breeze wafted the smell directly to her face making her stomach churn, Leah knew Gino wore the same offensive-smelling paste as his brother. She put her handkerchief to her nose.

His thick hands clasped in front of him, the carpenter and furniture repairman, Magliotti, stood just behind Sergio. He wore an expression of rigid calm and disciplined patience.

Leah remembered seeing him once through the window of his shop, planing a board with slow, elastic strokes, back and forth, stopping now and again to run his hand over the board, testing its smoothness. He came to the funeral from a sense of professional duty to another member of the businessmen's club rather than as a friend.

Magliotti had a strange way about him. His body was rigid. He held absolutely still, his muscles tense, like a cat ready to pounce, or like a tightly-wound clock. His perfect and studied politeness irritated Leah, and her irritation in turn vexed her because he was liked and respected. On her first visit to Scansansiano, Idrissa told her that as a kindness, Magliotti often bought the knock-off billfolds and belts Idrissa sold on the street. She had never seen this solicitous behavior on Magliotti's part, but if Idrissa said it, it was true. Leah watched Magliotti fidget with the button of his jacket.

To the left of Magliotti, toward the gate, stood the Innocenti brothers, Cristofano, who was tall and thin, and Gualfredo, short and portly. The two were a reflection of Sergio and Gino. Leah did not know them well; no one seemed to know them well. Always together, they dressed in similar dark suits and white shirts. They shifted back and forth on the uneven ground, in time with each other, staring intently at Leah and Elia.

Elia coughed. Leah lowered her eyes from the gathering and looked down into the grave. She remembered standing at Nick's grave, but with an effort, pushed the thought away and turned her attention to the graceful, gentle stream of the Hebrew prayers.

Grief and thankfulness were born as twins. After the onset of Nick's illness, she watched Nick and the other patients funnel their suffering into outrageous jokes, reams of laughter, and thoughtful acts of kindness toward each other and visitors in the infusion room. She thought of the shopkeepers watching her the night she had arrived. It was a silent gathering around her.

Two men stepped forward, lowered the casket into the grave, and the rabbi recited the prayers for the peace of Anna's soul. Finished with the prayers, the rabbi bent, took the shovel lying at his feet, and handed it to Elia for the shoveling of earth onto the casket.

Elia turned the shovel over, raised a bit of earth on the back curve of it, and tilted the handle. The earth pelted the lid of the walnut box. Elia read the words once more, "From dust you came and to dust you return," and stepped back. Standing erect, he emitted a deep sigh, turned his head, and looked out over the valley. He and Anna had lived their lives with little sorrow except the relentless longing for children. They had their secrets, it was true, but Elia felt they had forgiven themselves.

Leah and the others filed forward. By turns each one dropped a handful of earth onto the casket. With that last act of respect, they dipped their head to Elia and Leah and turned to wend their way upward between the gravestones toward the gate. Reaching the asphalt road, they trudged toward the hairpin curve that led to town.

Unsure whether or not to wait for Elia, Leah hesitated and looked back. Elia motioned her to follow the others leaning into the long, uphill walk.

When everyone was gone, Elia smoothed a place in the scant grass next to the grave and sat down, leaning against the giant cypress that rose above Anna.

Far back, in the shade of another cypress, Salvatore del Piano, the farmer Leah had seen crying, watched Elia, anger mounting in his chest. In a dance of nerves, he wiped his face of tears and sweat, stepped forward, and then back, rubbing his fingers against his palms.

Suddenly, he drew a deep breath, exhaled, and lurched forward, his arms stiff, his hands in tight fists. Striding out of the shadow into the sun toward Elia, his mouth twitched back and forth, and he pursed his lips, working them for the words that could express his rage, his grief.

Elia heard the snap of a twig and looked up to see Salvatore only a few paces away. Startled by Salvatore's threatening appearance, Elia braced his back against the cypress and jolted to a stand, emitting a sharp cry as Salvatore grabbed him by his upper arms and jerked him close, thrusting his face into Elia's.

"Why didn't you take her? I would've taken her! I could have saved her. It's your fault she's under the ground!"

24

Elia struggled against Salvatore's grasp, but Salvatore clung to his arms, crying like a wounded animal.

Finally exhausted, Salvatore dropped his hold, but faced Elia still, his body shaking with fury.

Elia rasped, "Even here, over her grave, Salvatore? Even now, after all these years?"

"Now and always! She wasn't for you! She was mine!"

"She chose a long time ago. She was happy; for God's sake, let her rest in peace! She didn't want to take treatment in some sterile clinic in Switzerland. She wanted to be here, in Scansansiano. It was the end. She knew it, and she wanted to die at home."

With an outcry, Salvatore raised his fist and punched Elia hard in the face, knocking him to the ground beside the grave. Trembling, pointing his finger at the opening in the earth, he shouted, "You belong there—you, not her!"

Turning away, he staggered toward the gate, yelling back in his anguish, "Not her! Not her!"

Chapter Eight

Grazia refused to attend the funeral. The insanity of her behavior at Elia's house embarrassed her, and she was afraid her emotions might overtake her again at the funeral. She refused to face the American woman.

"That bitch!" she muttered.

She stayed home and made lunch for Salvatore. The buglione, his favorite lamb dish, was ready and hot on the stove.

She saw the car drive in. Salvatore got out and the next minute was there in the house. He walked past her, silently, into the bedroom and in a few minutes, reappeared in work clothes. Without looking at the table, he said, "I'm not hungry," and left for the farm store.

Grazie shoved the dishes of buglione to the side and sat at the round oak table. She fanned herself with a piece of paper on which she'd sketched plans for a new flowerbed. Images of how Salvatore must have behaved at the funeral flitted back and forth through her mind. Her husband, crying his eyes out over another woman.

The smooth grain of the table glistened with a high polish. She noticed a spot she had missed. She put the paper down and pulled a cloth from her apron to rub vigorously at the mark. Satisfied, she stuffed the cloth back in her pocket, took a drink of water from the tall glass in front of her, and began again to fan herself.

That morning early, driven by her own demons and unable to sit still, Grazia had walked out to the fig tree in front of the house. She inspected the fruit on the fig tree: it drooped from the branches, had turned a deep purple, and was soft to the touch. She pulled one from the tree and split it open with her thumbs, taking pleasure in the inner soft white ring and the moist purple center. The figs were ready to harvest.

Grazie pulled a ladder from the shed, climbed to the top step, and, moving up and down to fill and empty her bucket, picked until she was exhausted. She reckoned there remained at least another hour's work. She could do that after a drink of water and a short rest. What she couldn't reach on the highest branches, she would leave for the birds. It would be done before Salvatore came home. He would have no cause to complain.

Sweating and thirsty, she walked back to the house, removed her heavy work shoes at the door, slipped into her thick-felt house shoes, and shuffled down the short hallway to the high-ceilinged kitchen.

From the table, she stared through the wide window that spanned the length of the counter and sink in front of her. She could see heavy clusters of grapes dangling from vines in the nearest rows of the vineyard. Farther off, Salvatore's cattle grazed in a small field that extended westward from the barn. Grazia always thought of the cattle as his, although she was the one who fed them and who mucked the stalls.

Grazia recalled a group of the neighbor children playing in the rows of the vineyard one day in late summer. She imagined she could see them there now. Conjuring them stirred the familiar ache of her years without children and brought tears to her eyes. She shook her head in frustration. In an instant, the frustration ignited anger.

The path to anger was always the same. She remembered something that happened in the past, and like the quick, erratic movements of a ferret, the memory changed to anger, and the anger scuttled and burrowed in the dim room of her chest, leaving her in an anguish fury. This was the anger that drove her to violent acts and frightened her even as she committed those acts. She had lived with this anger since before her marriage, but had never developed the strength to control it. It either lay as if dead, blocking the channels of her blood, or it blossomed in a burst of fury, without warning, shocking, surprising her. These "events," as she'd come to think of them, usually happened in the night when she prepared for bed, but often they came on her in the day as well. And in the past days, the anger came in public.

Whenever the anger struck, unwanted guest that it was, she was compelled to rise and move. At night, sleep evaded her. She spent long, dark hours walking the periphery of the farm, back from the road to the inside of the tree line, hidden from the neighbors.

During the day, rage constrained her to work at a furious pace, invisible twisting flashes of energy that pushed between her shoulder blades and up, against her neck. Anger tormented her while she milked the cows, trimmed the vines, planted, tended, or harvested the large garden, cleaned or cooked in the house. The beast was always there, hungry, foraging, pitching and plunging, driving her forward.

As a girl, before she had reason to be angry, she loved farm work: the soft clucking of the chickens in early morning, the crisp air of the winter months when vapor rose from the wide, wet nostrils of the milk cows, and the way the heat of the cattle, horses, and cats created warm, humid air that gave the barn an earthy smell. She could feel still the soft hide of her favorite milk cow as she leaned her forehead against the giant animal's flank, squeezing the teats in rhythmic motion, guiding the thick stream of creamy, frothy liquid from the fore udder pinging and foaming into the bucket.

People in town and in the countryside knew Salvatore and Grazia's farm for efficiency and order. Grazia's strength matched and, some said, exceeded her husband's. The neighbors exclaimed at her energy and attributed much of the farm's success to her work.

Their praise did nothing to quell Grazia's anger, and her face shattered in a rueful laugh at the irony of such praise. Hearing it, she shook her head, thinking a little truth makes the whole lie pass. The neighbors took this oddly nervous response as awkward modesty, which heightened their opinion of her, and to Grazia's chagrin, news of her odd strength and abilities spread throughout the countryside.

Sitting at the table, Grazia thought of how she had aged. She was weakening, and her anger had become tangled with inconsolable regret over the thoughts of what, as a young woman, she could have done differently.

She knew a time would soon come when she could no longer contain her anguish. The embarrassing acts in town were a prophecy of what was to come. Her hands shook as the memory of the incident at Anna's house flitted through her mind.

Grazia was frightened of herself, of her physical strength.

"Anna's dead, and I still want to kill her," she whispered. "He did this to me. And she accepted it. I'll kill them, and Salvatore, and I'll kill that damn bitch of an American woman too."

Tears of misery streamed down her face.

As a girl, at Confirmation, she stood with the others girls in her white dress and floral head wreath, listening to the priest.

"Buy the truth and do not sell it," he said.

She moaned. As a girl, she had bought a wicked, false truth from that bastard, and it would will out. Every day she feared and wondered how it would happen—in front of the whole town or in some secret but terrifying way.

Abruptly, Grazia hoisted her broad frame up from the table. The quick move sent her chair crashing backward to the floor. Seeing what she'd done, she grabbed the water glass and flung it full force across the room against the ceramic sink. The glass exploded in a loud crash, spraying a shower of diamonds onto the red tile floor. Ignoring the scattered shards, she tramped over them, out of the kitchen to the mudroom, wrangled into her work shoes, and stalked out to the fig tree to finish her task.

Chapter Nine

Sergio parted the beads that separated the living quarters from the store and stepped into the bathroom off the narrow hallway. Inside, he emptied his pockets, slowly unbuttoned his shirt, and with the shirt hanging open, regarded himself in the full-length mirror on the wall by the shower. A six-pack. He shrugged out of the shirt and studied himself. Next, he unsnapped the clasp on his wristwatch, rubbed his thumb gently over the gold links, and laid the watch on the stand by the sink, carefully straightening the band. Certain the watch was secure, he turned again to the mirror, raised his elbows, curled his forearms toward his head, and made fists so his biceps would bulge.

He smiled. He was sweating from the walk up the hill from the cemetery. But he was about to have a cool shower and a change from his stifling black clothes. He would be clean, dressed in his crisp khaki pants and his non-tuck sky-blue shirt. He would have lunch and would leave. His wife could care for the store while he sat with his friends in the bar enjoying a late afternoon drink.

"Even if she doesn't like it," he mumbled to himself.

"Hard as rocks!" His wife stood in the doorway of the bathroom, a derisive smile on her lips. She had heard what he said, but ignored it, as she always did.

"And you like it." He cast a prurient grin at the mirror, making sure she saw him.

She ignored this comment as well. "How was the funeral?"

"It was a Jew's funeral. They don't even speak Italian. Their priests mumble

30

and grunt."

He leaned to the mirror, opened his mouth in a grimace, and ran his fingers over his teeth.

"It's not grunts, Idiot; it's Hebrew. That's their language." She rolled her eyes.

"Well, this is Italy, not some Jew country. They should speak Italian."

She shook her head. "Get over it, Sergio. Your lunch is ready—and 'Polish' is here."

"Gino?"

"Unless you've got another brother."

"Don't call him Polish! He doesn't like it. Anyway, how'd he get here ahead of me?"

"How should I know?" She turned and left.

Sergio could hear her laying the table, mumbling to Gino, who would already be seated, waiting for lunch.

He stripped off his pants. His wife hated Gino. He couldn't blame her. Gino was a disheveled glutton and a mooch. Still, Gino was his brother. Sergio stepped into the shower and began to sing "Fields of Gold," an American song he'd heard on the radio.

From the kitchen, his wife heard him singing. She dumped his bowl of soup back into the pot and turned the burner to low; it would be another half hour of scrubbing and primping before he made it to the table.

Gino whined, "Do we have to wait?"

Her mouth filled with an angry 'no,' but she contained herself. She ladled a double serving of the thick soup into one of the larger serving bowls and banged it on the table in front of Gino.

His spoon was ready. She watched him slurp and grunt over the dish she had labored to make. The gorge rose in her throat.

Gino looked up, gave her a quick wink, and reached for the fresh loaf of bread that lay in the middle of the table. He tore off a huge chunk and stuffed his mouth until his cheeks bulged.

Finished, he wiped his fingers around the bowl, stuck them in his mouth to suck off the last of the soup, gulped down his wine, and emitted a loud

31

belch.

"I can't wait for Sergio." He scooted his chair abruptly from the table, sending a screech through the air.

"Tell him I've got business, and I'll be back."

"Yeah? What kinda business, Gino? I thought you were un-em-ployed."

Gino shook his fist at her.

"Just tell him. As for you, you can keep your nose out of my business."

He belched again, "Good soup."

She rolled her eyes. "Sure, Gino, I'll tell him. You're an important guy, can't spare a minute. It's a good thing you eat well and keep your energy up."

"Stupid broad." He made a face and hurried away.

When she heard the door of the shop close, she reached for his dish, but the air around his chair reeked so pungently from the fetid odor of his body and hair that she moved quickly to the window. She opened it and took long breaths of fresh air to stop the gorge from rising in her throat.

After siesta, Sergio dressed, ready to leave for the bar. From the bedroom, he heard the tinkling of the shop bell and poked his head through the beads to see who was in the store. Magliotti stood by the sale table inspecting a cappuccino machine. Leah Contarini had come in just behind him.

Sergio stepped through the beads into the shop. He ignored Magliotti for the moment and approached Leah.

"My condolences for your loss, Signora. I know what close friends you were. How can I help you?"

"That's kind, Sergio, thank you. I've come because Elia has broken his battery-run tool that froths milk. Do you have those? I thought I could spare him coming out to buy it."

Sergio smiled. "Life doesn't stop for death, does it? Come. I have several types. Just here." He indicated a table at the side. "Why don't you look through them. I'll wait on Signor Magliotti while you choose.

Leah nodded.

Sergio turned to the carpenter. "Magliotti, what can I do for you?"

Magliotti turned and smiled. "I want to buy this coffee machine." He held it up, a wide grin on his face.

"Why the big smile?"

"It's made in America. I wanted to buy one while I was there, but I didn't get around to it, so I'm happy to find it here."

"Ironic, no? That's why it's on sale. It's a good make, but it came to me by mistake. As far as coffee machines are concerned, no one here wants American; they want Italian. Are you sure you want American?"

Magliotti shook his head in disgust, "People here are as stupid as people anywhere."

Sergio's forehead creased. "Why do you say that?"

"Because I spent time in New York at a woodworking convention, and I could see that the American goods are very fine. They even have religious groups known for their elegant, sturdy furniture, much finer than we have here." He grinned. "Except my work, of course. "Truly, the Americans appreciate fine carpentry."

"Of course. And they have money to buy your work, yes?"

Magliotti laughed. "Plenty of money! They paid me very well for some of my handmade pieces."

"But this is a coffee maker, not a piece of wood."

"I was making an analogy. Now, may I have the coffee maker?"

"Your wish is my command! I'll wrap it up."

The two men laughed.

Sergio watched Magliotti slip through the door with the package under his arm and stepped back to Leah. She held up a long, thin tool with a small whisk on the end.

"This is perfect."

"That's what I want! Happy customers."

After they were gone, Sergio yelled to his wife. "I'm going to the bar."

She appeared through the strands of beads. "Every day the bar. So what did he want?"

Sergio grunted. "Idiot. He wanted the American coffee maker. I don't get it. Italian ones are so much better."

She hunched her shoulders. "On sale."

Sergio nodded. "I always thought Italian makers were better, but he's an odd duck – and smart. It makes me wonder if maybe the American maker is better."

She laughed. "Go on; go to the bar. You'll drive yourself crazy thinking like that."

Chapter Ten

In his rooms after the funeral, Idrissa changed clothes, drank a glass of water, and ate a banana. It was all he had. After a short rest, he gathered his heavy bag of knock-off goods and his blanket and carried them to the spot by Elia's shop where people from the old city passed on their way to market. Wadding the corners of the blanket tightly in his fists, he flung it out in front of him to settle on the street between Elia's textile store and the leather goods store next door. The faded-yellow geometric design of the blanket was worn at the edges. He bent to tuck under the frayed parts of the border in a neat fold to show his wares to better advantage. Once he had smoothed the wrinkles, he opened the big plastic bag he carried slung over his back. One by one he pulled out the knock-off belts, small backpacks, and Gucci purses he bought from the underground Chinese workers in Florence. He arranged his wares carefully in neat rows, then sat, crossed his legs, and leaned against the outer wall of the building to wait for customers from those passing to and from the market in the upper city.

From his vantage point, Idrissa could see in both directions. Most of those who passed this time of day were either women late to shopping, who scurried by with their empty carts noisily rattling behind them, or women who had finished shopping and were trudging toward home either with heavy bags of produce in each hand or tugging their heavily laden rolling carts over the cobblestones, in a sweaty rush to prepare the mid-day meal.

Idrissa noted the women's faces, red from the crisp air and from the exertion of shopping. Wisps of hair escaped from the buns at the back of their necks, leaving long, black strands tangling in the wind. These Italian women had white skin that turned red in the cool air, a different beauty from women at home. The African women moved more slowly and carried their vegetables and meat balanced on their heads. Italian or African, he thought, they were all beautiful in the way of women going about their chores, and they reminded him of his aunts and grandmother.

After the funeral, Idrissa had carefully folded his good clothes and laid them in a drawer to keep them neat for the rare public events he attended or, like today, for funerals. He was now dressed in blue jeans and a dashiki in red and orange with heavy gold embroidery. Around his neck he wore a thick chain of gold. This was the necklace his father had given him; it sparkled against his dark skin.

Idi, as some called him, put his hand to his forehead, in the manner of the Muslim washing ritual before prayer, and ran his palm down over the length of his face, his eyes closed. Today this gesture indicated not prayer, but worry. No one was buying his knock-off goods.

He thought of his father, a Haalpulaar tradesman who had died two years before, when Idrissa was seventeen. Idrissa thought of how different his life would have been if his father had lived.

He sighed heavily and chided himself. It was a worthless endeavor to imagine what could have been. If God willed it the way it was, that was the way it was. He was of a noble caste. His training, secular and religious, taught him to defeat weakening emotions. He struggled to console himself with the thought of his family's standing in Senegal. He had lowered himself by selling knock-off bags and belt, but had raised himself high by caring for his family. Any work that was honorable was good work. He would stay proud of what he was; he would endure what fate handed him.

Still, in the tension of two lives, he struggled to stop his imaginings. Some days his resolve was more difficult to grasp than on other days. On those difficult days, he daydreamed of Senegal, of a life he understood, of a community in which he was respected.

In the past months, he had been suffering an anger against Elia that felt heavy as a rock and burned in his chest. He was perilously close to losing control, and he feared how it might happen, how the anger might surprise

36

him before he could calm himself.

He wanted to continue his studies, like his father, a scholar, had done. Idrissa knew he had the mind for it. But rather than studying, rather than playing his *hoddu* with his musician friends around a campfire, or dreaming of his bride, he was here, in a foreign country. At home, he would have spent his evenings listening to the stories of the itinerant teller. Here, disparaged by strangers who knew neither him nor his family, he sat in the street all day. And at night, he sat alone in a barren room, with little money to care for himself, let alone send to his mother and sisters, the ones who depended on him now his father was gone.

He could see that his anger was a natural reaction to the randomness of loss. He was angry when his little sister died of a fever. Her death had seemed terribly unjust. Still, he knew that, ultimately, life is not unjust; it simply is what it is. Now that his father was gone, it was up to him to take care of the family. He knew these things, yet he struggled against his fate.

Idrissa took a deep breath, wiped his hand over his face again, and closed his wide, brown eyes. Memories of the world he had lost led to visions of the dangerous journey he had taken on the smugglers' circuitous route through Mali, across northwestern Niger, into Libya, and then the sickening journey over the sea.

He saw himself again on the barren road through the desert. Thirty of them packed into the back of the pickup. Attempting to evade bandits, the driver drove at breakneck speed. Approaching a steep hillock, he made a sharp turn, and a man fell from the back of the truck. Shouting in different languages, the other men yelled for the driver to stop. He ignored them and drove on. The one who had toppled off the truck was either dead from the fall or would die from the heat and lack of water if the next transport came too late, or came before he died but took no pity on him when it did pass by.

In Libya, there had been the ennui of long days waiting for the boat and, finally, the terrifying voyage in the little boat that bobbed like a cork in the water. Idrissa sat crammed in with other men, women, and little children, all of them debilitated by constant vomiting and a thirst that seemed unbearable. When one of the group died, the others gently lowered the body overboard.

The dead one's family would never know what had happened. The ones still living turned their faces from the others, ashamed to be relieved for the minuscule amount of extra room on the boat.

Idi had nightmares. They continued, night after night. In the dreams he felt the corpses' flesh in his hands, heard the sound of bodies plopping into the sea. He saw the curl of the water cover the chalky faces of the dead.

After landfall in southern Italy and what seemed endless weeks in a holding camp, Idrissa and the others who had been able to escape traveled north through Italy any way they could. They walked, failed at hitchhiking, and sneaked onto trains, ducking into the bathroom when the conductor moved along the aisles checking tickets.

Idrissa had been lucky. He saw several of his countrymen thrown off the train at small stops along the way. The memory of their pleas to the authorities for help still echoed in his mind, and he often wondered what had happened to them. Except for him, none of them had made it to Venice, where he had been fortunate to find others like himself and get started in business.

He pursed his lips. Ashamed to be the lone survivor of his group, he felt less a man than when he started the odyssey north. It seemed to him as if he had done something wrong.

Once Idrissa arrived in Venice, a fantasy city, he used his last funds to buy knock-offs from a boss-man from Mali. Carrying his bag on his back, he walked the stone streets until his legs ached, searching for a spot where people passed but where he would be unlikely to be chased by police. He soon became adept at swiftly grabbing the corners of his blanket, tying them in a knot, and running away with the heavy bag, purses, and belts banging against his backside. He hated running away; he hated feeling and behaving like a criminal.

Occasionally, he sneaked onto a vaporetto. It was difficult and never possible in the lengthening tourist season, when the boats were crammed and there was no room to tuck his large bundle under the seats and appear a normal passenger.

Anger over his situation rose again and again, seething, a live coal in his chest. The police had sent him, and many of the other Africans like him, out of Venice to the mainland. He and his friends, the *vu compra*, as they were called in a pejorative twist of the Italian phrase "would you like to buy?" went without a fight. It became a routine. They were chased away, driven out of the city, spent a day in Mestre on the mainland, and crept back into Venice that evening. By morning, they were back on the streets of the fabled city with their knock-off purses, bags and belts, leaning against walls with their blankets and goods spread at their feet, jerking their heads right and left so they could grab their merchandise and run if they saw police coming.

Idrissa hated this cycle of sneaking into the city and being chased out again. Before long, he saw the writing on the wall.

A new law fining both buyers and the *vu compra* has gone into effect, making it unprofitable and dangerous to stay in Venice. Ten thousand euros was a fine no tourist would pay for buying a knock-off purse. If a tourist had that much money, he could buy genuine Gucci, Prada, Burberry, and the other famous brands he craved.

The tourists' desire to buy seemed to Idrissa an odd, almost crazed, frenzy for acquisition, and it was now his living, his torment.

He made a decision. One day in fall, he waved goodbye to his friends and took a train south to Grosseto. He imagined life in the smaller Tuscan towns would be simpler, if his take less. From Grosseto, he headed up, into the Maremma hills toward Scansansiano, hoping there would be enough business to get by with enough left over to send home.

He banked on the thought that in a small town the police would leave him alone. He had been right; the Lieutenant did leave him alone. Idrissa and the Lieutenant had gotten to know one another; and if the Lieutenant asked him to move, it was only once in a while. Otherwise, he let Idrissa sell his wares in peace.

Social life in Scansansiano did prove to be easier than life in Venice. He had rooms of his own in town. He greeted and was greeted in turn by townspeople. But he had been wrong about business. Few of the frugal housewives who passed his blanket every day bought his goods. They were friendly enough, and they asked after his family, but with the exception of a few women, they walked to and fro without buying. He was forced to skimp on food in order to save enough to send home, and he often went hungry.

Frustrated as he was not to sell many purses, Idrissa wondered about the women. How could they walk in high heels without stumbling over the rough paving stones, so different from the soft dirt pathways of his village, where women padded to market barefoot or in flat sandals?

The thought of market day at home brought a smile to Idrissa's lips, lighting his handsome face with a fleeting moment of joy. These people of the outlying Italian towns were thrifty. Their thrift worked against him, but he delighted in the thought they were like his family. He could imagine his mother exclaiming, "Being well-dressed does not prevent one from being poor and careful with money." Idrissa saw that these Italian women were perhaps something very much like his wise mother.

From down the street, Idi saw the American woman approaching. He had seen her at the funeral and was happy to know she was back in town. Unlike the other woman, she carried a worn leather backpack, its straps lined with sheepskin, and she wore jeans, flannel shirts, and hiking boots. It was an odd way for a lovely woman to dress.

Approaching, she gave Idrissa a wan smile. "How are you today, Idi? Thanks for coming to the funeral. I know you and Elia don't always get along."

"Signora Leah, yes, but I wanted to pay my respects. I'm glad to see you back. I'm sorry you arrived in a moment of grief and have lost your friend."

Leah gave him a gentle smile. "Thank you, Idi. We go on, don't we. Grief changes shape, but it never ends, does it? I imagine you've had your share, no?"

Idrissa nodded. "Thank you, Signora Leah. You're very kind. But why are you out now?"

"I've been on a little errand, something for Elia."

They fell silent.

Leah liked Idrissa, but was saddened by and worried about the running argument he had with Elia over spreading his goods in front of Elia's shop. Elia would be especially upset if he saw him now, just after the funeral.

Idrissa broke the silence, attempting a joke in the hope of brightening Leah's spirit. "Would you like a fine Gucci bag?" He picked up a black, shining tote from the blanket and held it up to her, flashing a bright, white smile.

"Not today," she smiled. "Today, I need a coin purse." Understanding he wanted to cheer her, she pointed toward the corner of the blanket. "How about that leather one there, at the corner?"

"You have sharp eyes. That is not from the Gucci line," he laughed and took the little coin purse in hand, running his finger over the tight stitching before holding it up to her. "This is a purse my cousin made and my mother sent me, just to see if it would appeal to the market here."

Leah took it and brought it to her face to smell the leather, then opened it and inspected the inside pockets.

"Your mother was right; it's beautiful, and it does appeal. You should remember," she shook her finger at him, "mothers are always right."

Idrissa's laughter filled the air. "Yes, Signora Leah, I know this. I learned very young."

"How much is it?"

"Three euros."

"That isn't nearly enough, Idi! You can't make a living doing that kind of business."

"But for you—"

"No, no." Leah shook her head. "We'll keep the business separate from friendship; it's only fair." She handed him six euros and took the little multicolor purse. "It's beautiful."

"I'm happy you appreciate it. I'll tell my cousin."

"I do appreciate it; it's sturdy and beautiful. If your mother sends you a few more, you'll have better luck. They'd make a fine display." She ran her hands over the little purse. "I have to go. If more of these come from your mother, please hold at least five for me, would you?"

"Five! Of course!"

A few yards on, Leah heard Elia's voice behind her. She turned to see the

41

older man standing outside the door of his shop, berating Idrissa.

"I told you, get out of here! You disturb my customers! Get out! They won't come in the shop while you're sitting here!"

Elia had raised his hand to strike. When the blow landed, Idrissa, who had risen and was bending over his blanket to gather the four corners, was forced off balance. He toppled to the stone street with a loud offffffffh.

Leah yelled. "Elia! Stop!"

Idrissa was already on his feet and had grasped Elia by the shoulders. All the thoughts of home, of the dangerous trip north and across the sea, coalesced. This man was greedy over two square meters of space that didn't block his doorway. What he understood to be the meanness of it infuriated Idrissa. His eyes rimmed with red, and with all the force of an eagle making a kill on a lesser animal, Idrissa's fingers dug like spikes into Elia's flesh.

Chapter Eleven

L eah sprinted toward them.

Idrissa had Elia in a throw-hold.

"Idi, stop! You'll hurt him!"

She grabbed Idrissa's shirt in one hand and Elia's jacket in the other and forced her head between Idrissa's arms and Elia's chest.

"Let go, Idi! Elia, stop. Don't do this, not today! Not today!"

Leah's face was only inches from Idrissa's. His eyes had gone blank, as if he didn't recognize her or hear her pleas. She struggled to force her way further between them. Elia's strength was flagging, but he refused to let go.

"Please, Idi, Elia, please!"

To her surprise, Idi let go of Elia, dropped his arms, and stepped back.

With the sudden release, Elia stumbled backward against the wall of the shop.

Tossing curses into the air, Idrissa bent to gather his purses, belts, and bags, which had been scattered across the cobblestones in the fray. He piled them in the middle of the blanket, tied the four corners in a tight knot, and flung the makeshift bag over his shoulder.

"Tell him to leave me alone, Signora Leah." Idi hissed. "He's tormented me enough; my patience is gone."

He stalked away.

"Idi, come back! Let's settle it."

Idrissa called over his shoulder. "It's settled! Signora Leah. Tell him to leave me alone. He's not the only one who has lost family. I won't take it anymore."

Leah turned to Elia. He was panting in short bursts, his hand over his heart. She took his arm and led him into the store to a chair beside the counter. Red-faced, breathless with exertion and anger, he tried, but failed, to speak.

"Breathe deeply, Elia, as slowly as you can. Remember your heart. And today.... You should be home, Elia. Sitting shiva."

He stared into her eyes, gasping for breath, a look of disgust on his face.

"My heart! My heart! Shiva! I know, but I can't do it. I can't go back to the house yet. Let them wait. And Salvatore..."

"Salvatore? Who's Salvatore?"

He shook his head in sharp little jerks. "Never mind!"

Leah pulled away, surprised by the violence of Elia's response.

She drew a deep breath, her heart still pounding from the physical exertion and from the shock of seeing Idrissa's quick, violent reaction. His eyes were burning coals, and his anger strong as acid. In rage, he seemed a different man, capable of anything.

Minutes passed; the clock over the counter beat a loud tick, tick, tick against the silence.

At last, Elia inhaled deeply, sighed, and rose. "I'm going to Sergio. He can't deny me again, not after this!"

"But Elia...today?"

His voice softened. He put his hands on her shoulders, "Leah, I know I should be home sitting shiva, but I can't. I can't sit and think and remember. I can't bear the memories just now. I'm so full of anger, so full...."

Chapter Twelve

"'You Jews!' What does that mean? The boy pushed me down!" Elia stared at Sergio in disbelief. "And don't try to shame me about it being the day of the funeral! It won't work."

"Calm down, Elia. You're in an emotional state, and you're overreacting. Separate your grief from your problem with Idrissa. From what I hear, your business is doing fine. The kid wants to sell a few knock-offs; what does it hurt? Being so particular seems to be a trait with you people."

"'You people!' You insult me again so offhandedly?" Elia started to rise, but fell back in his chair. "There's no cure, no arguing against such ignorance. Let's just keep it on business. You got the Lieutenant to move him away from your store, and it's only just that you do the same for me."

"So go directly to the Lieutenant. And besides, my story with Idrissa is different. He really was blocking the way."

"You had the power of the Association behind you, that's why the Lieutenant had to help. And that's all I'm asking. Take the problem to the Association to get their backing. Idrissa does block access to my store, and now he's struck me. I insist you bring it to the businessmen's meeting."

"Okay. Okay. I'll bring it, but it's a waste of time." Sergio hunched his shoulders, palms raised. A slight smile touched his lips.

Seeing him smile, Elia shoved his chair back, stood, and leaned over the table.

"'You Jews,' you say! You're as bad as the ones who. . . Just bring it to the meeting and we can all talk about it. Maybe the others aren't such...."

Elia cut himself off before more angry words and accusations spilled from his mouth. He continued in a lowered voice. "Shame on you. You're the president of the organization, and you've got such ideas. Shame, Sergio, shame." He shook his head and stepped to the door of the shop.

At the doorway, a tall, lean man in a black overcoat brushed by Elia, knocking him off balance. It was Cristofano, one of the Innocenti brothers. Elia caught himself against the doorjamb and turned to watch him sit across from Sergio at the table by the cash register. Sergio whispered something to Cristafano, and they both laughed, lifting their heads to stare at Elia in the doorway.

Elia shook his head, "The perversity and the ignorance never end."

Across the way, the clothier stood in the doorway of his shop. He saw Elia leave Sergio's and wondered why Elia was flustered. He thought of the passionate case Elia had made to the city council when his son, disinclined to take over the clothier shop, had wanted to open a new bookstore in the old part of the city. Several of the council members balked at the idea.

"There are two bookstores there now. The area would be glutted with them," one of the council members argued.

Elia took the floor and, in his calm, emotionally powerful way, responded, "A gift shop with a few books is not a bookstore. This boy knows books. He'll be an asset to the whole community. Which one of you wouldn't like to have a better selection? Not only for yourselves, but for your children? And a place to buy books, books you can hold in your hand and look at, to read or give as presents? Not only a place for tourists' books, but a place for us, for what we might want to read. A bookstore where the books can be in Italian, for us, and not always have duplicate copies in German, English, and French, for the tourists."

In the end, the council agreed by one vote, and for the past four years, the barber had watched his son thrive, moving from strength to strength, smiling, making new friends, handling the books, and the ordering himself with aid on financial things from advisors at the bank.

When his son came to visit, the barber and his wife would take each other's hand in a hasty but gentle squeeze, the intimate touch signifying their joy in their son's success, a welcome development to them both. They had never noticed his head for business. They had even despaired when he refused to go to university or to help in the clothing shop, but wanted only to sit with his books.

Watching Elia walk down the street, the clothier wondered how he and his wife, the boy's parents, could have been blind to the skills of their son. He wondered too if this were the way of many parents, so intent on instructing their children they missed the most important things, things others could see if they had the vision of an Elia.

Lost in thought, the clothier started when he felt someone standing next to him. "Signor Magliotti! You surprised me. How's the woodworking business?"

"Not too busy, but consistent. I didn't mean to disturb your thought."

The clothier sighed. "It's Elia. So much sadness for such a good man."

Magliotti nodded. "The world seems unfair, doesn't it? It's like I saw on an old American tv show, the host said, 'Expecting the world to treat you fairly because you are a good person is a little like expecting a bull not to attack you because you're a vegetarian."

Laughing at the truth of the saying, the men stepped into the clothing shop.

Chapter Thirteen

The following morning, Leah rose early to go on a solitary hike on the *vie cave*. She headed for one of the longest of the trails, the one that began below town, snaked through a high stand of bamboo next to the river, wound upward through thick, deciduous trees and brush, and finally rose to the ridge on the other side of the valley. She sought the gifts of walking: the rise of forgotten memories, solace, insights on ways to maneuver the murky, narrow hallways of loss.

After the hike and a shower, and with the desire to keep moving and keep busy, Leah carried the small table Signora Vianello had given her down the steep steps to the car and drove the thread of road above the river to the older woman's house deep in the forested valley.

When the Signora answered the door, Leah noticed her purse in hand, but she wore only a light sweater.

Leah spoke before she thought. "Where's your coat?"

"My coat! My coat! You're just like the others. I don't wear it twenty-four hours a day, even if everyone thinks I do!"

Leah hugged her. "Please don't be upset. We love you for it, and that's not what I meant, anyway. I just think it's a little cool."

They walked toward the car.

"Well, the coat makes me one of the town characters, I suppose. But today it's not cool. The weather is fine, and I don't need a coat."

Her lips curved in a devilish smile.

"I can appear foolish and old whenever I want, you know, while all the time, I am observing, thinking, learning." She tapped her head with her finger.

Leah tilted her head and regarded her friend with a quizzical stare. "True, and maybe in addition, you're a bit scary."

"Good! I like to think people are a little afraid of me. They should be. I know many, many secrets!" She chuckled. "And the table?"

Annoyed with herself for having broken the gift, Leah made a face. "I hope it's not irreparable."

The Signora brushed her hand through the air. "Magliotti can fix it. He's quite good." She stepped into the car and pulled the seat belt over her.

"I should have been more careful."

"Don't fuss! Things happen." The Signora patted her on the arm.

Leah started the motor and backed into the road. The Signora turned her head, as if she were the one backing out, and repeated herself. "Things happen, and most things can be fixed."

"Most things, yes." Leah echoed in a sad voice.

Irritated by Leah's comment, the older woman wiggled in her seat. "Don't be maudlin, Leah. I'm looking forward to this outing. It's been weeks since I've been out of town, and I want to enjoy it."

Leah laughed aloud, delighted by the Signora's brusque love.

"Why are you laughing?"

"Because I was being maudlin, and you put me in perspective."

A smile flitted across the Signora's face.

The highway descended in broad curves from Scansansiano and passed over the bridge. They rode in companionable silence for a few minutes. On the other side of the river, Leah glanced toward the trailhead where she often walked.

"You never get tired of going out on your hikes, do you?" The Signora patted her arm again.

"No. There's something mysterious about the trails, something just a little dangerous that gets your blood going..."

"A little dangerous! You were shot! I'm perpetually astounded you continue to go out to the trails alone. If it were up to me, you wouldn't."

"The culprit's in jail, Signora; it was a coincidence it happened on the trail."

"It was not a coincidence. She knew where you were going, and she went there to shoot you!"

The Signora grunted, and Leah knew not to argue.

The pavement shimmered in light and shadow, given life by the fall breezes that meandered through the trees and dappled the narrow strip of asphalt with sunlight. They drove in and out of the shadows, upward through thick forests of ash, maple, beech, yew, and chestnut trees. Through the opened window, Leah imagined she could hear the satisfied grunts of *cinghiali* as they fed on fallen nuts and rooted for truffles in the surrounding oaks.

"I don't suppose Magliotti makes much of a living." Leah glanced at the Signora, who was staring out the window.

"Magliotti?" The Signora turned from the window.

"Yes."

"I'm sure he doesn't. There aren't enough people here, but I'm very glad to have him; I'm glad to have a shoe repairman too."

"I wish we still had shoe repairmen."

"You Americans always buy new! Houses only one hundred years old, destroyed. You must either be poor builders or extremely wasteful!" She shook her head in disgust.

Leah made a face. "Wasteful, I'm afraid."

At the T-intersection, Leah turned left, down a long descent, then back up a gentle hill into Casale. She pulled into the parking lot, a short walkway off the pedestrian-only main street.

Situated on a hilltop surrounded by forests to the east and fields to the west, Casale had been built over ancient Etruscan ruins, which still mottled the outlying land around the town. Like an invading army, a constant onslaught of thick brush and seedling trees threatened to engulf the buildings and streets of the town. Trees, grasses, and bushes crept through ditches and up hillsides into openings and cracks in walls or breaks in the pavement and cobblestones. This gave the villagers the sense of living in the middle of a forest, even as they sat at a table in front of the bar and drank their morning coffee.

The antique dealer's shop sat at the end of the main street, perched above a deep slope that gave onto a ditch and the road below. Across the road, in a thick forest, the broken walls and dark recesses of Etruscan ruins hovered and gaped in a sinister landscape of mounds, thick tangles of creeping vines, and shadows created by a twisted growth of trees and vegetation.

Leah had walked along the winding pathways of those ruins only once, when Secondo showed her how to find the unused trail that led from Scansansiano to Casale. Before everyone owned cars, the trail through the ruins was a heavily traveled path between the two towns used by people with business in one place or the other, donkeys carrying loads of wood, and dogs accompanying their masters.

Leah promised herself that when she had time, she would walk the little-used trail again. The heavy stone walls built around and over the maws of the Etruscan caves had fallen in a jumble of overgrown mounds and deep depressions. One misstep in the thick lace of vines that obscured many of the openings could send one tumbling into the musty holes where vipers made their nests. She was curious enough to make the walk, but only in daylight.

Leah pushed open the door of Magliotti's shop and stepped back to allow the Signora to enter ahead of her. A bell tinkled, and the glass insets rattled beneath the blinds. Inside, tables and chairs were stacked on one another, creating tilting pyramids that rose to the ceiling. Redolent with the smell of wood shavings, sawdust, and polish, the air in the room had a faint tinge of chemical odor, which Leah understood must be glue or stripping fluid. Untreated, the furniture yielded its natural grains to beautiful effect: pale, muted maple, the rich, wavy-tan grain of oak, and the lighter, flesh-like, tight grain of ash and golden yew.

The Signora spread her hands, palm upward, around the room in appreciation. The gesture ignited the memory of a similar gesture Leah's father made in his carpentry shop when he finished a project. The open palm, the arm outstretched, seemed to say, "Look at this wood, this beautiful wood." Leah spent many pleasant hours watching her father work the lathe, and sometimes working on her own amateur projects under his guidance.

51

A beautiful landscape painting hung on the wall opposite Magliotti's work-shelves. Leah and the Signora nodded to each other, surprised by his impeccable taste.

He appeared from behind a curtained door that led to a back room. A tall, lean man, he looked to Leah to be in excellent condition. His long narrow face, high forehead, with wisps of graying hair at his temples, gave him a distinguished look. But it was his hands that most attracted Leah's attention. As he pushed aside the curtains, she saw they were larger than most men's hands and muscular, strengthened from his work, she supposed. They were also hands covered with small scars, where he must have slipped with an awl or a chisel.

His voice was gentler than she expected. "Good day! And Signora…"

Seeing the older woman, who had stepped to the side to look at a little coffee table, he spoke with surprise and quiet delight. He extended his hand, taking the Signora's first, and then Leah's.

"Coffee?"

"Thank you. We've just had."

Not such a terrible lie.

Leah glanced at the Signora, who smiled and replied in a soft voice.

"Thank you, Signor. I compelled Signora Contarini to bring me along, and yet I have little time. We just thought to bring the table, but I did want to see you, and the shop, again."

Leah covered her mouth and coughed to hide her smile. The Signora was flirting with him. To keep from laughing aloud, she diverted the conversation by holding the table up for Magliotti's inspection.

"The crack is here." She drew her finger along a narrow line in one of the table legs. It's not too wide yet, but I'm afraid if it isn't fixed now, it will split even further."

Magliotti nodded. "Yes, it will, and don't worry, Signora. I can fix it easily, but it will take a day or two. Can you leave it?"

"I planned to. Tomorrow, then, or…?"

The Signora laid a hand on her arm with a slight shake of her head. Leah blushed.

"Sorry, I don't mean to rush you."

He laughed. "I understand; it's just that it takes time for the glues to set. Come any time after tomorrow. That will give plenty of time."

"I can wait longer, if you'd prefer."

"No. It will be ready. It's just the glue." He smiled.

Chapter Fourteen

Sweating, his heart pounding hard against his chest and a stream of saliva trickling from the corner of his mouth, he rushed down the trail from town, crossed the road, and entered a narrow left-hand path.

"My things! My things," he muttered as he scuttled up the rutted track.

Around a curve, across a small meadow, he came to a sharp bend. In his haste, his foot slipped, and he stumbled. Falling hard on his backside, he was thrown full-length and rolled out of control down the slope through the wet grass. Lurching for the branch of a young oak to arrest himself, he missed and screamed in frustration.

After a few more dizzying seconds, he came to a stop at the bottom of the hill where the land leveled. He brought himself up on all fours, staggered upright, and angrily brushed his backside with the palm of his hand.

"Fuck it!"

He wiped his shirtsleeve across his face to soak the drool dribbling from his lips. Nothing he did could stop the river of saliva. His clothes were soaked with it. Whenever he felt excited, or upset, or angry, or happy, he salivated. From early childhood, his mother had yelled at him for it.

"Look at you," she screeched. You're disgusting, driveling all over the tablecloth and your pants."

She slapped him hard across the face.

After the first embarrassing experience with friends when he was five and drooled in the excitement of playing with them, and they teased him, it had been impossible for him to go to a movie or to play with other kids. He learned to play alone.

Standing below the trail, remembering those earlier experiences, he gritted his teeth. The fall made the drool worse.

He hated his mother.

He looked down. His pants and shirt were stained and muddy, and he was bleeding from a cut on his hand where he had tried to grasp the branch. Anticipating the walk home through the streets of town, he started to sweat again, and saliva gushed from his lips. He would need an excuse for his filthy clothes.

Stomping his feet, he picked up his pack and checked to make sure the plastic sacks and small blanket were still inside. Seeing he had everything, he closed his eyes to still the last of the dizziness and looked up the valley toward the east and then down toward the west to get his bearings.

With the bag slung over his right shoulder, he started off again, stepping carefully along the side of the hill, moving toward the pathway a little above him. The pathway would lead him to the mastic bush he had marked with a few notches on one of the outer branches, a sign he was near his things.

At the bush, he ran his fingers over the notches. A small bit of resin stuck to his index finger. He had to get rid of it. His mother would yell if he got resin in the sink or on his clothes. It always stuck to his shirt and pants, and big globs clogged the drain.

He rubbed the finger with his thumb, then wiped it off on the grass and smoothed his hand lightly over the bush as if petting it. Lentisk. Schinos. Sergio had told him the story about Artemis, how she had turned one of her favorite nymphs into this bush so the nymph could flee from King Minos and remain a virgin. And here he was, petting her. He broke into a grin.

Standing quietly, he listened for footsteps on the trail above. No sound. Certain no one was about, he bent to take a thick stick. Holding it firmly in hand, he stepped around the bush onto the faint animal track he had discovered years earlier. Careful not to break the low branches or trample the grasses along the edge of the narrow trail, he leaned forward, moving up the hillside.

"My path," he whispered.

At the entrance to the cave, he stopped again, listening for sounds of movement. Errant *cinghiali* sometimes wandered into the cave, rooting in the dark corners. These wild pigs terrified him, but as frightening as they were, they were not enough to keep him away.

Nothing could keep him away. He pounded his chest with both fists.

Once, as a child, he had come to explore the trails after school and had crossed paths with a sounder of *cinghiali*. A small boar chased him, until nuts under an oak distracted it.

Back in town, he told his mother what had happened, how scared he'd been, but she only laughed.

"Stupid boy. Serves you right, running off to the woods."

That evening, his mother ordered him to put her soup on the table for supper. Carrying it carefully, not to spill, he paused in the hallway to lean over and let the saliva he could not control drip in her bowl. Smiling, he entered the dining room and set the soup in front of her.

The pull of his things would always prove stronger than fear. He knew this. His desire gave him courage, or at least compelled him forward, no matter the fear. Horror-stricken by the wild boars, he swallowed his terror and continued to go to his secret hiding place. For defense against the wild boars, he had hidden a large stick to use as a cudgel, the same one he now clasped tightly. His fingers turned white with the effort of wielding it.

Over the years, the smaller, native *cinghiali* had been overtaken by a larger species imported for the hunt. The big ones stood waist-high. Once, from a hillside, he watched a herd of them rooting the air blindly with their menacing tusks. Their sensitive snouts could ferret out whatever living—or dead—creature was close.

Since these bigger ones inhabited the forests, he developed a ritual of courage to help him. It was a simple but effective ritual, and he practiced it before each foray into the woods. Standing in front of his mirror, he stripped to the waist, flexed his flabby muscles, pounded his chest, and yelled a rhythmic chant at the image in the gold-framed mirror.

"You're strong and brave, and handsome!" he rasped, pounding his chest with his fist on each word.

After, he whipped himself to an ecstasy of self-confidence, dressed, took his handgun from the drawer, tucked it in the bottom of the pack he had carried since junior high school, and rushed toward the trail, drooling, his heart pounding. Compelled forward by the rapturous anticipation of touching the gold and silver, his urge never abated. He rushed away every afternoon on which he could escape without being detected.

Today, he had failed to perform the ritual. His desire to see his things had been too strong, like a fumbling lover who couldn't wait.

A light breeze wafted through the branches of the trees. Overhead, a kestrel emitted a loud klee-klee-klee. He took a deep breath, reached for his headlamp in the side pocket of his pack, and stepped into the cave.

The light of the headlamp cut through the thick darkness. He scanned the dirt floor, relieved to see only his own footsteps from yesterday's visit. Cutting a wide swathe of light across the darkness, he spotted the angular outlines of the large chest, sitting where they had placed it, in the recess of the rock. Moving slowly, carefully, he pulled away the heavy plastic sheet and swiped his drool-soaked sleeve once again across his mouth.

He sighed and emitted a crude grunt. Grasping the edges of the tarp as he would a sheet, he folded it in precise squares and laid it on a rock ledge to the side. His skin tingled; he inhaled hard, and when spittle oozed out his mouth, he sucked it in with a slurp.

Finally, he lifted the thick rug he had brought to cover the chest two weeks before and opened the heavy lid. In the light from the headlamp, the silver and gold objects gleamed in front of his eyes like the sun on the river in the summer.

What first?

He slid a large flat rock beside the chest, sat down, and ran his hand lightly over the objects, the way a spider crawls lightly over utensils in a drawer. When he came to a small silver cup worked with flowers and the flowing calligraphy of an ancient language, he clasped his fingers around the stem and brought the silver to his face and lips, moaning with the thrill of it.

Pleasure overwhelmed him.

Chapter Fifteen

The following day, Leah rose early. The day was warm, sunny, and free of humidity. Church bells rang through the limpid air. She had never learned the reason for the bells at the various times of day. They seemed to follow a ragged pattern, but she had yet to discover what the pattern meant. She would ask the priest. Someone told her she could gauge the chances of rain by the clarity of the bells, so she paid attention to the weather when they rang. Today, if she judged correctly, it would rain, although at the moment, rain seemed impossible. Rain or not, she wanted company, if only ambient voices in the bar.

Approaching the steps to the bar, Leah caught sight of the American and Secondo standing at the fountain across the piazza. Tall and thin as the trunk of a young tree, the American towered over Secondo. His dark brown hair, flecked with premature gray, glistened in the sunlight and curled at his collar. His smooth, tanned skin had the look of a man who spent most of his time outdoors.

Runner or swimmer, Leah thought.

A wave of jealousy passed over her as the American leaned close to Secondo in animated conversation. Secondo gesticulated in his usual way, pointing, and clapping his hands in lively emphasis. If she had not known better, Leah would have thought them old friends, standing comfortably in the bright light, the cool breeze at their backs, chatting while the early morning sun sauntered upward in the mid-fall sky.

Secondo looked up. Seeing her, he waved her over. Before she reached them, he flung open his arms in a broad, welcoming gesture. "Signora Leah," he indicated Stein, "this is an American!" Turning back to Stein, he gestured toward Leah and shouted again. "And this is Signora Leah!"

Leah and the American smiled, both delighted by Secondo's exuberance. In the ambience of his enthusiasm, they shook hands.

"Actually I have a name," the American said. "It's David, David Stein."

"I'm Leah Contarini. It's good to meet you; I'm always happy to meet Secondo's friends."

"Well, not friends quite yet. We met just yesterday, during the funeral procession. Secondo saw me on the street and asked me to come along, which perhaps I shouldn't have done, but Secondo's very persuasive."

Leah drew back. "No harm in going to the interment. Are you touring Italy?"

"I suppose you could call it that. Just now, I'm looking for the synagogue."

Leah noted how he avoided giving more information about himself. His face had flushed as if he were embarrassed, or, Leah thought, as if he were wary. His eyes shone, but they were dark. Unhappy? or angry? Perhaps sad or lonely? She felt a prickle at the back of her neck.

"Secondo saw me looking at this map." He waved the map in the air, as if to prove that he actually had been looking at it. "And he's promised to take me to the synagogue, plus tell me the story of his search for the silver and gold objects from the synagogue that were lost during the war. He says they're hidden somewhere nearby."

"Oh?" She glanced at Secondo. "He's told you a great deal."

Secondo hunched his shoulders and made fists in excitement. "Yes, and David's interested, very interested."

Leah spoke to Secondo, but looked at Stein. "Just remember, Secondo, it's your story."

Stein held her gaze. "Well, perhaps not his alone."

Leah regarded him carefully, enunciating each word. "Secondo has been searching for years, so I think maybe the search and possible discovery is his—and only his — story."

"I didn't mean to offend you."

"I'm not offended!" Leah spoke more harshly than she intended. "I'm careful. He's my friend—more than you can understand." Her voice was ice.

"You're right to be protective."

"I'm not being protective! Secondo doesn't need protection!"

"Of course." Stein smirked.

"You'll be in town long?" Her voice was steel.

With a small smile, Stein glanced away. "It depends."

Leah pursed her lips in frustration and turned to Secondo. "See you on the trails, Secondo. Be careful."

The two men watched her stalk away toward the bar.

Stein put his hand on Secondo's shoulder. "I think she's a little jealous we're talking."

Secondo beamed. "She's my best friend."

"I see that. I hope I can be one of your best friends too."

Secondo's mouth dropped open. "You do?"

"Yes."

"I saved Leah's life once."

"How did *that* happen?"

Before Stein could finish his sentence, Secondo, beaming with pride, began the story of how when Leah had been in Scansansiano, there had been a murder. Rushing ahead, Secondo told how he had been out for a walk on the trail and had come upon Leah lying in the trail, bleeding and unconscious, with a bullet in her arm. Stein's eyes widened as Secondo recounted how he had run to her, seen the blood, and had been afraid it was her heart, but then saw it was her arm.

"I remembered seeing my mother put a tourniquet on Marcella...."

Stein resisted the temptation to interrupt Secondo's story to ask about his mother and to find out who Marcella was.

"I watched her put it on Marcella, and I did the same thing for Leah. I poked a hole in my shirt and tore it to get a wide piece of cloth, not a thin piece, a thin piece is not good. And then I had to tie it in a place between the wound and Leah's heart. That took me a little while. Then I had to put a stick through the loop of the square knot I tied in the cloth, and I twisted it, a gentle twist. Gentle, not tight. That's how I did it. And I carried her to the bottom of the trail, and then Nick and the others took over, but they should have let *me* carry her all the way because…."

"Because you're the one who saved her! No wonder she's protective of you. You saved her life. But who is Nick?"

Suddenly sad, Secondo's face fell. "Nick is gone, and he can't come back."

As suddenly as Secondo had turned sad, he brightened. "C'mon I want to show you the synagogue."

Chapter Sixteen

Leah walked away from the two men, head down, troubled by the exchange. Approaching the bar, she looked up, pleased to see the Signora standing under a tree near an outside table. The Signora, which was all anyone in town ever called the older woman, was Signora Vianello, a Venetian who had come to the town years earlier and with an attitude of formal distance, was beloved by the Scansansianese and by Leah.

The two stood in the shade of a graceful manna-ash tree. Behind them, where the far side of the valley rose to a hilltop, a broad ribbon of brilliant green grass unfurled toward the north. Thick cumulus clouds had moved in from the western sky, but the sun had broken through, sending a single shaft of light glistening over the field. Leah glanced toward the field as she spoke with the Signora, partially as a way to stave off the tears of grief awakened by direct eye contact with her friend, and partially because the beauty of the scene drew her.

The Signora laid a hand on Leah's arm. "Anna knew how ill she was, Leah, and she didn't want it to drag on. She told me."

When the Signora touched her, Leah smelled the sweet, fresh scent of the older woman's soap as it rose from her wrinkled hands. Leah took a deep breath; it was the same scent her mother had worn on holidays.

"I know, Signora. Thank you for reminding me. She said many times she wanted it to happen fast. I'm just sorry I arrived too late to see her – and for her to see me, to know I was there. But there are other disturbing things as well. There was that strange woman outside Elia's house, and Elia, so distraught over Idrissa."

"And maybe Nick plays a part in your grief? You're just back. You must be flooded with memories."

"Of course, Nick too. I anticipated remembering all the good times. Maybe if Anna...I didn't expect..."

"We never expect. And old wounds can open and bleed when new wounds are made." The Signora shook her head as if to dispel the thought of too many painful, unexpected events in her own past. She changed the subject. "You said a strange woman? A name?"

Leah furrowed her brow, trying to remember what the neighbors called her. "I don't remember what they called her. It began with a 'grrr' sound, I think. She was a big, bosomy bottle-blonde woman, and she tried, literally, to fight her way in to look at Anna. It was strange! She charged the rabbis from Rome like a bull, batting and pushing toward the house. Once she got on the steps, she shoved me and elbowed her way toward the door to get inside.

It's created an aura over the whole funeral for me, as if not only is Anna gone, but everything is askew—and then that strange *American* standing around with Secondo. I feel like I've come to a troubled, darker place than Scansansiano has ever been. Nothing is like it used to be."

"It's probably the aura of the funeral, Leah. Or maybe you're just getting to know us better." The Signora raised her eyebrows.

"Know you better?" Leah looked across the valley again and sighed. "I'm not sure what you mean. My thoughts are jumbled, I guess."

"That's evident," the Signora mumbled.

Leah didn't hear and went on. "The funeral. Our times here, the memories. Nick's suffering all those months. And now, coming back alone. The angers...and that strange American man with Secondo...."

The Signora made a face. "You already said. You're jealous of anyone who gets near Secondo, American or not."

"Of course I am!" The words came harshly, not what Leah intended. Her face reddened, and she lowered her tone. "He saved my life—and he's an innocent, a child. Strangers could take advantage of him."

"Don't concern yourself. None of us know yet why the American is here."

63

Her lips parted in a little smile. "But we will."

Leah laughed. "You mean, *you* will! I thought so."

The Signora tilted her head, hiding the smile on her face. They stood in silence for a moment before she spoke again.

"About the bottle-blonde. Tell me more about the incident at the house."

Leah could see the wheels turning in the Signora's mind. By late afternoon she would have heard several versions of the incident and would have realized who the woman was.

"There's really nothing more to tell. Before the procession, the friends of Elia's from Rome, you know, the rabbis from the Jewish community, were expected at the house. I heard yelling. I opened the door and saw them struggling with this woman. If it hadn't been the day of Anna's funeral, it would have been funny in the realm of dark humor. She was shouting that she wanted in to see Anna. She fought them physically. I've never seen such a powerful woman, and in such a fury."

"As you said."

Leah ignored the comment and rushed on. "She was wind-milling back and forth. People leaned out the windows yelling at her to be quiet, then a crowd gathered, and they were all laughing. It was ludicrous, really—and sad. Magliotti was there, but he didn't do anything."

"Pffft!" The Signora sibilated. "Magliotti would never enter the fray, my dear; he's a bit farouche." The Signora shook her head in disgust. "I've served on various boards and committees with the man. The only thing he gets roiled about is his carpentry."

"He doesn't seem weak."

"I didn't say physically weak. All that hammering and sawing, but he has a mouse's spirit, and socially, he's awkward as a rhinoceros." The Signora waved her hand through the air, dismissing talk of Magliotti. "What happened then?

"Then she broke free, bolted up the steps, and pushed me out of the way. Strong as an ox—it took all my strength to resist her."

"Her name? Try. There are many bottle-blondes."

"A 'grr' something, but the full name didn't register with me. It was chaos, and I was too busy saving myself from falling off the steps. Anyway, she looked familiar; it seems I should have known her, but I couldn't place her. She had a sort of round face, dark skin, obviously in the sun a lot, hair dark at the roots but, like I said, bleached blonde, and ferocious dark eyes.

It was a real struggle to keep her out of the house; her muscles were like rocks. But as soon as I told her the casket was sealed, she stopped fighting, but she kept yelling at me."

Leah imitated her voice. "'Why you?' she screamed, 'You don't even belong here. I'm the one who sweated blood because of her all these years!'" And she was violent, as if she wanted to kill someone.

The Signora tilted her head, emitted a grunt, and started away. Leah put her hand on the Signora's arm to keep her from leaving.

"You know who it is, don't you?"

The Signora made a face. Leah noted how the older woman's hair glistened in the sun, with no trace of roots or gray. The Signora had her own hair professionally dyed in Rome every month; she disdained bottled dye jobs, and she would spot a bad one right off.

"There are many women in town with bleached-blond hair. Where did you say you might have seen her?"

Leah squinted. "You're trying to distract me. I didn't say, but I think near the grocery store, the little one just off the piazza. Or maybe I passed her on the street sometime."

"Why don't you go home and rest; you'll be ill if you don't."

The Signora's abrupt dismissal startled Leah, but knowing the older woman's resolve, she let it pass, kissed her on both cheeks, and stepped into the bar with the vision of the woman fresh in mind.

Chapter Seventeen

That night two men huddled in the dark next to the cemetery wall, listening. When the shorter, heavier one began to fidget with the heavy wire-cutters, the other man hissed and slapped at his hands. "Shhhhh!"

The short one grunted and made a face.

After waiting in silence a few minutes longer, the taller, leaner of the two grabbed the cutters, and the men rose to their feet. The short one held the gate firmly with both hands while the other snipped through the lengths of chain that locked the broad metal gates. The chain clattered to the ground. Propelled by its own weight, the gate squeaked open a few inches.

The tall, muscular man hissed. "Idiot! Why didn't you catch the gate?" He clamped his hand over the other's mouth and tilted his head, listening for footsteps or voices.

There was no sound but the wind in the cypress. He nodded and pushed the gate a narrow span wider and sidled through, followed by the other one, who twisted his torso back and forth like a dog struggling through a fence. On the other side, the tall man slapped the shorter across the back of the head and chided, "Open it wider next time, jerk."

"But the squeak—"

Slap!

They slinked into the heavy shadows along the wall and hovered against the cold stone, hidden from the light of the waxing moon. The smaller man wished he had stayed home in bed, but too cowardly to leave, he cowered like a child beside his taller, muscular comrade whining,

"You sure about this?"

"Idiot!" The taller man put both hands on the other's shoulder and shoved, tumbling the short man backward into the dry grass and dirt.

"Geez! Wha'd do that for? I only meant, last time—"

"Shut up about last time. We came away with jewelry, didn't we? So just shut the fuck up. I wouldn't be here if I weren't sure."

"I heard different about Jews, is all."

He had fallen on nettles that stung his cheek and was rubbing his face vigorously up and down.

"Then leave. Me, I say the Jews bury their dead with fistfuls of it."

"But why would they? Don't they love money and stuff? Why would they bury it? Besides," he puled, "How do you know? Maybe it's just a story. I heard that Leah woman—"

"Listen, Shithead! It's not a story. Forget about Leah. She's not from here. Somebody I know, who's from here, knows—"

"Who?"

The bigger man grinned. "That's for me to know, pussy, and for you to find out. And anyway, I saw them put something in next to her head."

"What did you see? And how'd you see it?"

He burped, and a cloud of stale air emitted from his mouth.

The bigger man jerked back in disgust.

"My god! Buy some mouthwash, for g-d's sake. Your breath stinks like pig shit!"

"I will. I will. But c'mon, tell me. Where'd you see it? What were they doing?" He sneered.

"Sometimes windows are open. Can I help it if I was walking by?"

"You peeked in? What'd they do? C'mon, tell me."

"I only saw the last bit. She was already wrapped up, but when they put her in the box, they put something next to her head and then some other little packet of stuff."

"Jewelry?"

"That's what we're here for, Dumbo; I bet it's diamonds or something."

He glanced in both directions, crouched down, and scurried ahead across a path of moonlight into the shadow of a cypress. Pushing himself against the trunk of the tree, he called over his shoulder in a rough whisper.

"If you're in, follow me. If not, get the hell out."

The shorter one lagged behind for a moment, checked to the right and left, then rushed to catch up, weaving carefully around the heavy stone markers and down the broad terraces of the cemetery toward the freshly filled grave of Elia's wife.

They worked at a frenzied pace, sweating, cursing under their breath, until the shovels tapped the wooden surface of the coffin. The taller man bent low, brushed the lid of the casket clear and, pushing against the sides of the grave, lowered himself. Maneuvering to straddle the casket, he raised his hand for the crowbar and stood with a foot on either side of the wooden frame while he prodded and jabbed at the lid. Once the lid was free, he wrangled it between his legs, shunted it up to the other man, and then hunkered down and shined his flashlight onto the corpse. From beside Anna's head, he took a shiny white object.

"An egg! A fucking egg!"

He threw it violently against the cypress at the edge of the grave.

The other man stifled a laugh.

"Shut your stupid face, or I'll shut it for you." He shook the crowbar at him. "And, anyway, jerk-head, there's something else in a little velvet bag."

He bent and pulled the tiny packet from a fold in the shroud, then holding it up to prove his point, snapped the delicate tie of the packet, and turned the bag upside down over his hand. A delicate river of ashes flowed from the bag into the night air and scattered on the breeze.

"Those damn shysters! They've been cheating us for centuries!"

He threw the crowbar, barely missing the smaller man.

Unaware of any danger to himself, the smaller man had dropped to the ground and was rocking back and forth, slapping his knee, laughing aloud.

"Shut the fuck up!"

The taller one screamed, and, in a fit of sadistic frustration, grabbed the shroud and tumbled Anna from side to side, yelling. "It's got to be here. I know they bury stuff with them!"

Overhead a cloud covered the moon. The shorter man sneaked off toward town.

Chapter Eighteen

Elia discovered the desecration at sun-up.

    After a sleepless night, compelled by loss and seeking the only closeness to Anna available to him, he again broke the traditional custom of shiva, the week-long confinement in the house, and slipped out into the early morning fog before the flow of friends arrived with food and companionship to help him pass the long hours of the day.

As he approached the gate, Elia chastised himself for forgetting it would be locked. He was surprised to find it standing ajar. Careful not to slip in the dim light, he descended to the lower tier of graves, gingerly skirting the gravestones. In this way, he came to the edge of the gaping hole that had been Anna's resting place.

The lid of the casket was broken, its boards in disarray, and the remains of the woman he had loved so dearly were sullied. Smudges of dirt profaned her white skin. Her pristine shroud, now disheveled and dirty, lay tangled around her, and her body huddled against one side of the casket, as if even in death, she had sought safety from the violence being done to her.

Elia's knees gave way. He staggered backward and fell against the cypress tree that rose next to Anna's grave. His hand swiped across the smear of egg. Understanding, Elia turned his head aside and emptied his stomach in the shadow of the branches.

When the nausea passed, he spat the remnants of bile from his mouth, fell back against the earth, and like a wounded animal, opened his mouth in relentless, high-pitched screams.

Gianni, the baker, who had been in his shop since 3 a.m., heard the wild howls. Leaving his bread to burn in the oven, he tore off his apron and cap, rushed down the hill, around the curve of the road, and plunged into the cemetery. He stumbled, picked himself up, and moved downward as fast as he could, weaving in and out the gravestones to the bottom tier. There, he came to the gaping hole, with Elia hovering over it on his knees, wailing in anguish.

Gianni grasped Elia's arms to pull him to his feet, but Elia resisted, weakly batting his hands against Gianni's chest in a vain attempt to push him away.

"I can't leave her," Elia cried.

The baker persisted.

"You've got to come away, Elia. We need help. Please, please come."

Once Elia was standing he quit resisting, and Gianni guided the sobbing man carefully by the elbow to the gate, coaxing him with soothing, compassionate words into the road and up the steep curve and around to the bakery, where he handed Elia into the care of his wife and ran to bring Leah.

Leah stared at the carnage in the ragged hole. She could hear her mother saying: Bad is never good, until worse happens.

Whoever had committed the desecration of Anna's grave had torn the earth away in an animal frenzy, fearing, Leah assumed, they would be discovered. They had scattered shovelfuls of dirt helter-skelter on the other graves, tromped on flowers, and smashed vases.

From the looks of the casket, Leah could see they pounded it open by brute force, spattering Anna with dirt and bits of twigs, leaving the body vulnerable to the night wind and to the mice and voles that lived under the roots of the towering cypress trees. In their savage search, they left Anna's body on its side, dirty fingerprints on her shroud and on her neck and arms where, Leah assumed, they pawed at her in search of jewelry.

Tears wove down Leah's cheeks. What ugly, debased world is this?

Suddenly dizzy, her head reeled, and she fell backward.

Chapter Nineteen

That afternoon, after the Lieutenant had spoken with Elia and Gianni, he interviewed Leah. Her voice was ragged with distress. Tears welled in her eyes.

"I wish I had more to tell you, Lieutenant, but I don't. We wanted to look after Elia first, and we wanted to guard the grave, so after Gianni took Elia to the bakery so his wife could be with him and Gianni could come to get me. I sent Gianni back to the grave and tried to call you, but Signorina MacCleod said you were out on a call, so I went back to the bakery to take Elia home and arranged with the neighbor to sit with him. Then I ran back to the grave to relieve Gianni. I asked him to keep calling you and to bring you as soon as he could. I stayed in the cemetery to make sure no one bothered the—I suppose it has to be called a scene now—and that's where you found me."

The Lieutenant listened intently, regarding Leah without a flicker of his wide chestnut eyes. He leaned toward her to catch every word, running his thumb over his ring finger as he listened. Watching her speak, the old emotions he held for her came back, and he wished he could give her the solace of an embrace.

A gentle man, reserved and proud of his station, the Lieutenant was immaculately dressed and groomed. Born and raised in a poor family of Scilla, he suffered from the prejudices many northern Italians hold against southerners, and his pride was mixed with the reserve and thoughtfulness a hurtful bias sometimes compels in the victim.

He was a man who moved cautiously, with an unflagging attention to detail. A characteristic of self-confidence ameliorated by personal experience of the meaner side of human behavior made him a good policeman. He had the quiet courage to go anywhere, the wisdom to go prudently, and the unfailing moral sense he had learned not only at home, but by the repeated blows of prejudice he had suffered at the hands of ignorant people.

The Lieutenant knew his own qualities, and he was proud of being self-disciplined, but he was unnerved by his attraction to Leah.

As she recounted what she knew about the incident at Anna's grave, Leah noted a shadow of horror flicker across the Lieutenant's face. His reaction elicited a tender yearning in her, and Leah let her gaze rest on his handsome face a moment too long.

Embarrassed, she coughed.

"I know you'll find out who did this, Lieutenant."

The Lieutenant's eyebrows raised.

"Thank you. I appreciate your trust, Signora."

"I've trusted you since the moment I met you, and I promise this time, I'll let you do your work. I won't get involved."

Even as she spoke, Leah knew she was lying.

"Don't make promises you can't keep, Signora." He smiled.

Leah blushed. "Well, I want to let you handle it, but you know that Anna was my dear friend."

The Lieutenant watched Leah pull a handkerchief from her purse. Youthful, beautiful, even with the thin scar that ran along the side of her cheek. He would have liked to touch her hair, to console her. Of course, not on this day. But other times. He silently cursed his steely adherence to his professional code. At the moment, the code felt like ropes around his chest.

The combination of natural shyness and professional reserve cost him the closeness he craved with the few women he had ever desired, and he knew the townspeople of Scansansiano assumed he had a cold temperament and preferred single life to the responsibilities of marriage.

The Lieutenant had not dared inspect his feeling for Leah too closely. To approach her was not appropriate when she had first arrived in Scansansiano with her husband, and now he thought perhaps it was too soon after Nick's death. He also wondered if his feelings were compelled by simple loneliness.

He was attracted to women other than Leah and had feelings of concern and friendship for many of the townspeople of all ages. How could he not? He had been at the center of their lives in the most trying times. He was there when they had been robbed or beaten, when families suffered the loss of a loved one by a road accident, or worse, as had happened when a loved one was murdered.

Leah was part of the mix, he told himself. He was lonely; she was a beautiful woman, now a widow. Their emails from the time she and Nick had left until she returned had been newsy, funny, friendly, and always reserved. Leah and the others could not know his seeming detachment hid a heart congested with emotion and desire, and the Lieutenant carried the niggling sense that they never would know, that he would never be strong enough or articulate enough to let them know.

He felt a sharp stab of longing for Scilla, for his sister, and for his boisterous friends, the young men and women he had laughed with at school.

"Lieutenant, are you okay?"

He shook his head to clear it.

"Sorry. I lost my train of thought. Yes, it's a 'scene,' a crime scene, and you acted appropriately. Sadly, this is not the first desecration of a grave."

"It's not?"

Leah's eyes widened in surprise. She waited for him to explain.

"Lieutenant?"

He cleared his throat.

"Lieutenant? You don't need to tell me—if you can't."

"No, it's not that…there have been others over the years, not here, but in the area."

"But why?"

"Because people are stupid and greedy. They think the bereaved bury their dead with gold and jewels. It's idiotic and ignorant." His words were staccato, bitter.

"It must be awful to see what you have to see."

"Sometimes I wish I could erase my memory. But it's worse for the families. They never get over it."

74

"I'm learning things about Scansansiano I never wanted to learn."

"The more often you come and the longer you stay makes it inevitable. If you live with us, you'll learn the bad as well as the good. It's true in any community. And what about last time? Didn't getting shot by a crazed murderer teach you a few things?"

"Of course. But that was a good, clean sort of violence."

The Lieutenant burst into laughter. "A good clean sort of violence! You've forgotten! You were bleeding out when Secondo found you, and you've forgotten the second attempt on your life later."

"Maybe. It was frightening, but well, it was a murderer. Do you know what I mean? It was the passion of love gone wrong; I never could have imagined the sort of degradation that leads to grave robbery."

"Do you think you'll stay?" The Lieutenant blurted the words and then blushed. The question had jumped from his mouth before he thought.

Leah touched his forearm.

"Don't be embarrassed, Lieutenant. You don't need to tip-toe around me. Nick is gone, and if I haven't yet fully accepted it, I'm in the process. For now, I'm alone and with no firm plans. As for moving here, I've fantasized about it since the first time we came. I've traveled most of my life and lived for years at a time in other countries. And, I admit that the U.S. has become a foreign country to me. But then again, Sara is there and if they have children..."

"You don't seem old enough to be a grandmother."

Leah smiled.

"Thanks, but I think you've kissed the Blarney Stone."

"The what?"

"Nothing...I mean to say I do feel at home here, and at home in Italy, but I also feel at home in the other places I've lived, places where I have friends. I'm not sure I really belong anywhere. The proverb says, 'Love to travel but don't make the road your home.' I guess I didn't learn that, and now I'm stuck with feeling alienated."

"I think," he blushed again and looked away. "I mean, the whole town thinks, you belong here. This could be your home."

"I'm gratified people here care for me that much. I still have hopes I'll find a place I can stay, where I can live and stop traveling."

"If it weren't for hopes, the heart would break.'"

"Lieutenant, you're a poet!"

He straightened his shoulders. "No, it's something my mother used to say."

"I'm surprised your mother read Thomas Fuller."

"She read everything she could get her hands on. All sorts of exotic things."

"'All things are difficult before they are easy.' Did she tell you that one?"

"Care and diligence bring luck." He shot back, but his smile turned to a serious look.

"I have diligence, but I'll need luck solving this. I can't get much from Elia just now, and your story and Gianni's are the same, with little new."

Leah's promise to herself dissipated. "I could help, couldn't I?"

"No!" With a smile on his face, he jabbed a finger at her. "Not again. I know from last time how impetuous you are. No interference, Leah. You've got to understand that. You know how dangerous things can get."

Leah rose and slipped on her jacket. "I'll act with care," she paused, "whatever I do."

"Don't do anything!"

Almost to the door, Leah spun around, "She was my best friend, Lieutenant."

The Lieutenant groaned and watched her disappear into the outer office.

Chapter Twenty

Leah walked back through the piazza to Elia's apartment. The neighbor sitting with him told her that once he took the medication the doctor had prescribed, he fell into a deep sleep and was sleeping still.

Leah left quietly and walked to the piazza bar, where she sloughed off her coat and took a seat at her usual table by the window. The cobblestone walkway that ran past the bar and into the piazza was crowded with housewives rushing to market, their shopping carts rattling along behind them. Leah watched them pass. The few coming home from the market were weighed down by heavy bags and carts.

Balancing a tray, the young barmaid eased around the corner of the bar and approached Leah's table. She gave Leah a hesitant smile. Uncertain about what to say to Leah, she had prepared Leah's usual order and set it in front of her.

"Your usual prosecco and an artichoke tramezzino."

"Thanks, Cinzia. It's just what I wanted," Leah lied.

Smiling, the barmaid stepped back to the cash register where a customer was waiting to pay.

Leah stared out the window, recalling the precise order of what had happened: Elia found the desecrated grave. Gianni, the baker, heard Elia howling and ran to help. Leah pictured it in her mind, envisioning step by step the aftermath of the discovery of the open grave.

It seemed clear, but she wanted to be sure. The Lieutenant would call her back to ask if she remembered more details. Would he be angry that she

77

took Elia home before coming to him herself? He had not mentioned it in the meeting.

"Aren't you going to eat?" The barmaid called across the room, interrupting Leah's thoughts.

Leah stared at the little artichoke sandwich. The bread was spread with a thick layer of mayonnaise on both sides. Leah peeled away the clean-cut layer of crustless white bread and scraped a large dollop of the thick, creamy sauce onto her plate. She glanced up to see the barmaid watching; they both flushed a bright crimson.

"Diet," Leah mouthed. It too was a lie, but she had no desire to hurt the younger woman's feelings.

Appeased, the barmaid nodded. "Don't deny yourself too much, Signora. These are difficult times."

Leah chastised herself silently for not eating the tramezzino as it was.

When she'd finished the sandwich, Leah sipped the prosecco and closed her eyes, glad for the warmth of the autumn sun, augmented by the glass of the window. Customers entering for a snack brushed by with a swish of their coats. Eyes closed, face tilted to the sun, Leah felt them pass in slight puffs of air.

A man from out of town leaned over the bar, pointed at Leah, and asked, "What's with her?"

"The barmaid whispered, "She's just like that, and we love her, so don't get any ideas!"

Leah's thoughts meandered from the vision of Anna's funeral; to the strange, violent woman who wanted to see the corpse; to the desecration of the grave; the Lieutenant's surprisingly gentle interrogation; to a dreamlike memory of the time before the infusion room, before Nick had wasted to skeletal thinness, his face pale, his lips cracked and scaly.

Before cancer.

The phrase seemed to describe another country, the fantasy of a *cuccagna*, place of perpetual joy and plenty where the lazy were king and food fell from the sky, where, in such a fantasy place, worries were nonexistent. If she had known what was coming, she would not have wasted so much time in what now seemed empty pursuits. She would have awakened each day with thanksgiving on her lips. "Would have…"

Chapter Twenty-One

Leah felt a touch on her shoulder. She opened her eyes to see Elia smiling sadly down at her.

"Not how long it was, Leah, but how good it was. True for Nick and now for Anna."

She cleared her throat. "You're right. Yes. But after what's happened… How can you be calm, Elia? The horror of it."

Her gravelly voice brought tears to Elia's eyes. He patted her cheek and indicated the chair next to her.

"May I?"

She nodded.

"I'm glad you're here."

He laid his hat on the table and wiped the palm of his hand over his face.

"I'm not as calm as I seem, but if I don't keep control of myself, I won't make it. The anger feels like acid eating its way through my chest. My grief is all mixed up with Idrissa, Sergio, and for that matter, all the people here.

People know me; they know the Jews. Since centuries they've known the Jews, and still there are those who carry these wicked, intransigent stereotypes and imaginings."

He shook his head slowly from side to side. "Drinking the blood of Christians, horns under our hair, all of us stashing riches in our mattresses, and these horrible imaginings that we bury our dead with gold and jewels. What other idiotic reason could whoever did this have to have done it? Such ignorance is unfathomable… but I know they didn't touch Anna! I've thought about it all night. Outrageous. But they didn't touch Anna!"

Leah was shocked to see how much Elia had aged overnight. Dull, straggly wisps of his once shining gray hair hung at his ears, and his shoulders, usually squared and strong, slumped forward in a deep curve, as if to protect his heart. His gray tweed jacket, rumpled and stained, sagged at his hips, and spots of grease dotted his tie.

"It probably was for the hope of jewels or gold."

"What other reason could there be?"

"I don't know. Someone who wanted to hurt you?"

Elia jerked and turned his head away, whispering, "Who…." His voice faded.

"Who…?"

Elia averted his eyes and reached to rub a spot on the table.

"Never mind. I came because I want to ask you to keep an eye on the apartment and to water my plants. I've decided to go to my sister in New York."

"Of course I'll take care of things. When are you leaving?" Her voice trembled.

"Tonight. I can't stay here, Leah. I can't. After the desecration and this ongoing trouble with Idrissa. I went to Sergio about talking to the council. He won't listen; he thinks I'm overly sensitive. I can't take it."

His face crumpled.

"I'm sorry, Elia. It's selfish of me to want you to stay. Maybe with your sister you can at least have some of the last of the Sukkot holiday with Jewish friends."

"She doesn't do much for the holiday, but I'm sure we'll visit friends and have a meal in the Sukkah."

As if, in that moment, the two of them felt the need for protection, they scooted closer to the table. The pellet stove did little to ease the chill from the room, and the sun had fallen lower in the sky, its rays no longer shining directly through the window.

"Giorgio has offered to drive me to Rome. I fly out at 10."

"Will your sister take you from the airport?"

He smiled. "Once a mother…."

Leah blushed.

"You'll be with her for at least part of Sukkot."

Elia nodded, recognizing both of them were stranded in the stupor of grief."

Leah fell silent, allowing the murmur of the other patrons and the hum of the stove to settle over them for a few minutes before she spoke again.

"I hope there'll be lots of stories from your childhood here in Scansansiano?"

A slight smile hovered on his lips. "Many. From the town, from the synagogue. All the acts of the beauty and bravery of two children, brother, and sister."

"Will you tell me?"

The sudden switch of topic propelled Elia into a lighter state; his smile broadened.

"I've already told them to you!"

"I know there are more."

Elia laughed. "Soap to the body!"

"What?"

"It's a Jewish proverb. As soap is to the body, so laughter is to the soul. In all this horror and grief, you've made me laugh, and I thank you for it. Of course I'll tell you more when I get back; I can see the ideas spinning in your head. Another article?"

"I'm that transparent?"

"You always have been!"

"You're just like my dad."

He took her hands in his and brought them to his lips.

"That's a great compliment."

"I meant it to be...we'll find out who did it, Elia, I promise."

Elia patted her hand. "Such spirit. But I'd rather think you were safe. Don't put yourself in harm's way—not like before, eh? Secondo might not be there a second time. And the Lieutenant couldn't take it if you got hurt again." He shook his finger at her, stood, and took his hat.

Leah wondered at his mention of the Lieutenant.

Elia bent to brush each cheek against hers. "I've got to go. I've got a packet for Secondo. I'd completely forgotten about it. I feel particularly guilty about it; I've had it for a few years and only rediscovered it today, when I was looking for something in the back of a drawer. I'll go to him now, to give it to him and apologize. Then I'll pack. Take care of yourself, Leah, and please, don't put yourself in harm's way."

"Wait...More about Sergio?"

"Sergio is just Sergio. And Idrissa? You saw. Nothing new. Except it's gone from bad to worse. Clients won't bother to walk around Idrissa, and the older women are afraid they'll trip on his blanket. Plus, he makes a hard sell that scares the women. To be truthful, I'm a little afraid of him myself."

"Of Idrissa? It can't be. He's not a violent boy, not really. He's tense because he wants to marry and bring his wife here, but it's expensive."

"Leah, you've been gone awhile. Idrissa is now a man, and he has the emotions and strength of a man.

"I'll talk to him. I'm sorry about Sergio, but from what I hear, you shouldn't expect much."

Elia shook his head sadly.

"I've left the key in the usual place."

He leaned to kiss her on both cheeks.

"Goodbye, Leah."

After he left, Leah wondered what packet he had for Secondo.

Chapter Twenty-Two

Elia and his sister, Rachel, sat in the back of a yellow cab, which was moving slowly through the stream of traffic going uptown from the Lower East Side. They were on their way to the house of one of her clients for a Sukkot party. It was near the end of the holiday, and though Elia knew he was admonished to give up his mourning during the eight days of Sukkot and be joyous in remembering the Exodus from Egypt, grief held too strong a hold. He would go to the party, but he had no spirit for celebration.

"Do you know these people well?"

"Only as clients. It's the first time I've been to their house. Why?"

"Just wondered. It would be nice to meet your friends."

"Later this week, and one or two friends will be there this evening."

"Ah, here's Willet Street." Elia sat up.

Rachel poked his side and pointed. "Now it's called Bialystoker Place, after the synagogue. Remember when we went?"

Rachel made an attempt to divert Elia's thoughts. Shocked by news of the desecration of Anna's grave, she had decided not to mention it, thinking silence may help the horror pass more quickly. She would wait for him to speak first.

"How could I forget? It's only been a few years. Remember? Anna and I went up through the women's galley to that break in the wall where the ladder is?"

"Of course I remember. You two were sneaking around like guilty children." She laughed.

"We didn't know if we were allowed. Anna was nervous as a mouse. She had such a strong sense of property."

"And propriety."

"I used to tease her about it."

He smiled.

Rachel shook her head.

"She needn't have worried. Everyone goes up; they want to see where the Underground Railroad was."

"The Underground Railroad?"

"Didn't you read any of the material they gave you?"

Elia shook his head.

"How unlike you." She scowled.

They rode on in silence. Rachel leaned against him and slipped her arm through his. She held him close, thankful she could give him respite.

The apartment overlooked Central Park. Their hosts, the Scarpes, greeted them at the doorway with warm smiles and ushered them into a large living room where other guests chatted in scattered groups, drinks in hand. A waitress with a tray wove her way through the room, while other guests milled about the room and on and off the broad terrace where the sukkah covered a large table set with china.

Comfortably furnished with overstuffed couches and chairs in deep, rich purples and blues, the living room bespoke great wealth. In the center of a glass coffee table sat a fragment of sculptural decoration in marble. Elia thought it looked like it could be the work of Agostino da Duccio, but could not imagine how these people, even as wealthy as they appeared, could have acquired a Duccio piece against the strict laws of removing such things from Italy. The walls of the apartment were hung with minor, but original, works of art: Matisse, Van Gogh, a small Picasso, and a strange sculpture by Dali that Elia could not identify.

He thought of his and Anna's modest apartment in Scansansiano. Anna would have appreciated this home with unenvious delight.

When Rachel ambled off to greet friends, Signora Scarpe, a tall, thin woman with wavy black hair and the dignified carriage of a Venetian, took Elia by the arm and guided him from one couple to another, introducing him to each in turn.

When she was called to the kitchen to see about the food, Elia excused himself and wandered alone from painting to painting, enjoying the relaxed luxury until the hostess invited the guests to come to the table in the sukkah. He rushed off to wash before the dinner.

Out of the bathroom, he turned to look behind him down the long, darkened hallway. To the right there was a bedroom door partially open, and in the dusky light he could see that on the walls were other works of art. For a better look at the artwork on the walls, Elia took a few steps past the bedroom, from which he could hear two people talking.

Suddenly, with a loud gasp, he pitched backward. Anger burned bright red across his face; he felt nauseous and woozy. When Rachel called from the living room, he swung round in a furious spin, stalked past her, and rushed out the front door.

Confused and embarrassed by his rude behavior, Rachel trailed behind, stopping with her hand on the doorknob to stammer to the hostess. "Forgive us. I think my brother must be ill."

In the taxi, seeing Elia was not ill, she flushed, furious at his behavior. "How could you be so rude? They're my clients."

"I know who did it! I know who it is! He'll pay for this! I swear he'll pay!"

"For what?"

Elia refused to speak.

In Rachel's apartment, he ignored her angry questions, brought up the Internet, and bought a ticket for Rome. Her anger gave way to fear. She pleaded with him to explain, but he said nothing, only paced the living room, muttering and breathing in short angry bursts, his hands balled into fists.

Chapter Twenty-Three

Secondo sat in his apartment looking out over the valley and, directly below him, the people coming and going to and from the piazza. He sank into the overstuffed chair and pulled mindlessly at the dusty tufts of stuffing that poked out of a tear on the armrest.

The only chair he had, the bulky piece of furniture stuck out into the room, compelling him to maneuver around it each time he crossed to the tiny galley kitchen or beyond to the bathroom, or to his narrow bed, which sat neatly made in the hallway. The chair had been his mother's. The thick cushions and back were comfortable, and as she had done, he sometimes sat for hours to watch the clouds or rain, or he leaned forward against the window sill to gaze at the river flowing gently toward far below on its way to the sea.

He lifted his glass of tea and took a sip. Of the many cups of tea he drank each day, this was the one in which he allowed himself honey and lemon. He drank it slowly, holding it wrapped in a handkerchief to retain the heat. He relished the warmth it gave against the chilly fall weather and the dead cold of the apartment.

Secondo tried to concentrate. For years, he had been looking for the treasures from the synagogue the older people said were squirreled away during the war. Nothing stopped his search. In the rain, in the snow, or on the sunny, muggy days of summer when flies buzzed around his head and sweat trickled down his chest, he searched the ancient Etruscan trails and caves. Even fear of vipers or of *cinghiali*, the wild boars with their long snouts and sharp tusks, did not deter him. His dream of finding the treasures urged him, obsessively, to continue looking.

His grandfather had spoken many times about the treasures—the Torah dressing in intricate silver and gold, the crown, the sash, the mantle, the pointer—certain they were in one of the caves along the trails that threaded the thick forests outside town. While Secondo's grandfather still lived, he would often finish his work at the synagogue early, and he and Secondo would scour the trails and side paths, poking through the thick brush, looking for the one cave, out of sight and reach of the Germans, that might have been a refuge for the ritual objects. His grandfather's dream had been to restore the treasures to the Jews, who had given him work when he badly needed it. Secondo embraced the dream himself after his grandfather died.

Secondo picked up the photos of the silver crowning attachments and of the breastplate of the Torah scroll. They had to be somewhere close by.

His thoughts turned from the treasure back to the letter Signor Elia had given him, the letter he had been trying to ignore since he first opened it.

He formulated the question with difficulty. Why was his grandfather not his real grandfather?

He sipped his tea, struggling to think under the influence of his medication, which he had begun taking again after stopping for several weeks. Unlike the roiled brain of his bipolar mind without medicine, his thoughts, under the influence of the pills, slowed and meandered, moving languidly through his head, plodding along narrow trails of thought. Arriving at a fork in the trail, his mind would trudge off in a new direction.

The process was the same, only faster, when he went off medication. Hypomania, or worse, mania itself, sent him reeling forward as if some invisible being behind were shoving him along his way, ramping up his thoughts. Barely able to keep balance, he bolted ahead, only to be thrown from depression to the heights: he sang, laughed, talked without cease to others or to himself.

Those were the days and nights the illness compelled him outdoors, in all weathers, to bolt up the trails that scored the sides of the valley, to wander through the piazza singing, or to stand, dancing from one foot to the other outside the bar, diving into conversation with anyone who stepped out and would stand for a while to listen to his pressured speech.

After nights of torment, finally blessed by a tinge of fatigue, he slept on the bench in the little piazza below the synagogue. There, in the broad bowl of a sky sprinkled with stars, he found the only shred of calm he could know in the chaos of mania.

Thinking on this, he set his glass of tea on the little table and took up the letter once again. He read it through for the third time. Even at this reading, his mother's handwriting elicited a painful yearning; and as he read, tears dropped from his eyes anew, just as they had on the first readings.

Secondo cried not because the letter said that the man who spoke so gently to him and let him watch as he patiently repaired woodwork or built new benches or fashioned a new cabinet for the Torah scrolls could not be his real grandfather. Rather Secondo cried because he missed his mother, and he wished she were with him to explain to him what had happened, even though it was all explained in the letter. He wanted to hear the story from her own lips, to ask questions, and, most of all, he wanted her to tell him what to do.

Could he still visit his grandfather's grave—or the grave he had known as his grandfather's? Could he still love him? He loved him so much. Did he now have to search for another family? And how would he do it? How could he ever find them? And even if he could travel and had the money to travel, how could he find someone in such a large place as a whole country, with hundreds of cities? And would that family want, as Secondo knew he was, a mental case for a relative?

Why had his mother given the letter to Elia? Why didn't she tell him while she lived? And why hadn't Elia given it to him sooner? The date on the letter was from long ago.

"I'm angry!" He jolted to his feet and yelled into the cold air of the apartment. "It was mean and evil to keep my letter! Mean! I hate you, Elia!"

The tears flowed. It was mean and bad that Elia had forgotten to give him the letter, yet Secondo wished he had never seen it.

He laid it beside the glass of tea. A look of determination crossed his face.

"I am a street sweeper," he said aloud, "Even if people I love don't tell me things; even if I get mad; if I can sweep streets, I can do anything."

He took his jacket from the back of the chair and headed for the trails to search for the lost synagogue treasure. Searching would help him think.

Chapter Twenty-Four

A few hours after Secondo had left his apartment, Leah too sought the solace of the trails. Below town, she crossed the bridge and stopped, undecided. To the left was Via Cava San Tomas. Straight up the highway and a quick dip down through the ditch and up again was the entrance to Via Cava Santa Maria.

She glanced from left to right and back again. A soft breeze played with the scarf at her neck, and a late-September sun wrapped around her shoulders and arms. Contrary to what Nick had called her "squirrel quality," she stood motionless, head tilted to take the sun full on her face.

On the return flight to Scansansiano, she had begun taking notes on an article about the local food for her editor, Melanie. After Nick's death, work had become her way of clearing a path forward. In work, she could divert her attention to the living, to the many ways humans manifest their creativity. She could sidestep grief and forget for a few minutes the gray wasteland of loss.

She was here, surrounded by Scansansiano's beautiful countryside, enveloped by the warm fall sun. For the space of the walk, she would concentrate on the grave robbery, the woman at Elia's, and the aura of secrecy that spread like a cloud through the town.

Later, among friends in Scansansiano, she could recall the details of her life in what had been among the happiest of times. She could wander with them through the past, where Nick was healthy and laughing and Anna was alive. She could elicit those memories to balance the images of his last days at home, when he was moving so fast toward the other world she couldn't keep up. And she would dive into the current situations in Scansansiano to be one of the community, not just a grieving widow and friend.

Arms dangling at her sides, she willed herself to stand still, to stop imagining Anna and Nick back, if only for a little. By the sun, the trees, the trails, the birds, she would block memories of other pain and loss as they entered her mind.

Anyone passing on the highway would have seen a woman nearing forty, standing in a little field beside the road in a languid stance, lost in thought. Her body appeared relaxed, but, unseen, her thoughts traveled in many directions through the great muchness of life, including the painful, perplexing events she had witnessed since her return to Scansansiano.

If it weren't for the asphalt road that led to and from town, empty for the moment but soon to be busy with traffic, Leah would have forgotten her hike to lie on the grassy spot below, by the River Beta, which flowed in lazy twists to join another, larger river, and then another, down to the Tyrrhenian Sea.

But she had a thing to do: untangle the snarled skein of the last days' events.

What was the thread running through it all that would make sense of what appeared to be separate events? She heard the rattle of a rock underfoot and looked up. Secondo appeared from the bend at the mouth of the trail. He waved, but his usual smile was missing.

"Secondo, hello!"

She thought of the day Secondo found her bleeding on the trail. Step by step, following an incident in which he had seen his mother set a tourniquet and then had seen the process again on a television program, he had fashioned a tourniquet from sticks and strips torn from his shirt, then carried her to the end of the trail for help. In the hospital and after, she came to know that although he lived hampered by a chemical imbalance and was socially quirky, he was an astute observer, capable of more than he was given credit.

He stopped a few feet in front of her.

"I've been looking."

Leah noted that his voice was angry, his face set.

"What's wrong? You look angry. Is it the American?"

"You're just saying that because you don't like him! He just couldn't come today. Well, I don't like Elia! And besides, none of it matters, someday I'll find them," he made an abrupt move to the left and slipped past her.

Dumbfounded by his angry words, Leah watched him stride up the berm to the highway, talking to himself.

"No one can stop me. Whoever…grandfather…and he better not keep my stuff…."

"Wait!" Leah called, but Secondo ignored her and continued up the hill in his awkward gait, one foot on the pavement, the other on the grassy berm.

Her calm broken, she turned toward the first of the trails. A long, gentle path, it wove a sinuous thread upward, wending through the sheer tufa walls like a high hallway through the forest, no wider than arms' length on both sides.

She would take the steeper trail another day, when she craved the challenge of a rough hike. Unkempt, rarely traveled, the steeper was a trail scattered with boulders that had plummeted from the tops of the tufa walls. An arduous climb, it leveled on the ridge above, provided broad, beautiful vistas, and ended conveniently near Rocellini's winery, where she could sit in the sun and drink a chilled glass of white wine.

Tempting. But as she thought of the trail's cracked and crumbling walls where fissures had widened in great spans sending boulders crashing to the trail floor, she decided against it and let it go. Too lazy today to clamor over the giant rocks, scramble up the initial steep incline, and fight the vines that had crept in and twisted around the boulders as the years passed, she let it go.

As far as Leah knew, she had been the only one to hike the higher trail in many years, and she felt certain when she did decide to walk it, it would be as deserted as ever. Like an abandoned house in the countryside, it held a certain mystery, and she took pleasure in being the only one to walk it. It was as good as hers; she could wait until another day when she felt more energetic.

Leah headed out, maintaining a quick pace, taking pleasure in the exertion of the gentle uphill climb, the cool enclosure of the walls, the dancing flecks of sunlight through the leaves, and the faint rustle created by the bows of holm oak and vine that dangled earthward from the rim of the walls. She relished the flutter of fear along her limbs that she always felt in the solitude of the trails.

As she walked, she mulled over what had happened since her return: Secondo's precipitous leaving just minutes before, Anna's death and funeral, the strange woman pushing at the door of Elia's house, the grave robbers, Elia gone to New York.

These events came back now in a flood of prescient warnings.

She recalled how, on her first trip to Scansansiano, she had come to these trails to take photos and had inadvertently photographed a murder, a quick shove off a cliff. The murderer had seen her, and now, moving along the trail, her heartbeat rose as she envisioned the memory of herself sprinting down the trail with the killer pounding relentlessly after her, only yards behind. Bursting onto one of the grassy openings, she had lunged down a dromos, one of the sunken passages that led into a burial cave, where she crouched under a rock ledge in a fetal position, swallowing hard to stifle the gorge that rose in her throat.

That moment she had heard the doglike panting of the killer as he stepped into the cave.

Nauseous, terrified, she had felt a crazy urge to laugh at the absurdity of it all: the impossibility that a one-second click of a camera, a million-in-one coincidence, would be the cause of her death, with no chance to say goodbye.

Leah's adrenaline rose at the memory of that flight from the killer, how she had narrowly escaped. Her thoughts skipped from the horrifying memory of the murder to the joyous wedding of her daughter and son-in-law, celebrated just days after the second attempt on her life.

The mélange life tenders to us all. She took a deep breath and filled her senses and lungs with the warm golden air and the fecund odor of foliage and fall leaves.

The encounter with Secondo gnawed at her. They were the best of friends.

Why was he evading her? What had he meant about not keeping his things? About his grandfather?

Chapter Twenty-Five

While Leah walked, the Signora sat in her usual place in the town library. Along the walls behind the stacks, space heaters poured shimmering waves of heat into the cavernous rooms. Forward, two of the mid-day patrons slumped in their seats, books slowly sliding from their laps toward the floor.

At the back of the library stacks, the Signora held a book on her lap, but it lay unread. Heat blasted from the radiators sending waves of dusty air throughout the room, making it impossible for the Signora to concentrate.

"What fool turned on the heat this early in the year?" she muttered.

She grabbed her purse and rummaged through it until she found a pen and a small pad of paper. Balancing the purse on her knees with the paper on top, she scratched an acerbic note to the library custodian and resumed reading.

Within minutes, the soporific effect of the heat took its toll, and her eyelids began to droop. When her head pitched heavily forward between her shoulders, she started and jerked awake, shaking her head in quick little movements. A shiver ran up her spine. She looked around the room to make sure no one noticed she had fallen asleep. The other patrons were busy with their books, so gratified no one had seen her, she settled back in her seat.

In the next instant, she became aware of two men sniggering on the other side of the stacks.

"Stubborn old Jew. You should have pushed him harder; maybe a fall would have knocked a little sense into him."

"He has plenty of sense. He's filthy rich; I'm sure of it."

96

Hands on the sides of the chair, the Signora eased herself out of her seat and sidled next to the stacks. The men were hidden behind a row of coffee-table books.

Donated by a long-dead citizen of the town, who had traveled extensively and returned from each trip with stacks of large-format picture books, the librarian had initially scoffed at the man's yearly donation of books. He had smiled without rancor and quietly responded, "Few of our children can travel; at least let them see the world with their eyes so they can dream of places beyond. Maybe their dreams will become a reality, and they'll bring new thoughts home to Scansansiano."

Hands on the edge of the shelf, the Signora smiled at the memory of the old man and was now happy for her own reasons about the big books. She rose quietly and tiptoed to the stacks, stretching as far as she could to catch a glimpse of the men who were talking. It was useless; she was too short to look over the books. Undeterred, she bent to peer through the shelf below, hidden at the lower shelf. She could see the bottom halves of the men's jackets.

"If he is rich, he didn't put any of it in his wife's casket, did he!" One snorted.

There was the sound of a slap.

"Idiot."

"Whadja do that for? Everybody knows what happened."

"You're a god-damned cretin; I don't know why I put up with you!"

The Signora felt a tickle in her nose and clamped her hand over her mouth to stifle a sneeze. A mouse-like squeak escaped her lips. She stepped quickly back to her chair, eased into the seat, and by the time she sensed the men peeking around the corner, her head was on her chest, and she was breathing evenly in a feigned sleep.

"Look at the old biddy. Musta been her snoring."

The Signora's hearing was exceptionally good, and she suppressed a smile. As soon as the men shuffled back behind the stacks, she stood and resumed her position peeking through the shelves of coffee-table books.

A little prayer of thankfulness wafted through her mind. How glorious to be old! She had been aware for many years that as she aged, people paid her no more attention than they would a lamppost or a chair, as if her age cloaked her in an invisible shield. Ignored and unnoticed by others, she heard and saw all sorts of private things about people that, as a young person, she had never imagined possible, and at her age, she had happily capitalized on this societal blindness.

During the economic slump, her age had become a particularly fruitful asset to business. Renovating a house she owned in the country for a bed and breakfast may have appeared to others to be a mistake, but following a thread of general gossip she overheard in the theater, she discovered that the most popular bed and breakfast in the area was closing because the owners were divorcing. She managed to approach the owners discreetly about buying the property. She promised to take the reservations of the summer customers off the couple's hands and offered the unfortunate pair half the deposits. Somewhat shocked she knew their situation, but happy to make the sale, they readily agreed.

"I'm glad to help," she had said.

The purchase of the bed and breakfast had been a risk, of course, but the Signora had done her homework. The couple's business had thrived for over a decade. The Signora trusted her hunch, and followed her instinct. It paid off handsomely for all three. The wife returned to Rome with ample funds; the husband had money to make the necessary repairs on the house before the sale, and the Signora acquired a thriving business. If she were a busybody, it was justified. Begun in gossip, the sale had been to everyone's profit.

She strained to hear what the men were saying and caught words that took a dark, horrible shape in her mind. Her mind reeled, and she was dismayed to think these men could be the acquaintances from the council that she thought they were,. It would be difficult to make sure.

Chapter Twenty-Six

Back from her hike, Leah showered and headed to the pharmacy to pick up vitamins and continue from there to meet the Signora at the bar. The Signora had phoned to say she had something to tell her, something she had overheard.

Just as she closed the heavy glass door of the pharmacy behind her on the way out, Leah heard a shout. She swung around to see a large woman raising a metal pail over the head of a man cowering at her feet.

Leah ran toward them. It was the same woman who had tried to enter Elia's house the morning of the funeral. Her shouts, clear and deep as a man's, pierced the air like nails.

"Stop moping and whining! She's dead! Dead! And I wish you were with her. You and Elia! Both of you!"

The man cowered in front of her, arms crossed in the air above his bowed head to protect himself from the blows the woman was raining down on him with the rhythm of a pile driver.

When the pail crashed into his elbow, he emitted an animal howl and begged, "Please, Grazia, please."

"Please? Please what, Salvatore? Thank you that I've lived a lifetime in the shadow of that woman? Or smile because you've used me, always thinking of her? I could kill you with my bare hands! Both of you. Dead. What a stupid, empty woman I am!"

"Everybody's looking, Grazia," he whined.

"Let them look, you bastard! Everybody knows! They've been looking at us, gossiping about us for years." She made a half pirouette and spread her arm in a wide gesture toward the crowd that had gathered around them. "Look at them! They can't help but know, given the way you stared pathetically every time you were within sight of her. The way I know you sobbed and blubbered at the burial. What? Surprised? I know it all. The gossip gets to me too. I eat it. I drink it. You and Anna. It's my only sustenance since"—she pounded him rhythmically with the bucket, enunciating each word— "since...we...were...young! Decades, Salvatore, decades!"

Leah rushed toward them. "Signora, please!"

Grazia ignored her, continuing to strike the man with staccato strokes. "You!....Elia!....Anna!...Anna!....Anna!"

Salvatore emitted a sharp cry at each strike.

Leah tried unsuccessfully to grasp Grazia's arm and shouted at the people standing nearby watching.

"Help me, dammit! Help me!"

Excepting a few, who called to Grazia to stop and go home, the motley group of men and women who had come from the bar and stores surrounding the piazza made no move to help. Some laughed, others chatted amongst themselves as if they had met at a fair.

Among the motley group that had gathered were the voyeuristic, those who had suffered unspoken betrayals themselves. Grazia's public beating of her husband reflected their own secret desires to wield a weapon against their own spouses. Others, more guarded, who happened on the scene, glanced surreptitiously toward the couple, walking slowly in order to absorb every detail for later gossip while trying to appear not to notice as they passed by.

Leah moved behind Grazia and caught her arm on the upswing, but Grazia twisted out of her grasp and whirled about to face her.

"Go away, Bitch! What business is this of yours? You and your precious Elia! Your precious Anna. I'll kill you and them."

She slammed the bucket at Leah, who jumped back just as the bucket wheeled past her face. Grazia twisted and struck at her again, again missing by only inches. Frustrated, she turned back toward Salvatore.

100

Leah moved in again, but before she could catch Grazia's arm, Grazia swung the bucket in a powerful, wide arc, slamming it once more into the side of Salvatore's head. He sprawled across the paving stones and rolled into a fetal position. Blood from the cuts on his face and head pooled onto the stones of the piazza.

Suddenly the Lieutenant appeared. He pushed his way through the crowd of onlookers, stepped in front of Leah, and grasped Grazia's arm roughly from behind. The bucket flew from her hand and juddered across the piazza. In one swift movement, the Lieutenant pulled Grazia's other hand down and cuffed her.

Grazia screamed. "Let me go! He deserves this, and Elia deserves worse! I'll kill him with my own hands! You know the truth, Lieutenant! You know it!"

She stumbled against him, forcing them both backward. The Lieutenant fell to the ground with a loud grunt, Grazia on top of him. Some in the crowd roared with laughter.

The Lieutenant shoved Grazia to the side and stood, his face bright red. He brushed his uniform then bent and took Grazia's arm, pulling her to her feet.

Leah could not have expected what happened next, and she silently praised the Lieutenant.

Upright, ignoring the crowd, Grazia slumped against the Lieutenant, sobbing in loud gasps of breath. Ruffled by the breeze from the valley, her hair spiraled from her head, Medusa's snakes. Mucus streamed from her nose, and she sucked it in with a loud intake, tilting her head against her shoulder in an attempt to wipe away her tears. With one last burst of fading energy, she clung to the Lieutenant and yelled at the crowd.

"They hurt me! Don't you understand; they hurt me! They've been hurting me for years."

She turned her face away, and in an exhausted hiss only Leah and the Lieutenant could hear, spat the words: "I'll kill them, all of them. And you too," she looked toward Leah."

Unable to support her broad weight any longer, the Lieutenant eased her to the ground, her hands at an awkward angle behind. Her flowered housedress fluttered in the wind, revealing thick, vein-ridden calves.

The Lieutenant hunkered beside her and turned his face to bark at the crowd.

"This is not a sideshow! Move along!"

They sauntered slowly away, some laughing, others already retelling the scene, elaborating, exaggerating in the way all humans have with gossip and stories.

When they had moved off, the Lieutenant took Grazia's chin in his hand, compelling her to look into his eyes. "Okay, Grazia? Can I take off the cuffs? Can you control yourself?"

With a tenderness that surprised Leah, he pushed Grazia's hair away from her face with his other hand as he spoke.

"You need to go home, Grazia, and take Salvatore with you."

At his words, she cried harder and leaned against him, susceptible to his kindness. Like a balloon, her body sagged and deflated, and her dress ruckled like a parachute around her. At his words, she cried harder, leaning against him.

The Lieutenant released the cuffs and laid his arm over her shoulder, waving away the few stragglers that had lagged behind to stare.

"I said go on about your business. Go on!"

Leah watched from near the fountain until Grazia lifted her head and, with the Lieutenant's help, hoisted herself to her feet. Once upright, she stepped back, looked the Lieutenant straight in the eye, and thanked him. With a sigh, she reached her hand to Salvatore, who still hovered on the ground, afraid of what she might do next.

But he took her hand, and she pulled him up. Averting his face from the Lieutenant and Leah, he dusted himself off, stopping to pat his facial wounds with a dirty handkerchief when the blood dripped down his nose.

Leah and the Lieutenant stood side by side as the couple walked slowly toward the entrance to the piazza, where they clambered into their car and drove away.

When the car was out of sight, Leah asked, "What was that?"

CHAPTER TWENTY-SIX

"It's a family thing."

She ignored his attempt to evade her question. "But what family thing? And how is it tied to Anna and Elia?"

The Lieutenant shook his head in quick little back-and-forth gestures.

Leah blushed. "I shouldn't have asked. I'm sorry."

He nodded. "Yes, better to let it be. I get called in on a lot of things, so I know details I wish I didn't. Knowing intimate things about families is part of the job. I can tell you only that, like so many things, it has to do with the complications of love."

The Lieutenant's voice burned with anger: "Love and selfishness." He shook his head again.

"But, the violence—"

"Grazia's strong as an ox; I've seen her rages before, but they're getting worse."

"And her threats?"

"This is the worst I've heard. And now she's threatening you as well. It must be from the incident at the house. There wasn't anything else, was there?"

"No, nothing.

Chapter Twenty-Seven

The following morning, Leah sat inside the bar at her usual table by the window. Still shaken by the incident with Grazia, she felt a sense of foreboding about whatever it was the Signora wanted to tell her. She sipped her coffee and stared through the window. Outside, women rushed through the rain toward the market, pulling their carts behind them.

The Signora stepped through the doorway, turned, and stretched her arm back out the door to shake the rain from the extended umbrella. Satisfied, she brought it back inside, clicked the button to close it, then slid it carefully into the umbrella stand before taking a chair at Leah's table.

"How are you holding up?" she asked without a greeting. "All you've had, and now this incident with Grazia."

"Sometimes I think life is best when there are troubles, Signora. It's like a challenge, but I wish I could choose my troubles rather than have them thrown at me."

"Doesn't everyone!"

"Anyway, I'm more perplexed about the 'aura' here in town than I am discouraged. You know me, I bounce back. At least I now know who the woman at Elia's was, and I can guess a little of her story, if not all of it. Can you tell me more?"

"Grazia. I could tell you more of the story, but I won't today."

"Why? She's threatened to kill Elia and her husband, Salvatore. And now me. Doesn't that make it ok for me to know more?"

"I'm halfway to thinking she would be justified—I mean to kill Salvatore and Elia, not you."

"You're so frustrating! Why won't you tell me?"

"There's no reason to tell you right now. One thing at a time. I have something else to tell you today since we're both working on the grave robbery. For the rest, you'll have to wait."

"How can I understand anything if I do nothing but wait? I want to act and not...."

"Think?"

"No! Of course I want to think, but I need material to think on. You won't talk, and the Lieutenant's always chastising me and won't tell me anything either.

"That's the way of a man protective of someone with whom he's in love, but can't find the courage to admit it."

Leah's head jerked up and she waved her hand through the air.

"Don't be ridiculous! Everything I do makes him upset or angry with me. I wouldn't call that love. And besides, there's Signorina MacCleod with her red hair and bombshell body. I can't believe she was hired for her secretarial skills alone."

"Ohhhhhh. Jealousy! A sure indication of love – or at least an interest. And my dear Leah, you don't know Signorina MacCleod at all. Her 'bombshell body,' as you so crudely put it, is paired with a very fine mind."

She gave Leah a look of disappointment.

"Youth really is wasted on the young."

"And wisdom is wasted on the old. And anyway, I'm not that young! And I'm not jealous! Or in love."

The Signora smiled, rolled her eyes, and patted Leah's hand. A rejoinder rose to Leah's lips, but she swallowed it. She did not want to get further entangled in her jumbled feelings about the Lieutenant.

The Signora signaled the waitress for coffee; Leah sipped from the cup in front of her, and they lapsed into a tender silence.

Outside, the rain stopped, and the sun broke through the clouds. Leah spotted a wide patch of perfect blue to the southwest.

"Let's let our disagreements go. I want to hear what you have to tell me.

I've thought and thought about what's been happening. Things weren't right when I arrived. Not just Anna's death, but a whole range of what seemed to be unconnected: Anna's death, Grazia's strange outburst at Elia's, and then that fracas in the piazza with Salvatore, the grave robbed, Elia's anger, Idrissa's outburst, Secondo's odd snub on the trail – I didn't tell you about that one—and that American, doing who knows what. All of it, besides you, now hinting about mysterious things you overheard in the library. Help me out, Signora."

"As I've told you before, you're just beginning to understand that every community has a dark side, as well as a peaceful one. You must think outside the box, like the businessmen say. You've been gone, and now you're back. You've changed. People here have changed, circumstances have changed. You can't help but be blinded by what still must be a heavy grief over Anna—and then remembering the times you and Nick had here. Am I right?"

Leah hesitated.

"You're right. Nick's gone, but I still have a relationship with him, and I guess I haven't yet learned how to fit that relationship and those memories into my life as a widow, especially here, where we had some of the best of our experiences.

I admit memories may obscure my vision. Still, I don't think confusion is all just in my mind. There's an aura here. I know there's a darker side to the town. There have always been adulteries, physical abuse, even the murder when I was here before, but I didn't know there was this perversity. Grave robbery, for God's sake!! And antisemitism, and a good, sturdy farm woman wielding a bucket in the middle of the piazza threatening to kill three people! It feels like some miasma of secrets and violence wafted in from Hell. Maybe not all these things are not directly connected, but I'm curious to know if they are—or at least if some of them are."

"You are an innocent!" The Signora laughed. "For you, it should still be the romantic village life of Italy, yes? I'm sorry, my dear, but I repeat: we are as good—and as bad—as people anywhere. Painful, but true. And you are particularly naïve for a woman you age, and you should remember that curiosity killed the cat."

Leah could not let it go. "But when I was here before: the murder on the trail. It was someone not from here, and now...."

Shaking her head back and forth, the Signora laughed again. "Oh dear."

Leah managed a weak smile. "Nick used to say naïveté was my strength—and my weakness."

"Nick was right about many things."

"And I should have listened more often, you mean?"

"He loved you as you were."

Leah felt tears welling in her eyes. She changed the subject to protect herself.

"Tell me what you heard."

"Yes. The library. But first, I want to give you a little history.

Chapter Twenty-Eight

"I t's a long story." The Signora watched for Leah's reaction.

"I don't have anywhere to go."

"Alright. Napoleon caused trouble."

"Napolean?" Leah grunted in surprise.

"Do you want to listen or not??

"Sorry. I do want to listen."

The Signora scooted back in her seat and stared out the window as if she could see Napoleon standing outside the bar.

"It was thinking about Napolean that I began to understand. We, I mean we Venetians, the nobility, that is…."

Leah smiled. Everyone knew the Signora came of noble Venetian stock and liked to remind people.

"We held back, and *La petit caporal* did whatever he wanted. We did make a weak effort at diplomacy, but when that failed, we simply accepted the incredible surrender conditions. The shopkeepers knew better. They tried to defend the city, but they were massacred by cannon fire from Rialto."

She sighed and shook her head, as if she had seen the event herself. "Then we were given to the Austrians. They weren't so bad. They played music and put up beautifully forged iron lamps."

"What has Venice got to do with Scansansiano?" Leah interrupted.

"Are you going to listen or talk?" With a little shake of her head, the Signora pursed her lips.

"Sorry." Leah blushed.

"Listening is a creative force, Leah. And you should do it with the will to learn."

"Sorry."

The Signora wiggled in her seat, made a face, and continued without acknowledging Leah's apology. "Alright. Here in Scansansiano, everything was different—and it still is. We're contadini here—"

"As you just pointed out, you're hardly a peasant, Signora."

"Again, you interrupt! And don't be silly! Of course, I'm not a contadina. I'm trying to make a point: When you think of Scansansiano at the time, you must think of the general aura of the town. Almost everyone depended on farming, and the same is true today. Even if someone like myself doesn't farm, I am part of the community. Now let me speak!"

Irritated, she gave another little shake of her head. The gesture reminded Leah of a wind-up toy, a little dog that shook its head when you twisted the handle.

"Where was I?"

"You were talking about Napoleon and how Scansansiano was a small town."

"Yes, well, in small towns, there was little distinction between the farmers and the townspeople. Everyone lived close to everyone else, and people were either supplying or buying from each other. Contadini were more than three-quarters of the population, unspeakably poor—oh dear! Just ineffably poor, and very religious. They wanted change, but they also clung to their traditions and their way of life and wouldn't hear of giving up their culture. The Catholic Church—which wielded so much power and, I believe, perpetuated superstitions—didn't like the French because they saw the French as immoral, against God. Anyway, it was all very different here than in France, and people revolted, not everywhere; nothing organized nationally, but spots of revolt.

Then there were the Jews. Napoleon gave them a certain freedom; he liberated the ghettos and gave them equal citizenship—here as he did in Venice. No more red hats, or yellow stars, or whatever badges Jews had been forced to wear—although in Scansansiano, they had stopped wearing them before Napolean anyway, and nobody cared. I think here it was Pietro

Leopoldo, or anyway somebody like him, who changed the badge business. He appreciated the Jews. In the 1780s, there was even a Jew on the town council.

But that's neither here nor there, and I've forgotten some of the details, but I think I'm getting it mainly straight. The Jews were happy about getting out of the ghettos, but that didn't mean all of them were pro-French. Part of the problem was that people assumed they were pro-French, and of course the Church had been talking against the Jews for millennia. All the standard, unfounded prejudices: Jews were rich, Jews were Christ killers, Jews were this, Jews were that. Ignorant stupidity!!"

She waved her hand through the air in disgust.

Leah shifted in her seat.

"Don't wiggle, Leah! I'm giving you background."

Leah blushed, and the Signora nodded her head as if to ask, "Did you think I wouldn't notice?"

All this combined meant that Jews were usually the first target in those scattered small group movements like the *Viva Maria, Sanfedismo, Vandea Italiana*...they were all anti-French, and since the Jews were assumed to all be pro-French, the Jews were targeted as much, even more, than anyone else."

The Signora fell silent, thinking.

Leah loved the older woman's enthusiasm, her seeming innocence, which obscured an exacting mind. And she appreciated the Signora's contradictions of character. Outwardly the Signora appeared to be a fussy, little old woman in a fur coat. Inwardly, she was a person of courage, spirit, and generosity, as well as, Leah knew, a woman who continued to learn.

Some moments passed. Leah stifled a yawn and wondered if the Signora had forgotten what she was saying.

The Signora lost her train of thought. Distracted in the way anyone, searching her mind for history, might turn a corner and find her own life. Leah coughed, startling the Signora, who bounced in her chair, making her hat jiggle like a rag doll.

"Now where was I? Yes, Scansansiano...it was different than most places.

People here had a long-time and very different habit toward the Jews than did people elsewhere. Here, Jews could own furniture, houses, and land. They were tailors and shoemakers, which means they came into daily contact with the rest of the population. They worked with the contadini and helped out in hard times. People knew them, and because the gentiles and the Jews knew each other and worked together, many of the laws against the Jews simply fell away well before Napoleon and no one, except a few, cared.

You see how contradictory and complex it all was? The mix of behavior and belief. Keep that in mind; no history is simple. We want to make it simple, to give it dates and heroes and bad guys, to say this started here on this date and ended there on that date, but it's not like that at all—and it's the same with criminals.

Except for brutes like the Nazis and their collaborators, who are no more than animals, the compulsion to crime is always complex. And we have to think of that when we think of what you are calling the 'miasma' wafting through towns. You're right about secrets. There are secrets in this town and, I agree, there may be some tenuous connections between all these strange events. Wrongdoing can arise out of a child's education in hatred by his parents or other elders, or by some strange genetic twist, or by an event that ruins a person's soul. Some terrible wound that festers so badly the person can't heal."

Leah cleared her throat.

"I suppose so; all of us have an animal side."

The Signora's face fell, suddenly sad.

"Yes, all of us."

Leah took her gloves from the table and twisted them impatiently in her hands. She leaned toward the Signora.

"But what does all this have to do with now?"

"I'm coming to that. It actually has everything to do with now, I think so anyway."

Leah pulled back.

"But how?"

"You're impatient."

"Yes...I just...I didn't know how to think about this."

"That's why history is important—including in solving a grave robbery, my dear."

Chapter Twenty-Nine

"You see… if you've been listening…." She narrowed her gaze.

"I *have* been listening." Leah sat up straight, like a student caught looking out the window during class discussion.

The Signora smirked. "Terrible things were going on, and Scansansiano couldn't escape them. Angry crowds attacked Jews, beat them, and some of the Jews who didn't die at the time of the beatings died later. Here in Scansansiano, the local authorities, mostly what you might call antisemitic aristocrats, arrested Jews and demanded valuable objects from the synagogue. And then the anti-French group, Viva Maria, came. They plundered houses, insulted men, terrorized children, and beat and did worse to Jewish women—"

"What about the sheriff, the police?"

The Signora patted Leah's hand. "Context, my dear. In certain contexts, hatred rises to the top and does whatever it likes to do, often aided by lazy, weak people—people in authority—who stand by and don't do anything, or who go along with whatever the leader—good or bad—says."

The Signora's face contorted. "Hatred is like slime; once it's spilled out of whatever scum bucket of a heart holds it, it oozes into all the cracks, all the organs, until it reaches the brain and gets interpreted as perfectly rational. It can go on for generations. Look around the world; it can even spill from mothers' mouths into their children's ears. Whole cultures worship hatred; they eat it like candy."

"What ugly imagery."

"An ugly thing provokes ugly imagery! You can't whitewash what is despicable! As for Scansansianese, within days, the Jews who had been arrested—there were some Christians as well—were released. According to the records, the townspeople began to realize this upheaval was not what they wanted. Things began to cool down a little, but in Siena, thirteen Sienese Jews had been killed, so you can imagine that the Scansansianese Jews were not only wounded, but terrified. They well knew that even if some Christians had been arrested, the spotlight was on the Jews.

"They were right to be worried."

The Signora ignored her and went on. "In early July a group of soldiers came into town, guided by someone from—I forget, but someplace nearby. They rode into town 'slowly, arrogantly, solemnly.'"

Leah made a face. "How can you know that, Signora?"

"Do you think I'm making this up! It's in the court records. What do you think I do at the library and at city hall, sit and contemplate my navel?"

"I'm sorry…it didn't occur to me—"

"I know, old woman in a fur coat! No, I imagine it didn't occur to you," she muttered and readjusted herself in the chair.

"May I go on?"

Leah cringed. "Of course."

"They continued up and down the main streets of town—our town—shouting 'Evviva Marie!' and, as you can imagine, it made everyone apprehensive. Things had been getting better, and now these men…

All of them came from outside, except four, who came from two separate Scansansianese families." She tapped the table, "Our own families! It appears that the actual orders of this group of soldiers, given by some Austrian general and the governor of Arezzo, were to gather men along the route south to liberate some town down in Lazio. The point is, they didn't have orders to do anything here in Scansansiano except gather whoever they could, on a volunteer, I repeat, volunteer, basis.

And I don't know how it is that the men from here hooked up with this group of soldiers, but they did, and all of them—the soldiers and the men from those two Scansansiano families who joined them—were antisemites to the core, and the people here didn't like their insolent attitude or their

114

loud-mouthed comments.

Still, initially they weren't stopped. They rode along to the synagogue, pouring out insults like water on the people of the ghetto, and they actually threatened to throw one Jewish woman over the city wall into the gorge, which of course meant they intended to sack the ghetto and kill the Jews."

"I don't get it. What were the townspeople doing all this time?"

"They were talking amongst themselves, wondering, I suppose, what course to take. But remember, they were intimidated and frightened. Soldiers with weapons. And, there was a good deal of confusion; some of our own people had joined in; others here weren't exactly sure how they felt. So, they hesitated—it's embarrassing to admit, but they did — and it's important to understand, as I said, they were afraid for themselves."

"What were the Jews doing?"

The Signora's eyes widened in surprise.

"What could they do? They weren't armed, and the massacre in Siena was less than a month old. Imagine how frightened and intimidated you'd feel."

With a little grunt at Leah, she settled back into the story.

"At any rate, the ruffians soon tied their own noose. They counted on politics and force rather than decency, and the worse the men behaved, the more our townspeople, including the priest – generally all the good people — were convinced that the soldiers and the men who joined them were nothing but scoundrels.

The last straw—I don't like that phrase in this case, because it implies a little thing ultimately made the problem, and this wasn't little. The last straw occurred at the synagogue. They called out the rabbi, taunted him by asking him to explain the Bible, and then one of them had the audacity to dismount, proclaim he couldn't think of any place better to do his business, and squatted down and did just that in the doorway of the synagogue, never in his ugly stupidity conceiving this act would be the end of him.

This crass, disgusting behavior pushed the townspeople over the edge. The soldiers' commander—I use the word lightly—made a show of disciplining his men for this, but it was too late.

News of the incident spread; the Scansansianese were now clearly convinced these men were serious and wanted to kill their Jews—that's how they thought of the Jews, as theirs—and this last revolting act pushed the townspeople beyond the bounds of toleration.

Groups of Scansansianese marched to the piazza, gathering others as they went. The day was getting on to late afternoon, and the group was joined by the men coming in from the fields with their tools—hoes and things—which worked just as well as weapons."

The Signora shifted in her chair, her face animated in the telling.

"And the priest joined them. I love this part!! It's exciting to think of everybody joining forces against evil, isn't it?"

"Of course, but Wow! I didn't know this side of you."

"I'm old, my dear. Like a prism, I have many sides."

She laughed and cleared her throat.

"The outsiders and the shameful locals who had joined them holed up in the house of the one of the locals, but it was useless. Someone set fire to the house. They were forced out into the open and when they came running out through the doorways, the community was waiting. Things turned violent, so violent some of the soldiers and the local men with them were killed.

Two of the men killed were ancestors to two families here, and it was one of Elia's ancestors who had pointed out the locals at the trial and stained the name of the families for generations."

Leah sighed, barely containing a smile. A long story to get to the point.

"I see the connection, but it was literally centuries ago."

"And I see you smiling behind your face! You needed to know the back story. I told you, you still have things to learn about us. In the ensuing years, the local men here in town whose ancestors took part in that shameful incident tried to cover up the history, proclaiming their ancestors were heroes against the French and the Jews.

But their bravado didn't work. The extended families lost face, and for various reasons, they also began to lose their money. They fell into deep poverty, and they've blamed and hated Jews since, passing that particular perversity, as well as others, from one generation to the next."

"Incredible! Carrying hatred for so long—and making a point to perpetuate it."

"You're much too educated to think it's 'incredible'! Haven't you read anything? Don't you keep up with the news? It's irritating that you call it 'incredible.' Think about it. You can understand that if whoever I heard at the library was from one of these families—or one from both of the families, we may not yet know to what depths of depravity they've gone, or will go."

"Grave robbing?"

"I don't know for sure; by the time I heard them in the library, everyone knew about the grave being robbed and knew that there was nothing in the casket, so the one who spoke may have simply been making a crass remark."

"So, who are the families?"

"The Landis and the Innocentis."

"Sergio?"

"And his brother, Gino. And Cristofano and Gualfredo."

"I can't believe it. Maybe the Innocentis, but Sergio? I've always gone to his store."

"So does everyone else in town. I'm talking about the subterranean life of people."

"Okay, but there are others who seem more suspicious to me. Like the American, like Grazia. She's threatened to kill three people! And the American is suspicious."

"We both know Secondo can't be involved, and that's who the American is always with."

"I don't know. You're right about Secondo. Still, why is the American here? He won't talk, and doesn't that make you think he's up to something? He's obviously not on vacation, and he couldn't have known Secondo before if what he says is true about this being the first time he's been here…and another thought about Grazia: it seems evident she is on the edge of sanity."

"You may have reason about the American."

"Tell me why you think so?"

"I think he's evasive and too clean-cut. He makes me think of an axe murderer who helps old ladies carry their groceries and then goes out at night and hacks people to death in back alleys. He doesn't seem the type to rob graves, but how many grave robbers do? But Elia doesn't know him. Grazia, she does have history with Elia; she's violent and strong, but is she that far gone? Murder seems more likely for her than grave robbing."

"She said she wanted to dig her up and kill her again, didn't she?"

"You're a regular fountain of knowledge, Signora. What's the history between Grazia and Elia?"

"I thought you knew." The Signora eyed her suspiciously.

"The Lieutenant said it was complications of love, but he didn't give details."

"He's too principled to tell you, although I think he wants to do whatever you ask."

"Not that again, Signora! Please," Leah pleaded. "Just tell me the story, ok?

"I see. How is it you Americans phrase it: You're pumping for information."

The Signora patted Leah's hand. "In this instance, I'm going to tell you more because I know you'll be ferreting around town relentlessly, which will create more of a stir than there already is. I also don't want you to think Grazia's a cut-and-dried bad woman. She says horrible things, and let's hope she never acts on them, but she does have reason for her madness. So I'll tell you, but not now; you'll have to take me to dinner tonight to hear it."

Leah laughed. "Dinner it is then, Signora. And a break works for me too. The rain has stopped, but according to the weather report, it will start again later. So, I'd like to take a walk and digest what you've told me. Meet me tonight at the Casalinga, and you can tell me the rest of the story. Eating out might also get me back at work on an article about local cuisine I promised myself I'd write.

Chapter Thirty

They met that night at eight o'clock at the Casalinga, the "Housewife." This was the restaurant locals chose on those rare occasions they dined away from home. The food was the same sort of food they ate at home, but was cooked by friends they had known for years.

A waiter brought menus. The Signora and Leah slumped over them, discussing each dish at length. How much garlic? What sort of mushroom? Which pasta would be best?

With characteristic discretion and grace, the waiter left them to their discussion. Leah made a mental note to write about this genteel behavior in the article.

Both women tacitly understood that ordering a meal was a serious task, which demanded care and thought. Both knew the meal would come first, to be ordered and eaten in a relaxed manner, before the end of the Signora's story or any other serious discussion. What one drank and ate was a decision that created an aura, an ambiance, to the evening, and it was important to take time to consider each person's tastes.

Leah thought of the service in American restaurants, where guests felt pursued and pushed to order, eat, and leave. She remembered an article she had read in a popular magazine written by a waiter. He admonished people going to a restaurant to study the menu beforehand and know what they wanted to eat before they entered the restaurant. He added that they should also be aware of the cost and decide on the tip before they came to the restaurant. This was for the ease of the waiter and seemed embarrassingly uncultured.

119

"Uncultured barbarian!" the Signora blurted.

Both the Signora and Leah relished the etiquette of Italian meals, which were leisurely social events extending for 2 or 3 hours, and they both anticipated this island of calm and peace in the midst of sad loss and the horrific knowledge of the grave robbery.

They studied the menu for fifteen minutes, then raised their heads and laid the menus on the table, a sign they were ready. With a genuine smile, the waiter came to stand beside them.

They began with an anti-pasta of mixed pieces of *fettunta* and *bruschetta* accompanied by a small salad of arugula and shaved parmesan with a delicate olive oil and lemon dressing. For a wine, they chose a gentle, local white.

Looking over the offerings for the first course, the Signora and Leah laughed in delight when they discovered that both of them loved *acquacotta*, "cooked water," one of the best Tuscan soups, made in the Casalinga with chard, the way they both preferred.

The second course was more difficult for each of them.

"So many choices, and I am famished. Are you thinking of fish, Signora?"

"No, certainly not. I may have left Venice years ago, but food habits stay. I'll eat my fish in Venice, fish 'country,' and I'll eat lamb here, in lamb country, so I'm thinking *scottadito*."

"And I'm having *buglione d'agnello*! We're on the same wavelength: lamb! And *contorno*?"

"Another difficult choice! I like every sort of vegetable, but tonight I'll choose *spinaci*, lightly sauteed."

"And I'll have *patate al forno*—as always, roast potatoes." Leah laughed at herself.

"We should do this more often."

Leah and the Signora took their time. They savored each course, chatted about trips they'd taken. Leah described the mountains and people of Montana, the national parks, the vast areas of wilderness. The Signora spoke lovingly about the area of Castello in Venice, where she had spent the early years of her life.

"It was so beautiful, so peaceful there when I was young. It's now overrun with tourists, as I suppose Scansansiano will be before long, but then the city was full of Venetians, not foreigners. The shop owners were Venetian, and we spoke Venetian rather than Italian. Today the children make a mixed mess of Italian and Venetian, and some can't speak even a word of it."

"Like a piece of home is missing."

"Yes." The Signora tilted her head forward with a sad look.

"I'm sorry, Signora. Loss of culture means grief to the people that live through it."

"Your historian, Toynbee, said, 'Civilizations die from suicide, not murder.' He was right. The problems and degradation of the city are our own fault. We should have done something much sooner to prevent the floods of tourists. Tourism got out of hand, and before we knew it ten, then twelve, then fifteen million people with no awareness of Venetian culture and artistry were coming every year. Soon it will be twenty million! Achhh, it's ruining the city."

"Signora, there's so much sadness around us. Let's finish this wonderful meal with a last few moments of escape from what's going on around us. Then, we'll go to our warm beds, get a good night's sleep, meet for coffee in the morning, and you can tell me the rest of the history."

The Signora leaned close and whispered. "When we stand up, I want you to turn as you're putting on your coat, and take a glance at the two men in the far corner. Those are the Innocenti brothers. It was their ancestors who joined with the soldiers I told you about. They've been staring at us all evening."

When they finished and paid, Leah stood, put her arm slowly into the sleeve of her coat, and pulled it around her shoulders. The two men were sitting under a light. It was the two from the funeral: one tall and thin, one short and portly. Both men wore dark clothes. Leah saw it had been useless to pretend she wasn't looking. They were staring directly at her, just as they had stared at her at the funeral. A shiver ran up her spine.

"I'll be right back, Signora." Leah straightened her coat and stepped around a large family group that sat at the table between her and the two men and approached the men with a smile. Startled, the brothers glanced at each other and pushed back their chairs with the intention of standing.

"Oh, please don't bother getting up. I'll only take a minute."

Leah had noticed their differences in height and weight at Anna's funeral, but now she studied their faces. The taller one stared at her with steel gray eyes. His jaw was lean and square, determined, as if he were clenching his teeth. His hair was dark and lightly oiled, and his smile false. He extended his hand, but Leah ignored it.

The other brother, shorter than his brother by at least a foot, started to speak, but with a quick glance from the taller one, closed his mouth and watched his brother. He rubbed his pudgy fingers back and forth nervously against his thumbs, looking back and forth from his brother to Leah.

"I just wanted to say hello to you both. I'm Leah Contarini; I believe we've met before, but it would have been some years ago, so you may not remember me. I came over because I don't understand why you're staring at us—or at me anyway—as you were at the funeral. I'm happy to answer any questions you have or …?" She held their gaze.

The taller one flushed bright red in anger, his eyes steel. "No, Signora. We have nothing to ask."

"Something to tell me?"

The shorter brother stuttered something, but the taller one put up his hand to stop him and spoke again to Leah.

"Not at all. Please forgive us if it seemed we were staring."

"It's a small matter, and there's nothing to forgive, but if in the future you do have something to ask me or tell me, please come to me directly. I'm always glad for a good conversation. Good evening, Signori."

Leah turned and walked away. She could feel their eyes burning into her back.

The Signora and Leah stepped into a cold nighttime mist and fog. They pulled their coats close around their necks.

Before they'd gone many steps, the Signora panted.

"That was a brazen thing to do, Leah! And please slow down."

"Brazen? I thought it was direct. It's creepy when they stare like that. If they have something to say, they can talk to me."

"Americans! You're so often like the proverbial bull in the China shop."

Leah laughed.

"I guess we are. But don't you like it sometimes?" she teased.

Chapter Thirty-One

The following morning the Signora continued her story about Grazia.

"When they were still children, Grazia and Anna were best friends, and so too were Salvatore and Elia. They played together on the teeter-totters at school and ran around the piazza while their mothers shopped. Like brothers and sisters. I remember them so well." Imagining the children, she looked away. Leah thought she could see tears well in the Signora's eyes.

"It's such a pleasure to watch children, to see the freedom, the joy of being alive, of living every moment in the present," the Signora said.

"I didn't realize you'd been here that long," Leah said.

"I haven't lived here that long, but I used to come for vacations, and although I was older, it's a small town, so I knew them. I decided to move here later on—sometime I'll tell you.

Anyway, when they reached adolescence, things changed. Like girls do, Grazia and Anna pulled away to talk and giggle by themselves; and the boys were standoffish, not knowing quite what to do about the girls, except show off by jumping on the fountain ledge or some other tomfoolery.

As they got to be young men and women and were sexually aware, they began to go to the movies with their friends, and take slices of bread to the bar to eat *supercrema gianduja*...."

"What's *supercrema gianduja*?"

The Signora laughed. "You're not going to let me finish my story are you? Full of questions and curiosity. No matter. This morning the stories are sad;

we can use the intervals.

Supercrema gianduja is what you know as Nutella. First it was produced in a bar form called *pasta gianduja* named after a famous carnival hero. It was hard times; chocolate was desperately expensive, so a Piedmontese man named Ferrero figured out how to make a good tasting substitute with hazelnuts. I forget exactly when—in the late thirties or early forties, I think. Anyway, he changed the form to a paste because the mothers were saying they wanted their kids to eat it *with* bread. In bar form, the kids just threw away the bread and ate the *pasta gianduja*."

She laughed. "He had to please the mothers, no? So he began making it in crème form, *supercreme gianduja*. And in those days, the kids took their pieces of bread to the bar where they could pay a penny or so and get the bread slathered with it."

"And now they make Nutella pizza with bananas!" Leah exclaimed.

"Yes, evolution! Hmmph. Back to the story."

The smile disappeared from their faces.

"Those four were like other kids their age; they wandered the streets in the evenings chatting about school and university and friends—things like that. Salvatore was crazy for Anna, and the two of them became close. Elia, feeling left out, I imagine, paired off with Grazia, disastrously so. Grazia was madly in love with Salvatore, with a fire only teenagers can feel, and everyone knew it, but since she couldn't go with Salvatore, she went with Elia."

The Signora shook her head. "It's a terrible thing, that passionate love of youth, so unreasonable and impulsive."

"I always thought it was wonderful."

"You're still young enough to be passionately in love. Give yourself time, and you'll see the other side of the coin."

Leah wondered if the Signora's comment reflected something in her own history. The moment passed and the Signora continued.

"Grazia liked Elia well enough, or anyway she convinced herself she did, convinced herself too well as it turned out. And Elia behaved impulsively.

Grazia got pregnant. Her family sent her to Rome on the pretext of staying with a recently-widowed cousin who needed the distraction of company. The baby was placed for adoption by the sisters in the church, and the following year, Grazia came back. None of the others guessed what had happened."

"Not Elia?"

"No—or, perhaps he did—but it seems not; I don't know. I think Salvatore guessed, but if he did, he was quiet about it, as far as I know.

During the time Grazia was gone, the friendship between the other three began to disintegrate. Salvatore and Elia argued; we all saw it on the streets and in the piazza, and sometimes they fought. Their behavior made me think Salvatore knew, and probably judged Elia for it. But nothing about Grazia was spoken aloud. Salvatore began to find fault with Elia for unrelated, nitpicky things, and Elia responded in kind, so the distance between them widened, and Anna, I think confused and in total innocence, veered away from Salvatore toward Elia.

And Grazia began to change; she turned hard, angry, and either it suited Salvatore, or since he couldn't have Anna, he took Grazia for second best. A great sin, I think. They were not well matched. They married eventually, but he either never wanted to give her children, or he was unable to. Ironically, Anna must have been sterile; it was clear that both she and Elia wanted children, and of course, Elia was not sterile."

So, from great friendships Grazia harvested bitterness. As the years passed, she remembered the baby she had birthed and that had then been taken away, and she realized with Salvatore there would be no children. She became mired in anger and frustration and, eventually, I think, real hatred. I don't know when the abuse started. Initially, Salvatore seemed to have the upper hand, but with time the tables turned, and Grazia began to abuse him."

"The scene in the piazza...."

"Yes, and the scene at Elia's house. Like the poet says, 'Heaven has no rage like love to hatred turned, nor hell a fury like a woman scorned.' She was scorned by Elia, at least to her mind, and then again by Salvatore. She was second choice and always would be. Over the years, she seemed to gorge on jealousy, living every day in anger until maybe it became a sort of madness."

"But do you think she's actually capable of such a heinous act as grave robbing?"

"I don't know. I do think she's becoming what she's brooded on, but I don't know whether or not she's passed the boundary into that level of degradation. She's certainly strong enough to have done it. And lately, she's been talking about wanting to bring Anna back and kill her again, which I think is such twisted thinking she actually did try it. She always was a big athletic girl, and she grew even stronger with work on the farm. I'd say she's as capable as anyone of going berserk. Having to give away a child and then being childless your whole life can harden a woman and maybe drive her insane."

"The underbelly of the town...." Leah's face sagged with sadness.

"Like every other place in the world, cara. Unrequited love, jealousy, betrayal, murder...we've got it all. And what I've told you is only part of it. Can you still love us?"

The Signora's question was surprisingly tender.

"Of course," Leah paused, "only now there's a strong dose of sadness in the mix of all the things that are wonderful about the town."

"Like there is in even the best of loves. Better to know the whole story. Maybe you can even be happier by knowing some of the sadness, some of the history. That makes a more genuine love, no?"

Leah nodded.

The Signora rose. "Don't be too sad, Leah. Things will work out, and if they don't, they will work out anyway. And with that little bit of wisdom from my mother, it's time for me to go home."

Leah laughed and stood. "Thank you, Signora. You and your mother keep me in perspective. But how did you know the whole story?"

The Signora smiled at her.

"Didn't you say you had an errand to run?"

Chapter Thirty-Two

Leah stepped out of the bar and drew a sharp breath. A cold wind had arisen. She cut around the corner of the building to adjust her scarf and zip her jacket. As she turned back around the corner to start home, she collided with the Lieutenant.

"Leah! You came out of nowhere!"

Leah looked at him with a quizzical glint in her eye. He had dropped the 'Signora'.

"Out of the wind. I stepped out of the wind to zip my jacket. It's cold!"

"But you're crying!"

"No, it's the wind; it makes my eyes water."

He reached to wipe away a tear running down her cheek, then quickly drew his hand away.

"I'm sorry. I shouldn't have done that. May I buy you a coffee or a glass of wine to keep you warm on your way?"

"There's no need to be sorry. I am upset, but really the tears were the wind's fault. I haven't been crying; I've been talking to the Signora. So many horrible things; we go over and over it all. I guess I need to be strong to be weak."

"Come with me."

He took her arm before she could refuse and guided her to the far side of the piazza, where another little bar was tucked in the corner. This delicately assertive behavior by the Lieutenant was new to Leah. She was enjoying it.

When they stepped through the door, the barmaid, who had been leaning on the counter flipping the pages of a movie magazine, tossed the magazine to the side and called in an unnecessarily loud voice, "Buon Giorno!"

"Two coffees," the Lieutenant said with a smile at the young woman before he and Leah took a seat in the corner.

After the barmaid set the delicate demitasses on the table and left, the Lieutenant leaned toward Leah.

"I can understand why you're, as you call it, 'a little subdued,' but tell me about it anyway."

"I'm not sure where to start."

"Start anywhere; we'll get to where we need to go."

Leah laughed.

"I guess so. Well, it's Anna's death, the grave robbery, Grazia, the American, and the Innocentis staring at me...."

"What do you mean, the Innocentis staring at you?"

"I'll get to that; what I'm trying to say is that recent events are like pieces of different puzzles put into one box. Nothing fits. There's no clear path to who committed the grave robbery. The Signora seems to think it's because of historic hatreds of the Jews that's filtered down through families here in town...

"The Landis and the Innocentis."

"Does everyone but me know about them? Still, it doesn't have to be them. It could be Grazia, couldn't it? She seems to hate both Elia and Anna, and for that matter, Salvatore. It's spine-chilling to imagine her sneaking into the cemetery at night and committing such a heinous act. It seems more likely it's the grave robbers you talked about, the ones from other places. I'd like to think it was someone from out of town, rather than someone here. Plus, I don't understand why the American is always around Secondo. It makes me nervous for Secondo. I'm not whining; I'm just confused."

She hit the table with the palm of her hand in frustration.

"Leah...."

He took her hands and spoke her name so gently Leah felt a surge of emotion and looked away.

They heard a gasp from the barmaid, turned, and saw she was staring at them, wide-eyed.

Leah and the Lieutenant smiled at each other and continued their conversation.

"Lieutenant, we're adding fuel to the gossip fire."

He glanced toward the barmaid, picked up Leah's hand, and kissed it. Leah laughed aloud; the barmaid turned away, blushing.

The Lieutenant continued.

"I know the Signora's told you this, Leah, and I've told you: we're no different here than people anywhere. Small town, city, farm—we're all the same. All of us have secrets, all of us hide certain things we've done or thought about doing, and most of us, when we have done something terribly wrong, are pressured by conscience and want to confess, or if not confess, to somehow unburden themselves so they can make amends. It's difficult to live with heavy secrets. This means that finally, things become known. It sounds naïve, but I count on normal people's desire to unburden themselves. There are almost always hints of some disturbance in a person, and when I'm observant, I see those hints. It works with things, good or bad. Murderers and grave robbers get identified, and an attentive friend realizes his best friend is in love before his best friend knows it himself. Most secrets come to light. I've got a good record, and I wish you would trust me and not put yourself in harm's way."

He ran his hand gently down her arm, then suddenly raised her hand and kissed it. It was an oddly old-fashioned but tender gesture. Leah didn't pull away.

"Lieutenant…."

He sat bolt upright, bringing his hands to his chest, making the face of one who has just made a terrible mistake.

"I'm sorry; I shouldn't have done that."

"Please. Don't say you're sorry. I'm not."

He coughed and pretended he hadn't heard.

"Back to business. I can tell you something about the American. I haven't figured out what it means, but it might ease your mind about Secondo. I just wish you would trust me and stop getting involved. You have a way of stirring the wasp's nest."

When the Lieutenant pulled his hand away, Leah felt a stab of loss. She wanted him to kiss her again, to kiss the palm of her hand, to embrace her. She wanted to bury her face in his neck, to hold him close.

She drew a deep breath and stumbled over her words. "The American...? Yes. I do... I want to know about him."

He gave her an odd look and wondered if maybe she had liked him touching her. He took a deep breath.

"I've done a check on him. I think you already know his name is David Stein. What I found out is that he works with a group of dealers in art. Art objects of various sorts, buying, and selling, that sort of thing. He has an extended visa, so it's possible he could be here—or at least in Italy—for up to a year. I'm tracking down the group that he works with, and I think I've got it, but I want to be sure. From the looks of it, the group deals in all sorts of artworks: paintings, jewelry, religious objects, even some of the crafts: furniture, exotic tools, fine woven or embroidered cloth work. Before long, I should have more information on where he's been and what he's been doing in Italy, but other than what I've told you, I don't know why he's here, and I don't know why he's so close with Secondo. My bet is that he's using Secondo for information."

"Or he somehow knows about the objects from the synagogue, and he wants to use Secondo to find them! That's got to be it. That jerk!"

Leah noticed the Innocenti brothers walk to the edge of the piazza and start down the trail.

"Leah?"

"I just saw the Innocenti brothers walking by."

"Shall I go on?"

"Of course, sorry."

About the American: don't jump to conclusions. Wherever the things from the synagogue are, Secondo and his grandfather never found them, and until his grandfather died, they were looking practically every day for nearly twenty years. Secondo's keeping that search going, but it would take a lifetime to search every meter of the forests around here. And as far as I know, apart from befriending Secondo and helping him look, Stein hasn't done anything illegal. His visit here may not have anything to do with religious objects."

"It seems evident to me. But you're right. How would he have known Secondo was looking for the things from the synagogue? Still, he put himself in Secondo's path from the first day—or was it really coincidence, and he didn't know anything about Secondo or the things from the synagogue.... From what you say, he's in the art business, so there's reason to be suspicious. Secondo told me that some of those things from the synagogue date back hundreds of years. Someone in the business would be interested, wouldn't they?"

The Lieutenant looked at his watch.

"Bored?"

"You know I'm not. I hate to leave you, but I've got to get back to the office. Can we have coffee again—soon?"

She touched his arm. "Soon, very soon."

They walked out together. The Lieutenant turned to say something, but decided against it, pivoted on his heel, and walked away, calling "soon" to the sky.

The Lieutenant's touch had sent Leah's emotions into a spin. She needed to get back to the *vie cave,* to be surrounded by trees, stone, silence, and wind, where she could think. To her other emotions, she now added a niggling sense of guilt. The Lieutenant's hands were smooth; she could still feel his lips on her skin.

She crossed the piazza. The wind howled around her and blew her hair in wild disarray. She stepped onto the trail that led down to the river and from there to the *vie cave,* where she hoped to calm herself.

There was no reason to feel guilty. She had not touched or thought about another man since Nick had died, but time had passed, and she was still young. A widow, single. What was it she felt for the Lieutenant? A purely sexual attraction? He was an available, handsome, and gentle man. Did she want a physical release with no ties? And what did he want? What about Nick? Did she owe him fidelity until she died? That sort of fidelity was a choice someone from her mother's era might have made, but Leah felt alive, ready to be touched and loved again. She could not erase passion from her life.

Below town, she crossed the highway and walked slowly through the meadow. Just as she entered the *via cava*, the sky darkened, and Leah felt the first drops of rain. Within minutes, it was raining hard. Heavy drops of water dripped from the trees overhead at the top of the slot trail, rivulets of water streamed down the tufa stone beneath her feet, and sheets of rain washed the trail walls and splattered, soaking her shoes and clothes.

This was what she wanted: to go straight into the heart of the trail, of the green, wild land and rain. She wanted to expend energy and take energy from the expending of it. Nick was gone. No relationship would ever be as excitingly tumultuous as the one she had with Nick. No one else would ever be a father to Sara.

She knew these things; she was wonderfully alive and sensate. What she felt for the Lieutenant proved that she could desire again, perhaps even love again. She hiked on, chilled, water sloshing in her shoes, her clothes weighing her down, happy for the moment.

At a fork in the trail, she spotted the Innocenti brothers in their dark clothes watching her from a few yards up on a steep arm of the trail that snaked in tight, hairpin curves upward to join a dirt road. The road ran through a large stand of umbrella pine to the west and to Rocellini's vineyard to the east.

They stood still, staring down at her.

"Leah?" the taller one called. "That's a Jewish name, isn't it?"

"Yes, it is."

"You're Jewish?"

Leah had never practiced Judaism, but had learned that her mother and maternal grandmother were Jewish.

"According to Jewish law, yes. Why?"

"We just wondered. And you said if we have something to say to you or to ask you, we should address you directly, no?"

"Of course. I'm glad you did."

He smiled, touched his brother's arm, and they started on up the trail, stopped, and turned back.

"Be careful on the edge of the field, Signora. It's a steep escarpment, very dangerous."

"I will; thanks for the warning."

They continued on.

Leah watched them curve back and forth upward.

"Thanks – I think." She made a face. "Okay, I'll go left," she muttered.

She kept on the left-hand fork of the trail, away from the brothers, stopping at intervals to let the rain fall on her upturned face and to take deep breaths of the cool air. After 15 minutes, the trail broke from the trees into an open field that ran along the edge of the valley ridge on the south. On the western edge of the field she could see a small shed, and beyond that, across two more fields, a tractor swept back and forth, plowing. To the north, a stand of umbrella pine stood dark against the clear blue sky, and a car sat at the edge of the dirt road that led to the Innocenti farmstead.

Leah crossed the field and stood on the lip of an escarpment, looking out over the valley.

Einstein said: "Look into the beauty of Nature and then you will understand everything better."

Leah thought of that now. There was a connection, a thread, even if only partial, through the things that had happened. She stared across the valley and far below at the line of trees along the river.

Grazia was the most likely for the grave robbery. She said more than once she would like to dig Anna up and kill her all over again. But was she truly a woman who could sink so low? And if she had taken such gruesome revenge, would she still be making a scene in public by beating her husband with a bucket? Wouldn't she be most likely to kill both her husband and Elia, what she had loudly professed, in public, she wanted to do, but hadn't done?

The timing seemed wrong for Stein to have been the grave robber. By his name, he must be Jewish; he would know there was nothing in the casket. His interest had to be in the lost gold and silver objects from the synagogue.

Nothing made sense.

The call of a hoopoe interrupted Leah's thought. Glancing downward, she saw she had stepped perilously close to the edge of the escarpment. She raised her foot to step backward.

Chapter Thirty-Three

David Stein stepped out of the leather worker's shop just as Leah and the Lieutenant left the little corner bar across the piazza. They seemed happy, intimate, and he wondered if they were a couple. He heard the Lieutenant yell "soon" to the sky. He wondered what it meant.

"Signor David!" Secondo yelled from a side street and came running toward Stein.

"Secondo, hello! What are you up to today?"

"I'm busy. I'm working, and I'm paying my bills. Come see where I'm sweeping. I sweep a different street every day."

Stein glanced across the piazza. The Lieutenant was walking in the direction of his office. Leah had turned to the edge of the piazza, where a trail led down to the river, toward the *vie cave*.

"Come! I can show you where I keep my tools and my map of all the streets I sweep."

"What?" Stein asked.

"You're not paying attention! I asked if you want me to show you where I work. I have to work."

"Sorry, Secondo. I can't go with you today. I've got business I have to take care of. Maybe tomorrow?"

Secondo's face fell. "Oh, okay!" As suddenly, he was happy again. "Tomorrow! See you!" He ran off across the open space of the piazza down another of the small side streets.

Stein headed for the trail that led from the edge of the piazza down to the river.

Chapter Thirty-Four

Leah's body catapulted into the air.

She landed hard and rolled crazily down the steep barren slope. Sky, dirt, forest, river, and rock flashed by her eyes as she spun downward. She bounced, hit, bounced again, hit again.

Later she remembered grasping wildly for a handhold, but there was no handhold, only the steep slope face, seventy nearly vertical yards of rock and dirt.

At the bottom of the escarpment, Leah's unconscious body rolled a few feet into the line of trees that bordered the river and wrapped with a dull thud around an errant fig tree standing a few feet into the shadows. Leah lay unmoving and quiet but for the shallow moaning that escaped her lips with each breath.

When she woke, she heard the low, throaty hu hu of a hoopoe from above her, and from farther away, she could hear the gentle ripple of water over stones in the river. The rain had stopped. A light mist was falling.

Cold and wet, Leah tilted her head. She was covered with mud. She tested her right arm. It hurt, but she could move it. She turned her head slowly and looked at her left arm, which lay against her body. Through the ragged tear in her jacket, she could see that her left arm was bruised and swollen; still, she could move it.

She tried her legs. They were the same: bruised, but she could move them. She turned her head to one side and then the other. There was blood on the ground beside her, near her face.

She laughed—and cried out in pain as she did. Broken ribs? Or bruised?

She laughed again and gasped. How absurd that she had seen a murderer shove someone off a cliff, and now she had thrown herself off a cliff. Or had someone pushed her? She wondered. Had she heard footsteps or felt a shove? She couldn't remember.

Who would want to kill her? For what reason? And how would they know she was on the trail? Had she told someone she was coming? She couldn't remember anyone else being on the trail or in the field.

The Innocenti. And they had warned her. Had they come back? Why would they?

Not much blood. She thought.

She lay still.

It had to have been a stupid accident. Too close to the edge. It serves me right!

Leah waited. She moved the fingers of each hand, then arms, then legs. In a few minutes she would try to sit up. For now she would wait, gather strength, get her bearings.

A hoopoe sounded once more.

Leah combed her memory for the shortest way back to town. She was not strong enough to climb her way upward; she would get to the river and follow it home. There was a trail on the far side that fishermen used. She had never walked it and did not know if it extended this far from town. On her walks on the higher *vie cave*, she had seen men and sometimes a woman or two fishing below.

She took a deep breath and gasped. The ribs hurt, but her neck was not swollen, so the ribs were either not broken, or at least had not punctured a lung. She remembered something her father used to say to her when she had hurt herself:

"Are you going to let a little pain decide what you do?"

"This isn't a little pain!" She mumbled.

But her father's words drove her on.

She put her palms to the ground and pushed her torso upward, scooting around to lean against the tree. Every part of her body hurt; blood dripped slowly from her face. Or was it a head injury? She was afraid to find out by touching herself with filthy hands.

The hoopoe sounded again.

A thought flitted through her mind: the murderer she had helped convict years earlier had escaped and come back for revenge. More likely, it was Grazia—or the Innocenti.

She laughed, grunting in pain.

Leah waited for the pain to subside, then rolled to her left on all fours. Taking shallow breaths, she waited, gathering the strength to stand. She thought of her brother. Once, when they were children, he dared her to jump out of the hay mow into the cattle feeder. She stood at the open mow, staring down two floors into the feeder, certain there would be pain when she landed. If she missed, she would likely hit one of the 2 x 4s that extended like stakes in an open V into the air. She would be impaled. Still, she knew she would do it; she would not fail in front of her brother.

Now she was staring into a certain pain again, but not as drastic as that jump from the mow. The fall had happened. She simply needed to stand up.

Had she been pushed? Had someone shoved her off a cliff and gone home to eat supper? She looked upward; the ridge was empty, full only of sky.

Maybe a goat or a sheep had butted her over the edge. She laughed again and groaned.

She chided herself. There was no murderer today, no Secondo, no Nick. Only her own foolish step into thin air. Breathing in quick, shallow breaths, she raised her hand to the tree for support, bent one leg, and, working her way up the tree with her hands, stood up, panting in tight little breaths, but there was no escape from the pain.

With a last glance up the slope, she shuffled from one tree to the next, inching her way toward the river, reaching from tree to tree for support.

Chapter Thirty-Five

Stein stepped to the lip of the escarpment and looked down, scanning the forest along the river. He called Leah's name and stood quietly, listening for a response. Except for the distant rumble of a tractor passing along the dirt road to the north, there was silence.

He stepped away from the edge and turned slowly in a full circle. No one. He was alone. Again, he moved carefully to the edge of the escarpment and looked down. Below him, the tops of the trees swayed gently in the wind moving up the canyon. Much of the forest floor was in shadow. In spots, through the shimmering lattice of the leaves, he could see the river.

He called Leah's name again and waited.

Silence.

Below, next to the river, Leah thought she heard a faint call, but the sound was obscured by the thick stand of trees and brush and the gurgle of the river over stones. She went forward, moving upriver toward Scansansiano, scanning the far bank for the trail she hoped was there.

Chapter Thirty-Six

L ate that evening, the bus from the train station on the coast jolted around the curves of the narrow road leading to Scansansiano. Its headlights splayed a swathe of light across the pavement into the thick brush. Rising above the bushes, a dense tangle of holm oak, beech, and clumps of blackberry crowded the edges of the asphalt, and branches on both sides of the road stretched toward the opposite ditch, as if little by little the luxuriant greenery wanted to obliterate all signs of human habitation and return to its wild, vegetative state.

Elia watched from the window as the bus hurtled through the tunnel of trees, sending him swaying back and forth at each curve. He had lost Anna, and now he had lost trust in the community he had always known. His heart constricted. He wrung his hands obsessively, remembering with a sick feeling what he'd seen in New York. Leaning forward in his seat directly behind the driver, he snapped.

"Can't you go any faster?"

The bus driver had known Elia for many years, and he had driven this road safely, with and without Elia, for as long. He sped ahead on the straightaways, slowed, and pulled to the center on the curves.

"Calm down, Elia. Even if you talk Swahili or Turkish, I can't go any faster than I am. You've only been gone a couple days, so relax; nothing's changed, and we'll soon be there."

He regretted his words as soon as they left his lips, remembering that Elia's wife had just died, but it was too late. Before he could apologize, Elia was out of his seat, shouting.

"Everything has changed! Everything!"

The driver's face reddened in embarrassment and fear.

"I'm sorry. Forgive me for what I said. Of course everything has changed. But you don't need to shout. I drive this run six times every day, and I promise you, compared to the speed I should be going, this is fast. It's not safe to push. You know that, particularly around these corners. There are too many idiots happy to try passing on the curve."

Compelled by his natural sense of discretion, Elia sat down in his seat and relented, embarrassed.

"I'm worried...."

"About what?"

"Just get on with it!" Elia leaned his elbow on the armrest and dropped his head against his hand.

The driver, a young man of thirty-five, married to the daughter of the barber, glanced in the rearview mirror and saw Elia slumped forward, head in hand. He let the question go.

Before the bus lurched to a stop in front of the bar in the lower part of town, Elia was at the door, shuffling from one foot to the other. When the driver pulled the lever for the door, Elia squeezed through before it was fully open, jumped awkwardly to the ground, and wrangled his suitcase in rough jerks from the belly of the bus. Through the dim haze of streetlights around the corner, he dove under the high archway onto the wide street that would carry him to the electrician's shop.

Chapter Thirty-Seven

Flushed, gasping for air from the walk up the hill, Elia banged open the door of the electrical shop. The glass in the door shuddered from the blow. Elia stalked into the shop, shouting for Sergio. "Thief! Pervert! Come out!"

Wheezing with each breath, the words erupted from his mouth in crushed syllables.

His entry shocked the other shoppers. Magliotti, who had been standing by a table of demitasses waiting for Sergio, gaped in surprise. He gave a wry grin, stepped back, and leaned against the window frame.

Signora Lucenti stopped short in the middle of pawing through a box of light bulbs and stared at the spectacle, her mouth pumping like a fish out of water. Oblivious to Elia's outburst and to all adults, Signora Lucenti's daughter pulled on a cord dangling from the display table. Motherhood trumped the woman's surprise at seeing Elia raging and cursing; she bent to slap the little girl's hands, which brought tears and howls.

"And stop crying, or you'll get another one!" The signora hissed.

The Innocenti brothers, always together, had been inspecting a coffee maker made in America. At the outburst, the elder one set the coffee maker carefully back on the table, and both brothers watched with nonchalant interest as Sergio burst through the long strings of plastic beads that separated the living quarters from the shop. His brother, Gino, followed, lagging behind with an eager sneer as Sergio strode toward Elia.

"What the hell are you...."

Sergio's thick dark hair, dressed with the usual cloying paste, hung in

144

oily curls at his forehead. Elia raised his arm. Sergio grabbed for his wrist, but Elia evaded his grasp, stepped behind him deeper into the store, then pivoted to face Sergio.

"You stole it and sold it! You damned antisemite! You wouldn't help with Idrissa, and now this. I'll tell the whole town. I'll tell them! Our parochet! I saw it in New York. I saw it, damn you!"

Sergio fumbled in his pocket for his cell phone. He punched furiously at the keys.

"I don't even know what the hell a pakit is—"

"Pa-ro-chet! Idiot! You were always fawning over and fiddling with our things when your family came to eat "the Jews'" food. We invited you, for god's sake—even Gino. The both of you."

Elia glanced at Gino, who was wiping the sweat from his forehead. The eager grin on his face repulsed Elia. He turned back to Sergio.

"Did you think I'd forget that time I saw you fondling the parochet in the synagogue, you sick bastard! I thought you admired it! And all the time you hated us. I'm ashamed of ever having been your friend."

With a quick step forward, he shoved Sergio backward.

"Even as a child I should have known better. As soon as I saw the parochet, I knew it was you."

"You've always been quick to blame, damn you!"

Sergio flushed. Raising a tight fist in the air, he stuttered. "Get out! Now!"

He brought his fist down with the force of a hammer. Elia swerved aside and swung his arm in a wide curve upward, a fruitless blow that barely scraped Sergio's ear.

The two stood back, panting. Gino emitted excited little squeaks.

"Hit him, Sergio; hit him! He has no idea! Hit him!"

"Shut your mouth, Gino!"

Seeing Sergio step back and drop his arm, Magliotti read this withdrawal as a sign of safety. Assured he would not be hit, he stepped forward to intervene and placed himself between the two men.

"Gentlemen, please. Obviously there's been a misunderstanding. This is no way to solve it. Consider the rest of us."

Elia stopped. The fury of the last two days and the fatigue of travel compelled him to forfeit his dignity. He was suddenly overcome with shame.

Deflated like a sail when the wind dies down, he dropped his arms.

"I won't raise a hand again. Hit me if you like, as Gino says. It will only increase the charges against you."

Sergio's face flushed a livid red.

"Get out of here, son of a whore!"

His eyes glistened.

"I wish I had your fucking "per ah cat" here right now."

He opened his mouth, then, as if holding a cloth to his face, he rubbed his cheek and let his tongue out, wiggling it lasciviously back and forth, rolling his eyes.

Gino laughed and mimicked him.

Elia stared at them. Whatever malevolence he attributed to Sergio was superficial compared to what he now read in the man's gaze. Sergio's eyes shimmered with lewd depravity that Elia could not have imagined and could not define. He was peering into eyes that held no soul, held nothing of the sacred, as if something had wrenched this man's humanness from his body and replaced it by black evil, which had taken root, flowered, and fed on corrupted thoughts.

Elia's anger melted as he watched Sergio's degenerate behavior. The anger was replaced by confusion and dismay at his own actions. He knew little of Gino, but he had seen Sergio perform gestures of goodness many times. Sergio attended Mass, served on the city council, gave alms. Could he be wrong about this man? Was the look on Sergio's face the leer of a profligate, or was Sergio simply angry, behaving stupidly?

Elia hesitated. The gorge rose in his throat. He had been a friend to this man. He closed his eyes and swallowed, again and again, to keep from vomiting. When he opened his eyes, Sergio was waving his palm in front of his face.

"Wake up Jew! Wake up! And get the hell out of my shop."

Elia ran out the door, bent, and vomited violently in the street.

146

Chapter Thirty-Eight

Elia staggered away from the shop toward his apartment. Pitching around the corner to his street, he glanced down the steps toward the tiny piazza above the valley. In the dim light he saw Leah bent over the parapet. She stood at an odd angle and seemed strangely old. He watched, but did not call her name. He had no desire to talk to her or to anyone.

Leah heard a shuffling sound behind her. She turned slowly and looked to the top of the stairs, surprised to see Elia standing there, staring at her. She held out her hand toward him and called, but he gave only a short wave and rushed away.

Too tired, too sore to follow, she let it go. There would be time to find out why he had come back, and she had no desire to explain her filthy clothes and bloody face.

She stepped away from the parapet and headed slowly in a step-and-rest, step-and-rest rhythm to the stairs. Leaning against the building, she rose one step at a time and, gaining the street, trailed haltingly toward her apartment, determined to seclude herself and spend as many days as it took to heal and to figure out what had happened to her.

In the hours before Elia had seen Leah leaning against the parapet, Leah had struggled along the river and up the hill to the piazza. She moved gingerly from tree to tree for a quarter mile, scanning the opposite river bank until she spotted the footpath on the other side of the river. She waded across a shallow section of the water, stepped up a small embankment to the trail,

147

and began the last tortured leg of the return to town. It was late afternoon; if there had been fishermen, they had gone home, and seeing no one in front of her, Leah sighed in relief.

It was late by the time Leah gained the lip of the piazza. She scanned the dimly lit space and was thankful that only a few teenagers, uninterested in her, were in the piazza. With her hood up, none of them recognized her, and none of them taunted her for her filthy clothes. A few had stopped to watch her slow progress with quizzical stares, but they said nothing.

By the time she was out in public again, she would have thought up an excuse for the cuts on her face and the slash across her head.

The moment Elia turned into his street, he saw Idrissa sitting beside the doorway of the shop, his knock-off purses spread in a neat array in front of him on a brightly colored blanket.

Elia bolted toward the younger man, his heavy suitcase banging his leg at every step. "I told you not to sit here! Go away! There are no customers this late at night anyway!"

Rigid with anger, Idrissa watched Elia advance.

Elia stopped short with his feet on the edge of Idrissa's blanket. He hovered over Idrissa, glowering.

Idi had stayed on the street later than usual. His monthly take was much less than he needed, and he hoped there would be some late afternoon tourists. When no one came along, he thought to rest his eyes and lay down along the edge of his blanket. When he awoke, in the minutes before Elia came, it was dark.

He stared at Elia, then, moving slowly, controlling his anger, he pulled the edges of the blanket from beneath Elia's feet, wrapped the blanket around his wares, and tied the corners in a large knot. Carefully testing that the knot was firm, he rolled to the side, pushed himself gracefully to his feet, and stood, hoisting the load onto his back.

The burden no more than a feather on his shoulders, he stood erect, and with a defiant stare that chilled Elia, he spoke.

"You have no heart, old man. But why should I care? You'll be dead soon."

148

Idrissa tapped his chest, then pointed at the spot where his blanket had been.

"And I'll still be right here, in front of your shop. Maybe I'll even move into your shop."

Shocked by what seemed a threat, Elia staggered backward. His suitcase fell from his hand, clattered to the stone pavement and popped open, launching a tangled mass of clothes, a razor, shaving soap, deodorant, and handkerchiefs onto the stones of the street in a chaos of colors, as if to mimic Idrissa's wares.

Idrissa laughed.

"Now you can be *vu compra.* You can sit all day in hopes of selling your wares; you can know what it's like to live on the street."

He turned, adjusted his bag, and sauntered toward the piazza.

"Macaca!"

Elia screamed. The slur he had heard in America tumbled from his lips without thought. He shook his head in a quick jerk, ashamed of calling Idrissa "monkey," wishing he could suck the words back into his mouth.

Idrissa had heard. His fists balled, and the word formed a stone in his heart as he walked away.

Elia kneeled on the worn street, snatched his things one by one, and crammed them back into the case. Finished, he unlocked the door to the shop, threw the suitcase before him and stepped inside to fall exhausted into a chair.

Sitting in the dark, gazing out the window at the dull halo around the streetlights, he thought of Anna, of the life they had, of early mistakes he had made and regretted. Idrissa was right; whether it was a threat from Idrissa himself, or whether Idrissa meant Elia was old and near to the end, what he said was true. He soon would be gone, and none of it would matter. What he had seen in New York, or Idrissa's blanket and wares stretched outside his door, or even Anna's death and the grave robbery, none of it mattered. It would all be over, all become just a tiny part of history. He would play his small part to the end, but first, he needed rest; then he could go on to find proof against Sergio. This was his small part, and he would fulfill it before he returned to the dust from which he'd come.

Chapter Thirty-Nine

Elia's battery was fading, and the flashlight cast only a faint glow on the narrow trail that led to the river. He had not been on the trails below town for years, but whoever it was who had written the note said they had news about the parochet, and Elia was desperate for proof against Sergio. It occurred to him as he walked carefully down the trail, that it could be Sergio, himself—or Gino—who sent the note, just to taunt him for his outburst at the store.

Elia heard the throaty hoot of an owl. In the next instant, the bird dipped across the path in front of him. With a sharp intake of breath, he stumbled and fell.

"Damn it!"

He pulled up on one knee and brushed at his jacket and trousers. Not ordinarily a superstitious man, the owl had unnerved him. It was cold and dark, and he wished he had not agreed to come, wished he had insisted they meet in the day, decently, in a bar.

"Elia, you're back so soon. Why didn't you stay with your sister in New York?"

An unfamiliar voice spoke from the dark in front of him. His speech sounded like someone with marbles in his mouth.

"I'm in no mood for games. Identify yourself! You obviously know I'm back, and you obviously know why I'm back, so tell me what you want to tell me, and we can get out of the cold. It's ridiculous to meet here, in the dark."

Elia's face was red with anger; he was sweating profusely and shivering in the cold breeze off the river.

"Something about a per–o–cat?"

"Don't act like you don't know. You're the one who sold it to her, aren't you?"

The man stepped forward, shining a flashlight upward from under his chin. He wore long sleeves, gloves, and a hood, and the light flowing over his face revealed a ghoulish mask.

Elia jolted backward.

"That hanging from the synagogue?" The other man asked, his voice calm. "No. No, Elia. Think it through. I wouldn't sell it to anyone directly; that's too dangerous. I would have worked with someone, wouldn't I? But, my goodness, what a coincidence you were there, at that very house where the cloth ended up."

Frightened now, Elia's heart pounded, but his anger compelled him.

"How can you speak like that, as if you'd sold her a pair of gloves or socks? It covered our Torah in the synagogue. It was made well over a century ago by hand by the women in the synagogue. It's precious to us."

The man gave a derisive laugh. "And it was precious to me. Several thousand dollars' precious. But c'mon, Elia, it's just a cloth. And an old one. Or perhaps we're here because of the way you treat people. Foreigners perhaps."

He put his fingers under his mask and wiped his face.

"Bastard! Is it you? Did I blame the wrong man? I've wondered. He's—you're? Crude, crude, and stupid, not smart enough to be involved in international art theft. But I remembered my journals: I remembered taking a group of tourists through the synagogue years ago, so I looked until I found the entry of that day in my journals. I told you. And there you—or the one you're protecting—were. You asked me if you could tag along on the tour. I agreed, and when we came to the little museum, and I spoke about the parochet, you wanted all the details. I wrote how I was excited about your questions; you showed such an interest."

The man emitted a loud guffaw.

"Maybe you didn't blame the wrong man entirely! Or maybe we're talking about something else? Or maybe I work for a woman? Or maybe it's just your time, Elia. You seem confused."

"What do you mean?"

"Oh, nothing." The man emitted a crude laugh.

"Tell me about your journal, Elia. I want to hear."

"Tell me who you are. Admit it. This is about the parochet. You're trying to confuse me. I told you the parochet disappeared long ago, during the war. You wanted to know how much it was worth. And I even told you that. $50,000 to the buyer on today's market, but it's illegal to sell such things. You smiled. I remember I couldn't understand why you smiled, but after rereading my journal entry, I understood. You knew even then where it was, didn't you?"

The man laughed again. "Of course. And it was me, wasn't it? Are you sure you've got the right man? It was me, yes? And I did know. And you're right, I smiled. I got $70,000 for it. You can't believe it, can you?" He laughed. "I knew if you ever found out, you'd be surprised, not by the price, but that it was me. It was me, wasn't it? I delighted in the thought that you'd be surprised, shocked. Are you confused, Elia? Aren't you wondering who I am? I've hated you from the first time I was introduced to you. Jews. You're always trouble, always poking into things, always crying about justice. But you don't give justice to everyone. Think about your history, Elia. Think about your own sins! Think about your ancestors' sins. Innocent men and woman."

"You're insane. We've done nothing to you, whoever you are. Nothing. How have we ever given you trouble? And if you hate us so much, why steal our religious artworks? Aren't they odious to you as well?"

"Elia! You can't be that naïve! Really! You don't have to love Italians to appreciate the Duomo. We steal your artworks because we can sell them for good money. But are you sure that's what this is about?"

"We?"

"Well, I had to have help, didn't I? Now the three of us have a secret."

"Who? Who are you?"

"That's for me to know and you to find out."

153

"But they're religious objects. How can you stupe that low? Don't you have any sense of ethics, of decency? It's like going into a church and taking crosses and candle sticks, and the vestments of the priest.

The man laughed. "It's not like that at all. Those are Christian things. Get with the program, Elia. Nobody cares about the Jews. Still, okay, I admit, if I could easily get to Christian things that were easily valuable, I'd sell them."

He threw his head back and laughed aloud.

"You're wrong. Everyone here cares about the Jews except for a few antisemites like you. You're a tiny minority in this town."

"Maybe so, but we're a strong minority. We run the show."

"You won't for much longer. When the Lieutenant and the others know it was you who sold the parochet, things will change. This is a good town, full of good people; they won't put up with what you've done—and neither will the police here or in New York."

The man slapped Elia hard across the face.

"The par–o–cat, the par–o–cat; that's all you think about. Are you so sure you know who I am?"

He slapped Elia again, and Elia pawed the air, trying to pull off the man's mask before he fell to the ground.

"Neither the people in town nor the Lieutenant will ever know about the parochet. I'm going to continue making money off your little knickknacks and your beautiful cloths with the funny language. There are hundreds of pieces here and from the villages around here, all to sell to people who appreciate the fine art of dead Jews. But maybe I'm mad at you because you betrayed a good woman, or because you're nasty to foreigners, or maybe it's just because you're a dirty Jew."

The man stood over him, tilted the mask forward from the bottom, and spat out the rocks he'd put in his mouth to disguise his voice.

He tore off the mask.

"Surprise! It's me, Elia.

"You bastard, I won't let it happen!" Elia pushed himself up and rushed away, up the trail.

Heavy branch in hand, the man caught up with Elia before he'd gone ten yards. Elia heard the step behind; as he turned, the man raised the cudgel and brought it down full force against the back of Elia's head.

Emitting a heavy groan, Elia slumped to the ground.

The man struck Elia's head again and then again until a white shard of bone showed through the matt of blood and hair.

Breathing hard, he looked down at Elia's body and shook his head.

"The trouble you've given me. Now I have to drag you out of here. I thought Jews were supposed to be smart. But here you are, dead. How is it you weren't smart enough to avoid meeting in an isolated place in the dark, late at night, without even knowing who invited you?" He laughed aloud.

Chapter Forty

Three days passed. The Lieutenant had called, Stein had called, the Signora and Secondo had called. Leah told them all that she had a cold and was staying in bed. She had tried to call Elia several times, but he was not answering his phone, and Leah decided to stop trying to reach him; she would wait until he was ready to talk. Whatever had happened, he must want time alone.

Her muscles still ached, but the bruises were fading, and she was thankful for how quickly the scrapes on her face were healing. The fall was not as bad as she thought when she first regained consciousness. She fabricated an excuse: a fall on the concrete steps just before she came down with the head cold.

Happy to be out and feeling fairly normal once again, she walked to the pharmacy, bought vitamins, paid, and stepped out the wide glass doors.

Looking up at the perfect cerulean blue of the sky, she considered the day. If she were to talk to Elia as she hoped, to pick up her table from Magliotti, and to contact Stein and set up a meeting with him—she was intent on discovering why he was in town—the afternoon would be too busy for a hike. She would wait one more day before she contacted the Lieutenant. She would hike now.

"Carpe diem! And a hair of the dog!" she muttered to herself, tucking the cream into her backpack and crossing the piazza to the steps that descended from the piazza to the river, the road, and the *vie cave*.

At the base of the hill, across the bridge, she stepped off the pavement onto

156

the berm just below the older and mostly unused trail.

Leah looked up again at the bright-blue sky and billowy cumulus clouds lower Tuscany provided in abundance summer and fall. She relished the warm sun on her shoulders and regarded the murky breach in the trees where the trail began.

Hesitant, she stood still, remembering the murder of Giulio: his body catapulted into the air, his scream faded like the last twang of a violin string—and then silence. She had seen the murder and was discovered in the next instant. The killer had turned, spotted her on the ledge below, and raced after her. She fled at full run, heavy footfalls behind her echoing her own.

The chase was still vivid in her memory. She ran to the ancient Etruscan burial caves and pushed herself against the back of a small recess, her heart pounding, while only feet away, the killer tapped along the wall and floor with a stick, prodding the crevices. Hovered at the back of a shallow opening in the rock, she struggled to match her breath with the killer's heavy breathing. Those moments, the terrified flight that led to them, and the fear that constricted her chest stayed with her.

If she remembered every detail, she was also determined those moments of terror in the cave would not stop her from the pleasure of walking these slot trails. Glancing behind her, she hunched her shoulders and shook her head to dispel the memory of her escape, to put out of her mind Elia's strange slight, and to erase for a while the history the Signora had recounted.

A flock of sheep grazed peacefully in the meadow across the river. She took a deep breath, turned to her right, and dropped into the deep ditch beside the road.

Chapter Forty-One

Wet from morning dew, the tall grasses soaked her jeans. She skirted a pool of standing water at the bottom of the ditch and leaned into the steep incline that would bring her up to the start of the trail. Huffing from exertion, she tugged at weeds for balance,

The opening of the trail and the first steep twenty meters to the sharp curve in the path above was strewn with rocks and boulders that had broken away from the tufa walls on either side and lodged in the leafy bed of the trail. Leah stepped over and around what she could, but as she moved upward, she was compelled to climb over the larger boulders, hopping from one to the other.

There were signs someone else had recently been on the trail. This was unusual; she bent down to study the marks. Layers of leaves accumulated over years undisturbed by any but her own tread were upturned, revealing the dark, moist humus beneath. She ran her hand over the warm curve of a boulder. It was scraped, as if someone had dragged a shovel over it.

Sweating heavily, she continued upward, smiling to herself as she remembered boulder hopping in the Tetons on the approach to Mt. Wister. She had leapt from boulder to boulder across the moraine to reach the beginning of the ascent. After summiting, the climb had ended in an exhilarating glissade to the lake, all five friends shouting for joy.

Twenty meters up, the trail turned to the left and broke abruptly from the tufa walls, opening onto a broad, level stretch of path bounded by thick oak and mastic brush. Long furrows gouged the deep blanket of leaves.

A sickening fear rose in her stomach.

She imagined *cinghiali* dragging her through the forest.

"Idiot!"

She chastised herself and began, step by step, to reason why the furrows could not have been made by *cinghiali*. The marks were too narrow, too consistent a drag. *Cinghiali* foraged at night, but it was mating season, so the nocturnal habits could have been disrupted to bring them out during the day. They were mostly herbivores—but not always.

Her mind wavered. Had the animals been disturbed while eating a rare carrion find? She stood still and listened. Her body cooled; a chill settled over her back and shoulders.

She imagined Nick laughing and taunting her: "Stop lollygagging! Either go back down to the apartment or go ahead."

She took a deep breath and moved ahead. Within minutes she was warm again. The sun wove strands through the foliage, flickering on the trail. The furrows zigzagged in front of her like shoe laces, winding right and left as the trail meandered, now flat, now upward.

She walked slowly, mulling over the marks. The wet leaves muffled the sound of her steps, and she felt herself moving as light as a breeze moves voiceless through the trees.

Chapter Forty-Two

Grunting, rooting at the earth, *cinghiali* circled the body. A sounder of ten, two mature sows, six sub-adults, and two little ones were sniffing at the man, but had not yet begun to feed on him.

Sweat broke out on Leah's forehead, on her chest, under her arms. Her heart beat wildly, and she panted in tight, quick breaths.

Fight or flight?

Suddenly dizzy, the gorge rose like a rock in Leah's throat; she swallowed hard and, from her spot lower on the trail, lifted on her toes in an attempt to see the man's face.

The animals obscured her vision. The man lay supine on the ground, obviously unaware of the *cinghiali*. Leah could not see well enough to tell if he were unconscious or dead.

The larger sows, black with thick, rough bristles, rooted under the man's shoulders and buttocks, rumbling contentedly. Their offspring, still young enough to carry faint stripes along their backs, grunted in imitation of the sows, pushing in and out the legs of the larger beasts to sniff at the man's head and face, at his legs and feet.

Leah stretched upward again in an attempt to see his face. Without going forward, it was impossible.

A quick movement in the brush startled her. She swiveled. The dark outline of a boar appeared in the brush two meters past the others.

Her quick movement and the slight breeze through the branches of the trees alerted the *cinghiali*. They lifted their grizzled heads and turned in her direction, probing the air with their snouts. Leah thought of a bear she had once come across in the mountains of Washington.

The young *cinghiali* males' budding tusks glistened in the sunlight. The much longer tusks of the sows jutted from their lower jaws like pitchforks. Unable to see her because of their weak eyes, but able to determine where she stood by her sound and smell, they turned from the body and stepped tentatively toward her, raising one foot, hesitating, then stepping forward, raising another foot, jabbing the air with their snouts, moving in her direction, step by cautious step.

Rigid with fear, Leah stood still, breathing fast and light through her mouth in an attempt to stifle any sound. Every instinct told her to turn back, to run down the trail and bring help. The odds were against her: the sows had young, some might be in estrus if the male were nearby, they were on the verge of eating, and they outnumbered her.

Too dangerous.

Still, she could not move. She could not leave the man, whoever he was, whatever had been done to him or whatever he had done, to be eaten, possibly alive.

She made a decision.

As she had done the time before in the burial cave, with the murderer standing near, she grasped the silver whistle that hung around her neck, brought it to her lips, and broke into a run, bounding forward, wildly waving her arms, the high-pitch of the whistle screaming through the clear air.

The *cinghiali* snorted in loud, sharp bursts and stood their ground.

In for a penny, in for a pound.

The absurd thought came to her mind. She may soon be on the ground next to the man, with the beasts at her flesh. She plunged ahead, straight into the musky smell of the sounder.

In one swift motion, they swung to and fled, bursting off the trail into the brush, crashing over bushes, squealing as they scattered.

Heart drumming in her chest, Leah listened as the chaotic sound of their flight diminished. When she was certain they were gone, and the boar with them, she turned to the body.

Chapter Forty-Three

Leah dropped to her knees beside Elia and gathered him in her arms. She stared into the lifeless eyes, the cascade of her tears falling across his face.

His skull had been bashed in. A jagged circle of blood-ringed white bone showed against his dark hair. She brushed gently at his stained, crumpled clothing and his dirty face. She rubbed vainly at the sleeve of his jacket where dirt and leaves had adhered to a swipe of something sticky.

From Elia's brain.

She turned aside, retched, then turned back. A fly buzzed and settled on the opening in Elia's skull. Swallowing her gorge, Leah waved the fly away with a quick, angry motion of her hand.

Aware she was acting against all rules of a crime scene and understanding the Lieutenant would be angry, she ignored protocol and lifted Elia's upper body further onto her lap and pulled him to her chest, rocking him rhythmically back and forth, cradling him like a child.

Death and then death again. Her thoughts wandered to people she had once known. They stood like bright posts through the flat plain of her history. Some had hurt her and were long forgiven; some she had hurt and then had hoped her pleas encouraged them to forgive her. Two she had loved with a passion she could not ease, a nagging longing, no matter where she went, no matter who else she loved. Some like Anna, Elia, and Nick were pure light that buoyed her on the violent waves of her own emotions, which at times threatened to destroy her.

Her legs grew numb. Still, she held Elia to her. As if in compassionate camaraderie, clouds moved in from the west, the sky darkened, and it began to rain in long, gentle strings that pattered on leaves and branches and shimmered down to earth. It soaked Leah and Elia and created rivulets of water that flowed against the legs of the living and the dead.

Trembling with the cold, holding Elia close with one arm, Leah lifted her whistle to her lips and blew again and then again: three short bursts, three long, three short. Again. And then again and again.

Chapter Forty-Four

L eah stared into the grave at the simple walnut box that held Elia. Done with crying, frustrated, angry, her gaze moved round and round the rough edges of the grave. She felt obsessed with the sense she must find whoever it was that had killed Elia.

At her shoulder, Elia's sister, Rachel, cried quietly, sniffing, blowing her nose in delicate spurts, while the rabbi intoned the prayers. Rachel muttered in intermittent outbursts, "What was it? What was it?" and Leah wondered if she had not understood Elia had been murdered.

Leah raised her head and looked over the group. These were the same people who had come for Anna's funeral, but now they seemed to Leah ragged imitations of the people they had been before. The men's dark suits, frayed at the cuffs, were spotted with grease. The women's black dresses wrinkled at their laps, and sweat stains circled their underarms.

What was the difference? Why were they all ragged, rough-edged, and spotted? Had she simply not noticed before?

Magliotti stood toward the back, his head down. Idrissa was missing, and Leah had not seen him along the way. The Lieutenant stood toward the back of the group just beside Magliotti, watching Leah with a sad, discouraged look. As she had anticipated, he was angry with her for disturbing the crime scene. His interview, after they took the body away from the trail, had been short and cold.

Leah was angry with him for being angry.

"It was Elia!" she spat back at the Lieutenant when he chastised her, "How could I not go to him, hold him? He was battered and hurt."

164

The Lieutenant's look softened. He stepped toward her to embrace her, but she walked away. He had not approached her since.

Standing next to Secondo, Stein stared with a look of surprise, almost as if he hadn't expected to see her there.

I'll find out about you. Leah pursed her lips.

All of the townspeople looked exhausted. Leah could read fear in their eyes and in their glances toward the cemetery gates that seemed to say, "Rush the burial; let us escape to the safety of the bar in the piazza or to the protection of our homes. "

Leah understood. Murder had come while Anna's desecrated grave still leaked into their dreams and troubled their nights. Murder had battered them all.

When the prayers were over, the family moved to one side, and townspeople stepped forward. Their heads lowered, their handshakes limp, they offered hasty condolences to Elia's sister, hesitantly yielding their words in soft murmurs before rushing away.

Rachel had been gone so long from the town few of the older ones her age remembered her. To those who did remember, she seemed a stranger, foreign, more American than Italian. They blundered in their attempts to share her grief, and they avoided her eyes, unable to take on even the small part of anguish they could have shouldered if she had still been one of them and they understood what she needed.

Within minutes after the prayers and after the townspeople and farmers had left, the gravediggers, shovels in hand, stepped from the shadows of the trees at the periphery of the cemetery and began to fill the grave. Loud thwooks of dirt echoed against the hillside as each shovelful dropped on the casket.

Women from the Catholic church, all of whom knew Elia from shopping in his store, had prepared a light meal in the foyer of the theater. In groups of twos and threes, Elia's friends and those he'd known in business filed into the open space to take a desultory drink of wine, eat a small sandwich, and then turn back to their shops and fields, relieved to have the ritual over and to discuss amongst themselves who could have killed Elia. Who was strong enough to have dragged him over such rough terrain to the top of the trail, and why? And if it could happen to such a good man, who might be next? they asked each other, leaning close.

After the luncheon, Leah and Rachel walked to the piazza. On a bench near the low wall that overlooked the valley, shaded by a tall acacia tree, they sat quietly until Leah broke the silence to ask what she had been wondering since the burial.

"At the interment, you kept repeating, 'What was it?' What did you mean by that?"

Rachel groaned, and Leah saw her hand shake as she reached into her bag to take a clean linen handkerchief. Tears tumbled slowly from her eyes, threading down her cheeks. Leah waited while Rachel turned away to delicately blow her nose and wipe her face of tears.

"When Elia was in New York, we went to a party, a Sukkot party held by one of my clients. I hadn't been to her house before, and I was happy to be invited because the hostess and I were becoming friends. I looked forward to seeing her house and meeting her friends, some of whom I hoped would also be mine."

She looked into Leah's eyes to make sure she understood. "We both knew some of the same people, and it seemed like things were going well. Elia was sad, and I was careful not to bring up the incident at the cemetery. We'd even laughed a little over memories of a trip to New York he and Anna had made some years ago. When we arrived, he seemed to ease right into the party and conversation with the others. And I could tell he was enjoying the artwork the hostess had on her walls and tables. The pieces were all originals, together worth millions, I imagine. Elia was impressed, and I know he wished Anna could have seen them.

Then, just before we sat down to eat, Elia went to the bathroom to wash his hands. When he came back into the living room he was furious.

I had waited for him by the entrance to the balcony, so we could sit together under the sukkah, but he didn't even look toward me; he stalked straight through the living room and out of the apartment with no explanation. I've never seen him so angry.

I made quick excuses to the hostess and followed him out the door and into the taxi, where I tried to get him to explain, but all he would say was, 'I know who did it! I know who did it.' He did mumble some other phrases. I couldn't quite make them out, but I did hear one clearly: 'He'll pay for this!'

When we got back to my apartment, he sat down immediately, made the return ticket to Rome, and early the next morning, he left, saying he'd wait at the airport for the flight.

"Without telling you what he meant?"

"Not a word. He didn't speak that night or the next morning except for what I've told you."

"It had to have been something he saw or heard when he went to the bathroom."

"Yes, but what? What could be in the bathroom that would upset him."

"Perhaps there was someone in one of the bedrooms? Someone said something?"

She tilted her head in thought. "Maybe. It was a large group, but I don't remember anyone else coming out of that part of the house."

"Something about Scansansiano? Or about someone living here?"

"That makes the most sense... I'm sorry. I only remember he kept repeating that he knew who did it."

"Did what?"

"He wouldn't say! That's what I'm telling you—and now it's too late. Leah, I worried; he was a man who could be quick to blame, and I thought he might hurt someone. Instead, he was the one who...."

Rachel began to cry again. Leah drew her close.

"I'm so sorry, Signora. "

Gentle as Leah's voice sounded, her heart was heavy as a rock in her chest.

Rachel wiped her eyes and sighed, pulling gently away.

"What did the Lieutenant say?"

"He's angry at me for making a mess of the crime scene, so I might not be the best one to report. We didn't speak except for the interview. I think he must be as befuddled as the rest of us. He doesn't know of any crime that's been committed lately, except the grave robbery. He told me a few bare facts after he'd talked to you. He can't imagine what Elia was going on about. It doesn't make sense that your client, in New York, could be involved in the grave robbery—and anyway, she's Jewish, right?"

"Yes…."

"So she would know there would be nothing to rob in a Jewish grave. And she's not from here?"

"She's been here before, but only driving through. It was before I knew her, and she'd never met Elia."

"If we knew the crime, maybe we could make connections, figure something out. The grave robbery is the only thing I can think of."

"I'm sorry I can't help. Elia simply refused to talk to me. He was angrier than I've ever seen him, and to tell the truth, I felt a little afraid of him."

Leah thought of the night she had been leaning against the parapet of the little piazza overlooking the valley. Why had he rushed away?

Leah gazed off across the piazza. The Signora was coming toward them. Leah waved. "Signora, hello!"

"You two have found a quiet spot."

"We've been talking about Elia. What could he have done, or what could he know that would arouse anyone to murder him? It's strange. What could he have found out? Except the grave robbery, nothing's happened."

Staring at the ground, the Signora considered the question and raised her head. "You don't think it had to do with the desecration of the grave?"

"No, Rachel said the apartment they were visiting belonged to a Jewish family."

Rachel nodded.

"Perhaps one of the guests? The Signora put her hand on her cheek.

"Maybe. Maybe something he overheard."

The Signora's eyes widened. "Or maybe it wasn't a recent crime?"

Leah nodded. "I asked the Lieutenant to go back several years in his records, but there was nothing—anyway nothing he hadn't already solved."

She smiled. "Handsome and efficient."

Leah ignored the Signora's remark. "There's got to be some connection."

The Signora grunted. "Of course there's a connection! But what? Perhaps the first thing is for Rachel to go back to her friend's, have a look around, and ask some questions."

Rachel started. "That's what the Lieutenant said, but I couldn't! The woman who owns the apartment is not actually a friend; she's a client, and I wouldn't know how to invite myself, especially after what happened."

The Signora responded in a gruff voice. "This is no time to be timid, Signora. Someone's killed your brother."

"But not her!"

"Perhaps someone she knows." The Signora opened both palms toward Rachel.

Rachel slumped against Leah, tears rolling from her eyes. "This is horrible."

"Leah!" The Signora's voice. "I know you have many things to do. Why don't you go on? I'll take Rachel to get something to eat and to have a good glass of wine. She needs strength." The Signora made a face when Leah hesitated. "It's all right; I'll be good."

"Is it all right with you, Rachel?" Leah asked.

"Of course. The Signora will take good care of me," she gave a faint smile, "and I think will make sure I get back on keel and do what I'm supposed to do."

Chapter Forty-Five

In the days after the funeral, Leah returned to hike the *vie cave* again and then again. The trails were her only solace. She remembered John Muir had said, "Between every two pine trees there is a door leading to a new way of life." She thought of this each time she labored upward through the narrow walls of tufa, past the cavernous burial caves, across the small, intermittent meadows. It was here, in wild Tuscany, where she experienced freedom and clarity, if not precise answers. The upward push through the thick forests along the river and valley sides and the ultimate break onto the ridge with a 180-degree of green rolling hills and vineyards cleansed her mind for thinking.

After, home again in the silence of her apartment, she read, or called the Signora to come sit with her so the two of them could go over all the same things they had already said about the grave robbery in previous discussions. After they would begin again on the enigma of Elia's death.

The Lieutenant neither called nor visited. Leah began to think their tete-a-tete in the little bar had been imagined. Secondo was busy with Stein, who also stayed away, and Leah wondered if Scansansiano would ever be a real home to her. In Montana, Sara was busier than ever and called only once or twice every two weeks. Isolated, distanced from her friends, and aggrieved over the loss of both Anna and Elia, she escaped by making notes, laying out possibilities.

One morning, Leah remembered the table she had left at Magliotti's. The twenty-minute drive to Magliotti's shop in Casale passed in lush visions of the Tuscan countryside. The dappled sunlight crossed her face as she drove through the tunnel of trees overhanging the narrow asphalt road.

Breaking into the open at the top of the ridge, she took in the beauty of the brilliant-green fields of winter wheat, like soft hair or fur, undulating in a breeze that wafted toward the north. Farther on, neat rows of grape vines angled across the breast of the hill. Leah's spirits lifted. She took great pleasure in the visual and physical intensity of the landscape. In recent days, her hope and faith in life diminished, as if a tap in her spirit had opened. Surrounded now by the fields, by the tufa outcrops, by the thick forests, and under the bright sun, she trusted that this beauty would renew her, would balance the inner confusion, sadness, and anger she felt over the painful recent events.

Magliotti's bell jangled against the shaded glass as Leah pushed open the door. The shop was empty.

"Signor Magliotti!"

She waited.

"Magli-ot-ti!" She sang.

"I'm in the back room. Be out in a minute."

His voice came from behind a narrow doorway to Leah's left. She could hear him moving about, dragging furniture.

She wandered along the shelves, brushing her hand over wooden knobs, chair arms and legs, clamps, vises, chisels, and sanding equipment. The pungent smell of wood permeated the air, and Leah breathed it in with pleasure, remembering the days her father had taught her to use the lathe in his workshop at the back of their garage.

Magliotti's shelves were laden with these materials, but were neatly organized, and this neatness in craftsmenship, a hallmark of excellence, signified to Leah that he must have done a good job on her table. She moved from shelf to shelf, anxious to see the beautiful little table, a gift from the Signora.

Every minute is a thin line, she realized as she waited. She would never again share with Elia her joy in having the table, he who had an eye for antiques. Tears came to her eyes. The most mundane happenings recalled Anna, Elia, and Nick. What the Signora had told her about Grazia and Elia made her sad; in the end, it only emphasized how human are even the best of people. It did not change her love for the older couple; it strengthened her compassion for Grazia. If she felt judgmental toward anyone, it was Salvatore, who had done a great wrong in marrying a woman he did not love.

The young Elia, Grazia, Salvatore, and Anna had been people with real passions, and they had made real mistakes. She had been the same. So many mistakes in her life, as well as joys and regrets, crowded her chest, just as they must have done with the four young friends. Most people must labor for years to forgive themselves and others, struggling perhaps with—or against—the threads of religion to understand how to make amends.

Leah could no longer imagine Elia and Anna as spotless beings. She had lost a useless innocence, the kind that forced her into a sense of false guilt, in which she envisioned people she loved and sometimes people she had newly met, were pure in a way she could never be.

It was a disservice to others to skip the destructive, or at least potentially destructive, side of their natures, to put them on such a tall, narrow pedestal they were sure to fall.

If she were stung by this loss of innocence, in return she had been gifted with a firmer love, one that encompassed the whole of the people about whom she cared, a love that instructed her in accepting the whole of herself as well—all with the challenge of learning forgiveness.

Elia had stormed through the town in a fury of anger. Why? What was driving him the day he snubbed her? She knew of the encounters with Idrissa and Sergio. There was the abrupt behavior the night he had returned, when he recognized her, but refused to talk and instead rushed away. And there was the ride on the bus on the way from the train station. The driver said Elia was nervous, distracted, uncharacteristically short-tempered. What had happened in New York? Would Rachel visit the apartment?

He could have, he should have, talked to her about all these things. He could have told the story of Sergio, how his family had tried to forgive

Sergio. She could have at least have listened, and maybe helped. Whatever had happened to Elia, his anger, his sadness was so great that he pushed her friendship away at the most crucial time.

The wound of that last spurn was like the wound she felt when Nick had sent her out of the room so she would not see his death. To be denied the most profound moments in a loved one's life was the worst sort of loss.

Most importantly, could she have saved Elia? Could she have saved Nick for a few more days? The sounds from behind the inner door signaled that Magliotti was still busy moving furniture in the back room. Leah continued along the shelves, picking up a piece of wood here and there to bring it to her face and smell it. To her, the smell of wood was perfume, a perfume that reminded her of her father in his workshop.

She moved to the next shelf, where there were pots and bottles of glue. Reaching to upright one pot, she tipped another over, and glue oozed onto the shelf.

Leah froze; her heart pounded against her ribs, her throat went dry. She remembered the white ooze across Elia's jacket when she found him on the trail.

Using her index finger, she touched the spot that had spilled onto the shelf and rolled the thick paste between her finger and thumb.

The paste on Elia's jacket was glue, this glue.

Chapter Forty-Six

"Something interesting, Signora?"

Leah started. His voice was right next to her ear. She swung around; his face was only inches from hers, so close she could see the pores on his nose.

Leah backed away. "You startled me. I've spilled your glue. I'm sorry."

"Why are you so pale, Signora? The glue is no problem. Do you feel ill?"

Leah sidestepped him and made motions of cleaning up the mess she had made.

"Not to worry, Signora."

He put his hand over hers and guided it firmly off the shelf. She pulled it from his grip.

"Oh, have I hurt you? There's really no worry about the glue; I can take care of it later; I use glue all the time and can clean it quite easily."

Leaning forward, he stared at her, holding her gaze.

"Why does it upset you so?"

"It doesn't!"

"But I see it does, Signora. You're shaking."

"No, I'm—"

"You are! Sit!"

A command. He motioned at a chair next to the shelf.

Leah sat on the edge of the chair.

"Lean back, Signora, relax. I'll tell you about the glue. It's really very interesting. Did you notice the color? It's light tan, almost white, the very strongest I can buy. Epoxy actually. Gorilla Glue!"

His laughter was a snarl; he pounded his chest with his fists, imitating the gorilla on the label. There was no delight in his unrelenting stare. His eyes were cold flint.

Suddenly he stopped laughing and, still staring at her, stood straight and spoke as if he were a professor giving a lecture.

"The glue should dry quickly, five minutes they say, but here in Tuscany—perhaps it's the damp climate—it doesn't dry quickly, particularly if it gets on cloth. I'll show you."

He pulled a cloth from his pocket.

"You see, here…." He took a rag from the lower shelf and pointed to a spot on it where a bit of glue had made a smudge.

"Signor, I have to—"

"You have to nothing!" he screamed.

As suddenly as he had screamed, he spoke softly, but his voice was the purr of a cat hunting a mouse.

"I can't help but wonder why you are shaking, Signora? I don't like to think my customers are uncomfortable."

Leah stood and moved toward the door.

"I have to get back. If the table's not done, I'll come tomorrow or the next day."

Magliotti followed her. When she reached the door, Magliotti leapt in front of her. Speaking in a sickeningly sweet voice, he grasped her shoulders and turned her back toward the shelves.

"I insist. Sit down," he guided her back into the room, "and we'll discuss your table. It's just here."

He gestured toward the back room.

"I have it ready. Oh dear. Your face is flushed."

He put his hand on her arm.

"Are you too warm? Not still worried about the glue I hope?"

He slowly shook his head back and forth.

"Are you ill? Or…."

He stared down the length of her body.

"…perhaps you find me attractive?"

175

He fluttered his eyelashes in an exaggerated imitation of a female lover. Leah glanced toward the door.

"You can't think of leaving? You've only just come, and we have things to discuss. I can't, just can't, let you go."

Leah bolted toward the door, but Magliotti moved faster. He grasped her wrists and pulled her roughly against him, encircling her waist with one arm and clamping his other hand over her mouth. She twisted, beating at him with her fists. When his hand slipped a fraction of an inch, she bit him hard between the thumb and forefinger. Blood spurted from the wound.

Magliotti yelled in pain and grabbed her wrist. Taking the chance, Leah ducked, spinning toward the door, but Magliotti caught her by the hair, jerking her sharply backward. As she fell, he leapt forward and threw himself on top of her, straddling her, grappling for her wrists.

Leah wrenched one hand free and slapped him with an open palm against his left ear. His head tilted to one side with the blow, and he yelped in pain, but clung to her left wrist. She writhed under his weight, shoving with a jolt to the left. Magliotti fell to that side, still holding her wrist, and before she could gain purchase, he was up, bending her arm behind her back with his forearm across her throat.

She struggled against him as he dragged her, kicking, into the back room of the shop and pushed her face down to the floor. With a knee in her back, he tied her wrists and her ankles, then flipped her on her back and ran a rope around her neck, tying it to a post.

Once she was secured, Magliotti leaned over her, breathing hard in spurts.

"You little vixen." He panted. "No screaming, or I'll have to dispense with you now rather than later. And we don't want that just yet. I do admire your toughness. I've wanted to get rid of you for a long time. My goodness, you're as tenacious as a bulldog. I learned that lesson when you first came here years ago, and I saw that it was because of you that young woman's naughty doings came to light. I thought to myself then that eventually you and I might tangle; I hoped not, but how I worried you'd find me out!

You're the type that digs and digs and never lets up. Not necessarily smart or logical, but persistent, a real bulldog. I hoped and prayed that after you left, you would stay away. But you didn't! And now here we are!"

Terrified, Leah watched him ramble, twist his face, and shake his head. He was crazy; he was Jekyll and Hyde; he was going to kill her.

Magliotti sighed heavily, still shaking his head back and forth as if he were scolding a child.

"Just like a bad penny, you turned up again, and when you stuck your nose into the grave robbery business, I knew that as far as you're concerned, a stitch in time saves nine. You needed to be taken care of.

I tried on the escarpment that day. My goodness! I was within a hair's breadth of getting caught by that American—"

"Stein was there?"

"Oh, yes. And I'm so thankful he was whistling as he approached. I had to run like the wind to get behind the little shed before he saw me. He was looking for you. I think he may be a little in love with you, Signora. He stood there at the edge and called and called. Like a lonely dog howls in the night. But you didn't answer. I'm much stronger than I look, you know. One shove and you flew into the air. Boom! Just like you'd been catapulted from a cannon. I was certain you were down there dead."

"What luck I've had lately! I was in my car smoking a cigarette on the dirt road at the top of the field, and the Innocenti brothers walked by. They mentioned you were coming that way. Imagine how the fates smiled on me—and again today!"

Magliotti laughed with delight and flexed his muscles.

"You bounced up and down so many times against the rocks and the dirt and must have smacked hard against a tree at the bottom. I lost sight of you, but I couldn't wait because of Stein. I was sure you would have broken your neck!

Naughty girl. I walked around town for three days, waiting to see if you would show up. I asked the barmaid—no one else. I didn't want your friends to connect my name with you. But since the barmaid hadn't seen you, I was sure I had succeeded. The little bulldog was gone!

Then, just like a jack in the box, you jumped right back up and began nosing around again. Such trouble you make for me – and for the Lieutenant, always getting involved when you shouldn't."

"I can see by your face, you didn't know it was me." He laughed. "You thought it was an accident?"

Again he laughed aloud and slapped his thigh like an old man hearing a good joke.

"But you get the last laugh—'last laugh'! I'm so witty today - by knowing Signor Stein almost caught me. He was following you, Signora. I don't know for what, but I can imagine!" He cackled and wagged his finger at her.

Everyone loves you. Maybe they appreciate your tenacity, but I think you're just too observant, too tenacious—although I admit I was a little careless about that glue."

When he leaned close, Leah banged her head against his. He pulled on the rope around her neck, choking her.

"Calm yourself, Signora. I can't kill you, not just yet. There's not just the killing, you know; there's the disposal, and I have things to do."

Leah felt the darkness closing in as he pulled on the rope. Her arms had gone numb, the sockets in her shoulders ached. She could feel the strength draining from her body.

He loosened the rope around her neck. She gulped air.

"Well! That was good exercise! Whoever could have imagined. Such a coincidence that you would make the connection right here in my shop and by happenstance."

"You bastard! What did he ever do to you?"

"Another happenstance. I had nothing against Elia. I don't know what to say. Coincidences for which one can never account. Too bad for both of us!" He shook his finger at her.

"What happened? Tell me!"

"I didn't want to kill him. It was just another unfortunate circumstance. A little bird told me—oh, that's a lie—Elia himself inadvertently told me that he happened across a cloth hanging I sold to an American, a hanging from the synagogue. There was a go-between, of course."

"Inadvertently?

"I can't explain now. Something I overheard."

CHAPTER FORTY-SIX

"You're talking about the parochet."

"I think it was called something like that, yes."

"But why kill him?"

"Dealing in artworks is one of my very best, but lesser-known," he grinned, "businesses. It's also one of my most lucrative. And I am not licensed. Bad Boy me!"

He shook his finger at himself.

"I'm afraid the authorities would call my dealings illegal. You know that, Signora. Don't play dumb. If Elia had made his way to me, which he almost did—but he blamed the wrong person—I would have lost everything, and probably been sent to jail."

He sighed.

"Like everyone, Signora, I need to make a living."

"You filthy pervert! Murderer! Grave robber!"

"Oh, no. Don't blame everything on me. I don't do those perverse things, and I certainly wouldn't treat dear Anna's corpse in such a grisly manner. No. I made a simple sale, and then…" he blushed, "just a nice, clean murder. And since you were so unfortunate as to tip over the glue, I guess with you, it's in for a penny in for a pound! And now I have yet another body on my hands! Shame on you!"

He waggled his finger at her, giggled like a girl, and suddenly was serious again.

"But I think I would have killed you anyway—probably when you came for the table—just like today!"

"Bastard! Where did you get the parochet?" Leah lifted her head and spat at him, but missed.

"Such fury and spirit. I like that!"

He leaned forward and brushed her cheek with the back of his hand. "If there were more time… You really are quite attractive. But, alas, no time!"

From the window ledge, he took a roll of tape and taped her mouth.

"I have my sources for artwork, Signora, but I'm not a tattler, even though with you it wouldn't matter at all."

He wiped the sweat from his forehead. "My, you are a strong woman.

It's taken a good deal of strength to get you in here, and I'm all sweaty. Elia wasn't easy either. What a mess of blood and oozing stuff—and then dragging him up all those boulders and along the trail.

After I—what shall I say?—'deposited' him, I spent the rest of the night washing my hair and body and destroying my filthy clothes. I was exhausted. And now you... What am I going to do with you?"

He shook his head and sighed.

Leah struggled against the bonds on her hands and feet, breathing heavily through her nose from the exertion.

"You may as well relax, Signora. The tie is very strong; you can't escape. Seeing you like this, knowing you haven't got long in this beautiful world, and since you asked, I'll break my rule and give you a hint. You won't be around to tell anyone.

"'A soldier's daily duty to his uniform and shoes.' Is that enough for you? I know it isn't, but it's all I'm going to say. It will give you something to think about until...well, you know."

He laughed and tousled her hair with a heavy hand.

"I'm sworn to secrecy."

Opening his eyes wide, he put his finger to his lips and rolled his eyes.

"I'm very sorry I didn't finish your table. You must admit it was a great deal of work lugging your friend up that trail. I was exhausted. That and then getting clean—so tired, and I still had to keep up appearances, being seen in town and whatnot.

Now I must leave; I'm expected at home. But not to worry. I must go now—you came at a most inopportune time—but I'll be back tomorrow morning to give you something to eat, your last meal, as it were. Would you like anything special?"

Leah made no move.

"No? Well then, I'll leave you to think about your very last night on earth. If I didn't have a meeting tonight in addition to all I've got tomorrow, it wouldn't even be that, my dear, but one must keep up appearances. And, well, it might be fun."

He bent to stroke her cheek again. Leah recoiled, her eyes furious.

180

"I'm so glad you're tied up, Signora, but even though you're angry, I keep thinking what fun we could have if there were only time. Maybe...."

Laughing, he slapped his knee again and left the room.

Chapter Forty-Seven

The barmaid had just set the Signora's coffee on the table when David Stein stepped into the bar. Seeing the Signora, he made a slight bow in greeting.

"Good day, Signor Americano."

Stein groaned. "It's David, David Stein."

"I know your name. But we've all been calling you 'the American' since you got here. It's become a habit."

Stein grimaced.

"Such a face! Don't get upset. We call you that because you're a mystery to us.

"I'm unwillingly one of several mysteries in town, it seems."

"Or perhaps just a part of just one?"

"Meaning?"

"I'm not sure."

"I can promise you, Signora, I am in no way involved in grave robbing, beatings in the piazza, troubles with Idrissa, or any other nefarious doings."

"What about art treasures?"

Remembering his last call to his office, Stein blushed and cleared his throat. To avoid the Signora's eyes, he tilted his head and rubbed his neck. The Signora had seen his eyes shift right, a sign to her of his discomfort and perhaps a lie.

"A question you'd like to avoid, I see."

A slight smile crossed her face. His discomfort amused her, the more so because he seemed too disingenuous to be bad. In fact, she liked him and believed him innocent of any wrongdoing, but his silence about himself piqued her. The Signora had a decades-long belief that she was entitled to know the life and secrets of anyone who had been in town for longer than a week. She let him squirm under her gaze.

"I actually came in looking for Leah. I stopped by her apartment, but she wasn't there, so when I saw you here, I thought perhaps you'd know."

"She called and said she was going on an errand, but that she would come by my house tonight. You could see her then if you'd like to come by."

"I don't want to inconvenience…."

"If it were an inconvenience, I wouldn't have asked you," the Signora interrupted. "I'm much too old for such niceties. And, I rather like you—those wide eyes, your unadulterated Americanness, if not quite as naïve as most of them, and the way you retain a kind of stubborn arrogance of being always in the right. You have a certain charm—an innocence. That said, I find it insolent of you to be so closed mouth when such terrible things are going on. This is not a time for you to be secretive about yourself, Signor; there are too many worries, too many fears. People feel uneasy."

Stein emitted a little laugh. "Please, please call me David—and I'm sure you also have many secrets, Signora."

"As a matter of fact, I do. But they are not about me. My personal life is an open book—well, not quite all the way open. The secrets I hold are mostly those of others, and as the Arabs say, 'A secret is like a dove; when it leaves my hand, it takes wing.' So you see, I must be very careful to safeguard what I know, not for me, but for others. I must take care not to damage innocent people. But your secret is about yourself, no?"

She shook her finger at him.

"And in the current context of murder and grave robbery, it seems your silence can do damage."

"Well said. It might help you be easier on me to know that I have some of the same considerations toward other people, particularly toward one other person. And I would say too that sometimes to be in on a secret is a great blessing."

She nodded her head, considering what he had said.

183

"You make me even more curious and, strangely, more patient toward you as well. Come to my house tonight. And bring your sidekick, too, if you'd like; he and I know each other well. Leah will be there. I know that will be a reason for you to come."

"Secondo's not my sidekick, and why would Leah be a reason for me to come?"

"Perhaps you're his sidekick? And don't play innocent about Leah. I'm old, but my eyes are perfectly fine. I've seen the way you look at her."

"Signora. Please, I'm begging you. Don't keep this up. I'm not Secondo's sidekick, and he's not mine. We're acquaintances, becoming friends. I hope. If people would just let us be."

"I see you are. Still, strange, don't you think, that a man comes all the way from America to this particular village to befriend another man most people believe is simple-minded? You can't really blame us for being suspicious and wary."

"I know my behavior seems strange, and perhaps overly mysterious, especially given the unfortunate circumstances of the grave robbery and the murder."

"Your Italian is excellent, but your choice of words off. These are more than 'unfortunate circumstances,' and you have skirted any response about Leah."

Stein's temper frayed to breaking. "Damn it! I don't want to talk about Leah—or Secondo. I am not involved in anything unseemly or illegal, and I'll explain it all when I'm ready. I apologize for using the wrong words. Perhaps my Italian is not as good as you think it is."

He turned away.

The Signora called after him.

"Do you know where my house is?"

He threw the words over his shoulder.

"I'll find it!"

She watched him cross the piazza and disappear, then whispered one of her favorite proverbs to herself.

"Time and chance reveal all."

Chapter Forty-Eight

Stein walked away, forcing himself to a slow pace and breathing deeply to suppress his anger. He crossed the piazza opposite the trailhead and leaned against the parapet to look out at the green hills across the valley, the vision of the bridge spanning the river far below, and the deep blue sky, where a few puffy clouds lumbered toward the northeast.

His office in the New Art Consortium called at least twice a day now, badgering him with questions. When would he be back? When would he finish the meetings in Florence?

He had put off his boss with one excuse after another, assuring both him and his colleagues he would be back soon. Their persistence and roadblocks to his own goals were making it take much longer to find the right moment to act.

The art world rushed ahead with a few steady artists producing consistently fine, if little-known, work. Still, new fads cropped up every few hours, and a small number of precious treasures, hidden sometimes for years until chance brought them to light, were tucked in obscure recesses of the world.

His colleagues and bosses wanted those obscure pieces. They were ever more intense on profits for the business; they wanted more: more pieces, more unusual pieces, more old pieces. They walked a strictly legal line, but it was more a tightwire than a line in the sand. Stein felt like his partners had changed for the worse in their desire for 'progress,' whatever the hell that meant. He remembered the beginning; they had been excited to find and bring lost or stolen artwork to light, to return it to the true owners. Now it was all about business. Beating the competition.

There were days he wanted to extricate himself from the business of art, to get back to enjoying in freedom the works that passed before his eyes thinking of nothing but their beauty. He emitted a bitter laugh; he had bought into the American frenzy of work, to the detriment of relationships, and he was too trained, too involved, and he told himself, too much in need of the job. There was only one thing that might lighten him on this trip. If it turned out as he hoped, his life would change forever.

He stopped thinking about his hopes. Added to professional pressures, his exchange with the Signora upset him beyond what she had guessed, and he was glad to have his back to her. By evening, he would regain composure. He could talk to Leah, and perhaps if he were subtle enough, he could learn more information from her.

Chapter Forty-Nine

Stein rapped on the Signora's door at eight that evening. She answered the knock with an expectant look that changed to disappointment when she saw him.

"It's you."

"Did I mistake the time?"

"No, it's just Leah hasn't come; I was expecting her earlier."

"Shall we make it another night?"

"Of course not," the Signora snapped. "She's simply been delayed."

She stepped aside for him to enter, indicating the living room through a large archway.

The floor of the entryway shone with a recent polishing. Stein stepped carefully, following in the footsteps of the Signora, through the wide opening into a living room of simple but elegant taste.

A large, comfortable sofa in heavy, soft dark-brown material, two large easy chairs in tan, a glass-topped coffee table that sparkled in the light, and a cherry wood dining table gave the room an aura of comfort and welcome. On the walls hung good reproductions of the Venetian painters: Tintoretto, Tiepolo, Carpaccio, and several others, plus some contemporary originals from D'Este Widmann and Zennaro, who, Stein knew, worked in small studios in Cannaregio.

"You like them?"

"Very much. You have eclectic tastes, classical and modern, representational and abstract. I particularly like the Zennaro and the D'Este Widmann. They're gifted artists, not nearly as acknowledged as they should be."

"You seem to know quite a bit about them."

"I've been fortunate enough to meet them."

"I knew of their families, but not them really; they are much younger than I, and" she hesitated slightly, "of another class."

Stein was surprised to see her blush.

The Signora rushed on. "They're cousins, I think, or nearly so."

"And good friends."

Her gaze narrowed. "Did you know them professionally or personally?

"Both."

"Both men?"

"Yes, both men, and I also meant I know them both professionally and personally. They were kind enough to invite me to stay for a few days after I had met them at an opening of their work."

To distract her from any discussion of his own work, he rushed on. "They took me into the lagoon for a day in Gianni's boat. It was a perfect outing. We stopped on the way back for a glass of wine in a bar in Burano. Red wine and delicious cicchetti."

"'Gianni'? You know them quite personally, then. They must have liked you. Zennaro too?"

"Pino? Yes. You sound skeptical. Couldn't I be likable?" He laughed.

The Signora grunted and let it drop.

"Please sit down."

She motioned to one of the overstuffed chairs. Stein sank into it and leaned back.

"A glass of wine?"

"Prosecco?"

"You do know Venetians."

He smiled. "I assumed."

"Just so. I always have a bottle in the house."

She parted the long strings of beads that divided the living room from the kitchen and soon returned with two delicate flutes filled with the pale, sparkling wine. They raised their glasses.

"Cin cin!"

The well-chilled wine pleased Stein; he let it play on his tongue, dry and light.

"What do you think could have delayed Leah?"

The Signora set her glass on the coffee table. Attentive now, he could see she was worried.

"I don't know. It's odd. She's so intent on finding Elia's killer, I can't tell what she'll do next. She knows nothing about finding killers. Her method is to be nosy and curious, stumbling around until she gets into trouble. We were going to talk about things tonight. 'Put our heads together,' as Leah called it."

The Signora smiled at the memory of Leah's phrase.

"The Lieutenant is stopping by as well, but he said he would be late, not before ten."

"Maybe knowing the Lieutenant was coming, Leah wasn't in a rush?"

"You don't know Leah. She said early. That means she would have been here by 7 at least, and I had laid out a few things for a light supper. Would you…"

"Thanks. I ate early," he lied.

The Signora glanced at the clock on the wall.

"It's a quarter past eight."

Stein started to rise from his chair. "I'll go to the apartment; maybe something came up, and she's late, or just can't get away."

"Don't bother." She motioned him to sit. "I've called there."

"Then…."

"Then, we must wait."

The two of them chatted for what seemed to both an interminable two hours. Stein was amazed at the amount of conversation one could have on the weather of this part of Tuscany.

By 10:30, they lapsed into silence. Stein pulled a photo book of Venice off the coffee table and slowly flipped through the pages. The Signora pretended to read from a book she had taken off the end table.

When the phone rang, she jumped to answer it, listened, and hung up without speaking.

"The Lieutenant."

"Not coming?"

"No. Something about a broken door at the supermarket."

Stein stifled a yawn.

"I think we can be sure Leah's not coming now."

"It's unlike her."

The Signora had aged with the night. In the muted light of the lamps, her skin sagged, yellow and mottled.

Touched by her age, her concern for Leah, Stein felt a tenderness toward her, "I'll stop by her place on the way home tonight to see if there are any lights. If not, I'll pass by again in the morning around ten or eleven and try to rouse her. If I still can't find her, I'll go to Secondo to see what he knows. Maybe he's seen her."

"I'm surprised you didn't bring him tonight."

Wrapped as he was in concern over her and Leah, her abrupt tone surprised him; he responded with equal pique.

"We're not joined at the hip, Signora. As I've had to explain—it seems like hundreds of times—he's a friend."

"Very new friend, I'd say."

Stein groaned. "Meeting Secondo has been one of my keenest pleasures."

He took his coat and stepped toward the door, leaving her to wonder what he meant.

Chapter Fifty

When the Signora answered Stein's knock the next day, she was startled to see the worry on his face.

Before she could ask, Stein exclaimed, "No lights last night and no response this morning. I've looked everywhere, and I can't find Secondo."

Brushing by her without waiting to be invited in, he stepped straight through to the living room and began pacing back and forth.

The Signora blinked at his rudeness.

"American." She muttered to herself.

"What?"

"Never mind. You have no clue where Secondo could be?"

"No clue. I've checked his apartment, the bar, the little piazza off his street.'"

"Hmmm."

The Signora tilted her head, thinking.

"We've got to do something," Stein said. "After everything that's happened and her being the one to find Elia...."

A slight smile flitted across the Signora's lips and vanished. Another one in love with Leah.

"After I left last night, I remembered Leah mentioned there was a table being repaired for her," Stein said.

"That's the table I gave her! I forgot about it. We should go to Magliotti!"

The Signora was suddenly excited.

"He'll know something."

"That's what I intended to suggest before you interrupted."

"Forgive me, Signor Stein. That was rude. I was surprised. I'd forgotten all about the table."

Stein pursed his lips; her apology was pro forma, and it amazed him she could even think about manners when Leah could be in trouble.

She was embarrassed. Her offhand apology had been purposeful, and yet he deserved no more. The information about the table was important, and he obviously didn't know they'd taken it to Magliotti. Plus, her worry was no less than his, and he had been rude when he entered.

"I'll get my coat." She hurried off through the archway.

"Of course, your coat."

He lumbered past her and sat down, his face flushed with a mix of embarrassment and frustration.

Chapter Fifty-One

Stein pushed open Magliotti's door. The bell gave a loud jangle and banged against the glass of the door. The Signora stepped in front of him and entered the workroom where Magliotti sat at a worktable, sanding the leg of a standing jewelry chest. He looked up.

"Good day, Signora, and…."

The Signora gestured toward Stein.

"This is David Stein, an American visiting Scansansiano, though none of us quite know why."

Stein scowled at her and extended his hand to take Magliotti's.

"A pleasure, Signor. My presence is no mystery; I'm sure many people visit Scansansiano simply because they like the area and the town."

Magliotti nodded.

"Of course, and there's much to like. You know that, Signora, no? Why be rude?"

"Of course I know that, and I'm not rude!"

Exasperated that Magliotti failed to join in her jibe at Stein, she made a face.

"Pleasantries aside," Stein continued, "we're here to ask if you saw Signora Contarini yesterday and if you did, about what time."

A loud crash sounded in the adjoining room, followed by a low growl.

Magliotti jumped up, sending the jewelry chest smashing to the floor as he did. The delicate legs of the chest broke and skittered toward the shelves on the wall.

Stein dove to catch the chest, but Magliotti yelled, "Leave it! It's the dog!

I'll be right back."

He hurried to the door and slipped through into the back room. The Signora and Stein waited. When Magliotti reappeared 10 minutes later, his face was red with exertion.

"Forgive me. I promised to take care of my friend's dog while he's away for a few days."

He laughed nervously.

"I wish I hadn't agreed. I can't let him out, or he runs away, and he's always causing trouble. But, never mind. I did. Yes, I did see Signora Cantarini yesterday. She came by to pick up her little table. Unfortunately, I didn't have it ready, so she wasn't here long. She mentioned a walk. Let me think…hmmm…I believe she said she was going up the far *via cava* toward the caves, past the church."

"On the far side of the river?"

"Yes, Signora. Why so startled? She often walks there, doesn't she?"

"Not unless she gets a very early start."

Magliotti grunted, "But it wasn't late! I'm sure she said that specific trail." The Signora snapped at him.

"It was late, Signor, for that walk; it takes a full day even for a fast walker. She couldn't have gotten back before dark."

He snarled. "She assured me she is used to walking."

"I'm sorry to be abrupt." Her face reddened. "We're worried about her."

"As you would be. Myself, I wouldn't go into – or even past - those ruins alone, early or late, but perhaps I'm not as brave as she is."

Magliotti's smirk seemed out of place to Stein, but before he could say anything, the Signora grabbed his arm and rushed him out the door, calling over her shoulder, "Thank you, Signor."

They heard Magliotti's laughter behind them.

Stein hurried along with the Signora. She was babbling to, it seemed, herself.

"We've got to get the Lieutenant and some of his men to scour the trail. She could have fallen into one of the deeper caves; the ground isn't secure in any of them."

"But wasn't Magliotti right? From what I've heard, Leah walks those trails all the time."

"Does her stubborn insistence on exercise make the trails less dangerous!"

It was a reprimand, not a question.

Confident the Signora and Stein were out of hearing range, Magliotti opened the door to the back room. Anchored tightly to a short rope at the wall, Leah jerked furiously against the binding on her hands and feet.

"Your friends are worried about you, Signora."

Chapter Fifty-Two

When she heard the voices of the Signora and Stein, Leah kicked a little table with her feet. The lamp, precariously balanced on the table, tilted, and crashed to the floor. She heard Magliotti say he was watching the neighbor's dog. Sidling through the door, he had reached for a chisel from the top shelf and hissed into her ear.

"Listen, bitch, one more sound, and it's them as well."

A few minutes later, she heard the door close behind the Signora and Stein. The cloth over her mouth, tainted with furniture polish, had given her a stabbing headache that clouded her mind; combined with growing panic, the smell made her nauseous. She breathed heavily through her nose to keep from vomiting and choking and closed her eyes against the headache.

Magliotti stuck his head in the door.

"Resting peacefully. Good girl. And remember, I'm here in the next room, and I can hear every little sound you make. We'll just go on pretending it's a normal workday, shall we? No one the wiser."

He closed the door; the catch snapped.

The day passed in excruciating discomfort. Her body ached, her arm muscles were pulled taut.

Leah heard Magliotti sawing, intermittently waiting on customers, singing, and laughing. Before he left for the midday meal, he banged the shutters of the windows and door to a close and, releasing her from the rope that tied to the post, shoved her through the dim workroom to the bathroom so she could relieve herself and take a few sips of water. After she drank, he tied her hands again and gagged her tightly.

Late afternoon he was back. Exhausted, Leah fell into a fitful sleep at the sound of his light hammering. When she woke, it was dark outside. Magliotti was standing in the doorway.

"I'm off to have my supper. Too bad you can't come along. You must be very hungry."

He laughed. "But remember, we have a *big* date tonight—and you wouldn't want to die on a full stomach. That would be so messy."

He laughed and closed the door. Footsteps, then the key twisting in the lock of the shop door.

Earlier, in the dim light, Leah studied the layer of rolled carpets next to her, below the window. She looked at the rope that anchored her; it would reach, she judged. In the ambient illumination from the town, with her feet and hands bound, she began to twist her body, snakelike, back and forth, inching toward the carpets that rose about a foot off the floor. Once moving, her breathing settled, and she concentrated on making it the few feet to the pile of carpets, resisting the pain that wormed through her temples, shoulders, and legs.

At the hump of rugs, she took a deep breath and, like a beached whale, heaved upward, only to fall back. Panting, she tried again and then again to hoist herself onto the rugs. Exasperated, she lay still to catch her breath.

Step by step.

She forced herself to move slowly, to think clearly.

Her breathing softened. Rested, she puffed hard through her nose, lifted her head, and laid it on the first roll of carpet. Planting her bound feet flat on the floor, she pushed her way up until her shoulders were over the bulge. Slowly, she thrust her body upward, inch by inch, like a slug, onto the carpets until her torso was raised on them and she could swing her legs up and over.

Chuffing from exhaustion, but less nauseous now, she rolled toward the low window and raised her head to look out. It was too dark to tell the exact lay of the land. She could make out the forms of bushes below. Scooching around like a June bug on its back, she pulled her feet upward and, with her head down, tensed her core and raised her feet to the ledge. She drew one deep breath through her nose, then exhaled and, simultaneous with the out-breath, threw her bound feet and legs crashing through the window with blunt force.

The effort robbed her of strength. Drawing long, anguished breaths, she dropped back, head and shoulders, against the rough weave of the carpets. She squinted, concentrated on her breathing, and gathered courage for what she had to do next.

Leaning into the wall for balance and using her head against the wall to gain purchase, she hoisted herself onto her knees, her back to the window. Her arms felt like they were being ripped from her shoulders, but she forced them upward and began to saw the ropes against the jagged edge of broken glass jutting upward from the window frame. With each back-and-forth motion, she cut a long slash on her hand and arm. Blood dripped onto the sill in little rivulets. Fear numbed her pain; she continued to saw until the tethers fell away.

Once her hands were free, she tore the cloth from her mouth, emitted a heavy groan, bent and untied her legs.

The narrow window was just big enough for her to squeeze through. It was the drop to the ground that worried her. Darkness stole her depth perception. She could see the outline of bushes, but not the ground beneath them.

There was no choice.

After knocking the last embedded shards from the frame with the side of her hand, she made one swift twist of her body, lifted one leg out, and then the other, grasping the frame as she lowered herself down the side of the building.

She had misjudged. A few jagged shards of glass were entrenched in the frame, and as the full weight of her body hung from the window, the serrated fragments sliced her hands. With a cry of pain, she released her hold and fell.

The distance was greater than she thought. The bushes broke the fall, but gave way under her weight, and she crashed onto the rocky ground, grasping at the branches of the thick brush for purchase. Slick with blood, her hands slipped off the branches, and she tumbled head over heels down a steep, rocky face into the ditch at the side of the road.

She lay still, sucking air to regain her breath, then moved her arms, her legs, her neck, and finally, twisted her back.

"This again," she muttered.

Every part of her hurt; this fall was like the one on the escarpment, only worse. Nothing was broken, but the cuts on her hands were bleeding heavily. She pulled off her shirt and, using her teeth, tore at the pocket to make a hole, so she could rip the full length of the shirt.

When her hands were wrapped, she sunk into the grass, took a deep breath, and willed strength into her body for the long walk home.

Above her, stars glittered in the night sky. A fingernail of moon rose on the eastern horizon, and Leah thought how sweet it would be to simply lie there, cradle her wounded hands, watch the night sky, and wait for someone to come.

An angry curse from above broke her revere.

Go! Go! A voice in her mind.

Pushing herself to her hands and knees, she stifled a howl of pain and crawled upward to the road, where she rose shakily to her feet and hobbled across the asphalt into the ancient ruins of caves and pits. The musty smell of the long dead made her gag; she dry-heaved as she ran in wobbly, pathetic zigzags away from Magliotti.

Chapter Fifty-Three

Magliotti leaned out the broken window and stared into the dark for some sign of Leah. "Fuck!"

He jerked inside, slammed his fist against the wall with a string of curses, then spun round, yanked open a drawer, grabbed a hammer and a flashlight from the neat rows of tools, and rushed out of his shop, leaving the door banging in the wind.

A thin crescent in the sky, the moon provided only dull light. Magliotti rounded the edge of the building to the steep slope at the back, stumbled, and barely caught himself on the broken branch of one of the large bushes. Hunkering down, he slid on his backside from bush to bush down the incline until he jolted to a stop at the bottom of the ditch. By the dim light of the flashlight, he could see the shadowy depression of a body in the tall grass. He cursed again; she had fallen here, but was able to move.

The faint light of the moon and the ashen illumination from the buildings above were barely enough to distinguish anything but outline. The flashlight's narrow beam refracted light, distorting details, and ended abruptly in darkness.

He leaned into the dark, listening. The snap of a twig sounded from somewhere across the pavement.

"The ruins. Damn that bitch!"

Magliotti scrambled up from the ditch and loped across the pavement, descending on the other side to the narrow pathway that led into the moss-covered rocks and mounds of the ancient city.

The waning moon cast just enough light to distinguish the trail from the mossy edges of mounds that opened in gaping maws, one on top of the other in a jumble of rock and cavity.

Fleeing through the depths of the trail, Leah slammed into a low tree trunk that jutted sideways from a crevice in the rock. She jerked back. A branch caught on a rock, slapped out, and sliced her cheek. Gasping from the pain, she scrambled forward, her heart pounding like a pile driver in her chest. Underfoot rocks covered with moss, wet from a recent rain, sent her wobbling forward, tilting side to side like a woman drunk. Leah bit her lip to keep from crying out.

Over her shoulder, she caught the glimmer of Magliotti's flashlight, but the sound of his footsteps was muffled by the short, sharp bursts of her own breath. Up a side trail that she thought was a shortcut, she came abruptly to rock face. No way around. Turning, she bolted back to the main trail. Blood oozed down her cheek, and her hands throbbed with each beat of her heart.

Remembering the walk she had taken with Secondo to learn this little-used trail that ran from Scansansiano to Casale, she turned opposite than her instinct told her, always to the right. In quick erratic movements, she darted ahead, from one footfall to the next, stumbling against rocks that had tumbled onto the trail, the bottoms of her feet bruised and painful. Sucking air so loudly it seemed to her Magliotti would surely hear her, she jerked ahead, praying his curses, and the intermittent sounds of rocks tumbling underfoot behind her, meant that he did not yet know where or how far ahead she was.

When she felt the trail slope downward and broaden, and the path become less rocky underneath, Leah knew this was the way to the field. She had remembered. The smell of fresh grass wafted to her from below. She rushed on, panting, her body one long ache.

Magliotti reached the top of the trail and scanned the field in front of him. He spotted Leah's form and her wobbling walk, moving slowly through the flatland below him.

She heard him laugh.

He yelled at her through the night air.

"I see you, Signora!"

Leah took one deep breath and yelled back.

"Catch me then, bastard."

She rushed ahead, into the broad dark of the field forgetting the pain in her body, determined to best Magliotti, determined to win.

Chapter Fifty-Four

"She hasn't gone to the caves! Listen to me! She told me herself a few days ago she wanted to walk the trail to Casale, through the ruins!" Secondo jerked his arms up and down in frustration; his hands waded in tight fists. He could see by the look on their faces they didn't believe him.

"I know Leah! I know where she's gone. It's to the Casale trail. I taught her the trail! She and I walked it, and she wanted to walk it again. It was next on her list."

"That trail is just as bad." The Lieutenant pursed his lips.

The others smiled. The Lieutenant professed to be angry with Leah; she had interfered again with his work, but everyone knew in truth he was afraid for her, afraid this time the bullet would take her from him, from the town.

Unaware himself of how profound his feelings were for Leah, the Lieutenant's stomach clenched.

"This is not a woman's place!" he hissed.

"What?" Gianni, the baker, asked. "What's not a woman's place?"

"I meant to say that Leah is stubborn. She should have stayed put and let the authorities deal with things."

Gianni laughed. "You give yourself away, Lieutenant. Your face is bright red. By the authorities, you mean you."

"I'm worried, that's all. I worry about all the people in town when I think they're in danger."

Gianni patted his shoulder.

The Lieutenant thought of sitting with Leah in the little corner bar.

Courageous, astute as the Lieutenant was as a policeman, he possessed an incurable innocence of heart. The only love he had known before Leah had been a high-school sweetheart. When she ran away with a swarthy young man from Rome who came to Sardegna on vacation with his parents, the Lieutenant swore off love, or thought he had until he kissed Leah's hand that day in the bar. He admired her courage, her beauty, and her ability for single-minded concentration, but the idea that he might truly love her—and not merely desire her—had not entered his mind until that day.

This lack of introspection and self-awareness drew other women to the Lieutenant like bees to honey. They gathered around him, yearning, their breasts falling and rising in desire when he spoke to them.

With a quick greeting and lost in an internal deliberation on the most recent theft or break-in, he passed these women by, missing every hint of their liquid eyes, their heaving breasts, and their flushed faces.

Stein was listening closely to the exchange between Gianni and the Lieutenant.

"Stop talking! There's no time to wait!" Secondo shouted. "Tell them, David! They don't believe me! Tell them!"

If Secondo had known the story of Cassandra, he would have known what she felt like. He could see, with certainty, that catastrophe was close by Leah at that moment; he could feel it, and they refused to believe him. His fear, coupled with anger, made him desperate.

On the narrow streets of Scansansiano, Secondo had heard the sighs of pity, the whispered "simpleton" and "orphan." It did not matter to most of them that he had proved himself by bravery, by quick action. Except for the few who knew him well, the townspeople formed their ideas about him while he was still a child, before he was even seven years old and already suffering from bipolar illness. It didn't matter he had long been treated for his illness.

Through the light of their prejudice, they painted him as a weak-minded boy. He could have told them until his voice failed that mental illness was not stupidity, not mental deficiency, not idiocy. He knew what was wrong with him, studied, learned, but they would never, had never, erased their preconceptions by actually learning about the illness, actually reading about it to come away with understanding and compassion.

He was the one who had applied the tourniquet and saved Leah's life once before. To others, it was an anomaly; they simply rearranged their prejudices.

No matter what he did, when he walked into a store or stopped to greet someone in the piazza, the brief look of fear in the eyes of the others taught him he would always be strange, unpredictable, and potentially dangerous. In Secondo's experience, most people were like the pupil of an eye: the more light a person tried to give, the more they contracted. He looked around the group. A heavy sigh escaped his lips; he fell silent, enervated, and angry. Tears of frustration and fear for Leah made his body tremble.

Stein clapped his hands loudly and called for everyone to stop talking. When they were quiet, he put a hand on Secondo's shoulder. Squeezing slightly so Secondo would feel it, Stein spoke directly to the Lieutenant.

"Secondo knows better than anyone what Leah would do. He's the one she always talks to about her walks. He's gone with her dozens of times, and they've discussed the trails repeatedly."

The Lieutenant rubbed his neck, stared off above the trees for a moment, and then nodded.

"Stein's right. Secondo does know better than any of us."

Secondo burst ahead of the group, jerked open the door of Stein's rental car, and sat in the front passenger seat, yelling at the others to hurry. Stein started the car in silence.

"Go! Drive fast!" Secondo yelled at Stein.

Gianni took a place beside the Lieutenant in the police car. Following closely one behind the other, they turned out of the piazza parking lot, swept under the arch, and down the switchbacks to the bridge and the narrow pull-off where they could access both arms of the *vie cave* that eventually joined in the crux of a rough-shaped Y farther up the cliffside.

The Lieutenant and Gianni took the closer branch of the trail, and Stein and Secondo stepped high through the weeds of the ditch to the further one.

After a steep uphill climb, the trail leveled out over the last four hundred meters, and with easier walking, Stein and Secondo arrived first at the point where the trails joined, the others only a minute later.

The Lieutenant took charge. "Space yourselves and meet again at the top of the ridge, on the road. From there, angle toward the ruins. Gianni, you know the ruins, right? The old trail? Stein, I know you don't, but Secondo you do, and the Signora"—the Lieutenant shook his head as he said it—"is meeting us on the road up above."

"What!" Stein croaked. "Why did you let her? We'll have to take care of her."

The Lieutenant made a face.

"The Signora does what she wants. Don't worry; we'll go at our pace, and she'll go at hers."

Secondo slipped by them shouting.

"Stop talking and go!"

The others scrambled after him into the dark.

Within half an hour, they broke off the trail onto the road and veered eastward for a half-mile until they came to Signora Vianello, waiting in her car.

Seeing the glare of their flashlights and their dark forms, she clambered from the car and jostled from foot to foot on the berm just where it dropped toward the trail that led across open fields into the ruins.

A dark stream of bodies, the group flowed from the berm like a beast with many legs onto the trail, fanning their flashlights back and forth, cutting narrow pencils of yellow across the thick winter wheat and grasses of the fields.

Secondo, the Lieutenant, and Stein moved ahead of the others by fifty yards, emerging finally into the rocky area that spanned a little rise before it dropped into a shallow valley and stand of trees 800 yards from the edge of the ruins.

They stopped to catch their breath.

"David?" Secondo's voice pierced the dark. "Listen."

"What?"

"I don't think we should go straight."

The Lieutenant broke in.

"It's the quickest way."

"But what if there's someone besides Leah?"

"Who?" Stein questioned.

"I don't know. It feels strange."

"What would you do, Secondo?" Stein asked.

"Go on the sides of the trail, so nobody can see us."

The Lieutenant grunted his assent.

"But turn off the flashlights. Our eyes have already adjusted enough."

Heeding Secondo's advice, they moved forward through the darkness, spacing themselves on either side of the trail. Weaving in and out the trees of a small beech grove, they kept their distance from the path, but were still able to see the outline of its snake-like meandering through the field. From the stand of beech, they maneuvered behind bushes across another field until the trail took a hairpin curve around a stand of yew and into open space.

Startled by what they saw ahead of them, the three men jolted to a stop.

Ahead, Leah sat on a large rock at the edge of the trail, breathing hard, her head bowed, her hands held palm up in front of her as if she were reading an invisible book or as if she were making a plea. She sat unmoving, unaware of them and unaware that twelve feet behind her, a man was approaching, his arm and weapon raised.

With a violent yell, Secondo rushed at an angle toward the trail, screaming, his hands flaying the air. In one swift movement, Magliotti turned toward the yell, cocked the hammer of his gun, aimed, and fired at Secondo, who crumpled to the ground.

The next salvos volleyed wildly into the air in rapid succession.

"Secondo!" Leah screamed. Stumbling toward him, she dropped to the ground beside him, crying out, "Secondo! Secondo!"

From behind, Stein and the Lieutenant leaped around Leah to fling themselves on Magliotti. On impact, the pistol flew from Magliotti's hand. He fell backward under the two men's flying weight, and all three fell heavily to the ground.

Once they disentangled themselves, Stein and the Lieutenant rolled off and grasped Magliotti by the arms.

Magliotti twisted and turned, whimpering, "Don't hit me, please don't hit me."

Stein slugged him in the face once and then again. With a loud crack, Magliotti's nose shattered, and blood spurted over them.

Magliotti spluttered and began to cry.

"He hit me. He broke my nose, Lieutenant. Arrest him!"

The Lieutenant grabbed Magliotti's arm and shoved him forward.

"Stop whining, Magliotti, or I'll let him hit you again."

The others, with the Signora surprisingly close behind gasping for breath, came running and jolted to a stop just in time to see Stein hit Magliotti.

"It's Magliotti!" the Signora, whom no one had ever seen act surprised, blurted.

The Lieutenant snapped cuffs on Magliotti.

The Signora knelt beside Leah, who was leaning over Secondo.

"I can't see his wound! Give me a flashlight!" Leah yelled.

Gianni handed her his flashlight. Shining it on Secondo's side, Leah saw that blood had stained his shirt and was pooling on the ground. Gianni threw off his jacket, stripped off his shirt and white T-shirt, and handed the T-shirt to Leah, who pressed it against the wound.

"Give me a stick and tear the shirt. Here! Quickly!" She threw it back at him. The Lieutenant handed a stick to her and Leah set the tourniquet.

"As soon as I tie the knot, we run. It's faster to go into town to my car rather than back to Scansansiano."

"But your hands and face, Leah!"

"Forget about my hands! We have to go. Now! He's bleeding badly."

She brushed away the Lieutenant's hand.

The Signora directed them to take his arms and legs and to support the head. Leah walked alongside, holding the t-shirt over the wound. Secondo moaned in pain as they wound back up over the rough terrain through the ruins and along the winding trail to the final ascent into Casale and Leah's car.

The Lieutenant, with Magliotti in tow, watched them disappear in the ruins, then turned in the direction from which he had come to take Magliotti back to the Signora's car.

Chapter Fifty-Five

Y ou're a magnet for murder, Leah. You've got to stop! Look at your hands; they're torn to bits, you can barely walk, and your face is a mess."

She stifled a smile. The words were angry, but the Lieutenant couldn't carry it off; his eyes showed he was proud of her.

The night they found Leah and caught Magliotti, the Lieutenant felt torn between anger and relief. She had intruded again, endangering herself, which frightened him more than his tightly-corralled emotions allowed him to admit. He felt an urge to hold her, to protect her.

At the moment he was staring into her bright eyes with such a forced scowl, Leah barely kept from laughing.

She retorted. "But I didn't meddle, Lieutenant! I know you think I did, but I didn't. I went to Magliotti's shop to get my table. That's all. I didn't know it was him. Anyway, you've caught him. And he's confessed. I had no idea he was the killer until I saw the glue."

"Yes, the glue…."

He said nothing about being impressed by her awareness and obvious courage, instead, he jabbed his finger at her as he would a child.

"Okay, you didn't meddle. I'm just wondering how many murders we'll have to deal with as long as you're here? Or will have to when you come back?"

"I hope you'll never have to deal with one again." Her voice shook.

The Lieutenant rushed to apologize. "I didn't mean to be flip about it. But really, only the glue?"

"It was enough. When I found Elia, there was a smudge of it on his coat, under the collar. I told you about it. I wouldn't have noticed, except I took Elia in my lap, and when I reached around to lift him, I touched it. Magliotti told me himself he was working with it when Elia came into his shop. And I recognized it when I went to pick up my table. I was meandering along the shelves waiting for him to come out of the back room, and I accidentally tipped over the bottle. It was circumstance. Really, I forgot about the glue until I went to pick up the table."

"A dangerous circumstance."

"Magliotti guessed immediately that I knew. He told me then about the parochet, but said he didn't rob the grave. He seemed shocked I would imagine he could do such a base thing. I guess he figured I'd be dead, so it didn't matter if I knew he was the one that killed Elia. He also said he's the one who pushed me down the escarpment."

"What!? When were you pushed down an escarpment? You didn't tell me!

"I didn't tell anybody. I thought I fell. I couldn't remember exactly."

"Damn it to hell, Leah." He caught her in a strong embrace and kissed her on the mouth.

She struggled to free herself, but he pulled her closer and kissed her again. She felt herself sinking in the warmth and sweetness of the kiss.

A loud knock sounded at the door. Leah and the Lieutenant jerked apart.

"Damn it," they said in unison.

"What is it?" the Lieutenant yelled at the door.

Signorina MacCleod stuck her head around the door.

"The papers you wanted to sign, Sir."

She stepped in and handed him the papers, glancing from one to the other. She smiled.

"Is there anything else, Sir?"

"No, we're almost finished. Thank you, Signorina. I'll get them back to you before you leave for the day."

She looked from Leah to the Lieutenant.

"No hurry, Sir. Take your time." She left.

He looked at Leah.

"Please don't say anything. Please. Can't we just continue where we left off?"

"Where we left off? You mean where we just left off?"

Leah looked as puzzled as a five-year-old, and the Lieutenant gave a loud laugh.

"I mean where we left off our discussion of Magliotti. We'll talk about your fall down the escarpment later. We'll continue with other things, as you call it, later."

"Oh," her shoulders slumped.

"Another circumstance. And yet another that Elia ended up in the house of the person who bought the parochet. Magliotti got a fine price from a black-market dealer in New York. The woman that bought it collects artworks, including religious objects, but knew nothing more than that the hanging was from Tuscany. She's adamant that she got it from what she thought was a reputable dealer. Of course, Elia would have recognized it immediately."

Leah interrupted, "He recognized not only the theft, but the ethics, or lack of ethics, in buying it; I'm sure it infuriated him; it is illegal as well as unethical."

"How do you know that was what upset him?"

"I know Elia. And I'm sure Magliotti will confess, because he's hoping for gentler treatment."

"I don't think he'll get it. Rachel dragged her feet at first, but was ultimately willing to go back to her client's house and take a look around, by excusing herself to use the bathroom. Personally, I think the client probably knew it was black market and wanted it anyway."

"No matter what, Magliotti shouldn't get gentler treatment! Where did he get the parochet in the first place? And what's going to happen to it? Will that woman return it? She should, and get jail time too! Besides the parochet, there must be other things."

"Slow down. We don't have all the answers; Magliotti's not telling everything—yet. For the rest, I've turned all the information over to the police in New York, and they'll funnel it to the appropriate authorities."

"You have hopes Magliotti will talk? He had to have had an accomplice from here."

"I'm sure he did."

"How'll you find out?"

The Lieutenant pleaded. "Please, Leah, leave it to us! Take care of Secondo."

"I am taking care of him. I stayed the night in his room, and he slept well. It was a flesh wound, a deep one, but he'll heal well, the doctor says, and he'll get back normal use of his arm. I think he's enjoying the attention."

She wrinkled her nose; the Lieutenant laughed aloud.

"He deserves it. It was a brave move. He's saved you a second time. He… and Stein."

"Stein!" She made a face. "Who is he really? Do you know yet?"

The Lieutenant was heartened to see Leah's response. "All I know is that as far as our records show, he's not a criminal and has never been one."

Leah smiled. "I thought you would push further to check him out. When did you do it?"

"As soon as he came to town. You know that—"

"Did I?"

"Yes, and I've done more since. That's how I found out he's got a clean record."

"Wow, I thought I was suspicious." She stood. "I'm going to get some sleep."

She paused at the doorway. "That reminds me: Grazia?"

"The Signora will let you know."

"Can't you tell me even the short version?"

"The Signora will let you know. Go home and get some sleep."

Chapter Fifty-Six

Outside the station, the Signora was hobbling across the piazza. Leah jogged ahead to catch up with her.

"Signora! Did you hurt yourself?"

"Hurt myself!" The Signora jerked her arm away. "Hurt myself! I ran all over creation last night looking for you. Have you forgotten that? All of us were there, stumbling around in the dark, getting shot at, and your stubborn, impetuous behavior has made us all sore and tired—it almost got you killed!"

The Signora's eyes glittered with incipient tears.

A wave of tenderness for the older woman rose in Leah's chest; she reached forward and gave her friend an awkward hug with her bandaged arms and hands.

"I'm sorry, Signora. It really wasn't my impetuous behavior this time. I had simply gone to pick up the table and, by a weird coincidence, realized it was Magliotti. Unfortunately, he realized I knew at the same moment I realized it was him."

"Nothing is simple about you, and I don't like your almost being killed. I don't like it." She stamped her foot, and tears spilled onto her cheeks.

Leah took the Signora's arm. "Why don't we have a glass of prosecco? It will do us good."

In the bar, they took the table next to the window. While the Signora shrugged out of her coat, Leah ordered. Returning to the table, balancing the tray awkwardly on her bandages, Leah noted again the dark circles under the Signora's eyes and how the skin of her neck sagged in folds. Leah felt a pang of guilt that she was responsible for the look of deep fatigue on the Signora's face.

The Lieutenant told Leah that the Signora ran to her aid, actually ran, her coat fluttering out behind her. It was a strain on her heart and, seeing the Signora slouched in the chair, Leah understood the deep toll of that run.

They clinked glasses. The Signora sighed. "So wonderful this drink. It calms me."

"You need it. I hope you were able to sleep once you got home."

"Of course. Just the excitement, you know. You?"

The Signora had regained her gracious demeanor. Leah felt a twinge of regret for that small distancing.

"I'm fine. They bandaged me, and I spent the night in Secondo's room."

"Not a very comfortable night in a hospital chair, I think."

"It was fine. The hospital has those new couches that make out into beds, and they brought me two of the warm blankets they use in the maternity ward for new mothers after birth."

"Better then." She nodded. "Secondo?"

"He's fine. He has a flesh wound, bad enough, but not life-threatening. I told the Lieutenant that I think Secondo's enjoying the attention. And in addition to the good news on Secondo, from what the Lieutenant says, Magliotti has confessed. I suppose you already know why he killed Elia."

"I talked to the Lieutenant before you did, earlier this morning."

"Ahh. But we still don't know where he got the hanging."

"No."

The Signora shook her head slowly from side to side.

"The men you heard in the library, maybe?"

"I don't know. Their remark was offhand, in bad taste, but not proof, and the more I thought about it, the more confused I was. I can't really identify the voices; they were whispering. I thought maybe it was the Innocenti brothers, but now, I don't think so."

"What about Stein then?"

"Seem out of the question. He would have an interest, but by all accounts, he's never been here before. Otherwise, why would he have Secondo showing him around?"

"Not Grazia!"

"No. Given certain circumstances, she could have murdered Elia I think, but I think her threats were only words. I talked with her. She's been suffering for years. But from what she said in our conversation, I think maybe she'll soon have a breakthrough. She's hit rock bottom, but she'll get through it. She knows how strong she is, how strong she's been all these years. And because she knows, she understands she can change the situation. As for the wall hanging, she wouldn't have an interest in it or the chance to take it.

Before we caught Magliotti...."

Without noticing Leah's smile at her use of the plural pronoun, the Signora continued.

"....I certainly thought...well, as I said. She definitely has troubles, but I see now they would not have led her to murder, although they may have led her to some drastic action."

"Like?"

"Well, I'll tell you the rest of her story."

"When?"

"Don't be impatient. Drink your prosecco."

Leah shook her head. "How are we ever going to find out about the parochet?"

"We will."

"How can you be so sure?"

"We need only eliminate the impossible. What remains, however improbable, is the truth. Isn't that what your famous writer of detective stories says."

"Arthur Conan Doyle?"

"Yes."

"I wish he were ours; he's British."

"Well, you never should have left the realm! At any rate, we need to eliminate the impossible."

She swallowed the last bit of her prosecco.

"We'll tell stories and ramble around until we figure it out. Just like we've always done. We'll be like your Inuit."

"My Inuit?"

"Don't you know who the Inuit are? It's your country, my dear!"

Leah bristled, "Of course, I know who the Inuit are, but it never occurred…"

"It never occurred to you that I would know about them! Hopeless. It's hopeless. Impossible ever to fathom the depths of human….what shall I call it? Human misconceptions…an old woman in a fur coat, with an empty head…."

"No…"

"Don't! I love you dearly, but I haven't got time. I want to tell you the story; it may help."

Leah's deep blush rose to her hairline.

The Signora continued.

"I heard a story once about an anthropologist and some Inuit friends who were lost in a snowstorm. The Inuit made a little tent out of animal skins they were carrying, and they all got inside and started talking about snow. They talked about different kinds of snow and stories about how they had been caught in the snow, and wind, and ice. To the amazement of the anthropologist, they spent several hours talking about snow while he was in a vice-grip of fear about being lost in a snowstorm, sure that if they didn't starve to death, they would freeze to death.

After some time, the Inuit men stood up, broke camp, and headed into the storm. He tried to reason with them to wait for clear weather, but they ignored him and went on. There was nothing for him to do but follow. The Inuit men walked straight back to their village, seemingly not lost at all."

"How…?"

"Evidently, as they talked, they were going over all the information they knew about snow, and they were comparing it to the snow they were in, the direction of the wind, those things, and from all those stories, they figured out which way to walk. We'll do the same, and the answer will come. All of us: you, me, the Lieutenant, Secondo, Stein, Gianni, we'll all be thinking about the parochet, keeping our receptors open, and something will turn up."

Chapter Fifty-Seven

Early the following day, approaching Gianni's bakery, Leah closed her eyes and drew in a deep breath, anticipating the warm golden scent of fresh-baked bread.

"Do you always walk around with your eyes closed?" Stein's sudden appearance from an alleyway startled her.

"The bread." She stammered.

He laughed. "You're not alone. To tell you the truth, I do the same thing when I'm on my way to buy bread. Now I get two pleasures: the bread and you. I was hoping to run into you."

"I thought I'd see you at the hospital, but you were gone before I got to Secondo's room."

"Your hands?"

She held them up for him to see the bandages.

"Have you got time for a coffee?"

The offer surprised her.

"Here in the piazza?"

"Sure." He gave her a quizzical look, wondering why she had asked if they would be in the piazza. They turned toward the central bar.

Stein ordered two coffees at the counter and took a seat across from Leah at the table by the window.

"I've been wanting to tell you my story, but…."

"After all the intrigue, I finally get the story? Why tell me now and not before?"

Stein laughed aloud.

"Patience, Leah. Sorry for the wait, but I promise, the story's a good one, although it's long. I couldn't tell you the story before because someone else was involved, and I needed permission."

"I'm an impatient, suspicious woman, but I owe you an apology, so I'll sit through it."

"You had reason to be suspicious. I hope now we can start again. Maybe dinner some evening?" A faint blush spread over his face.

Thinking of the Lieutenant, she evaded his invitation.

"Listen. I'm not in a hurry, but I do need to get to the baker's before the bread is gone, which will probably be about three hours from now."

"Three hours should do it," he laughed.

She settled into her chair, delighted at the prospect of having her curiosity satisfied. Stein's laughter enveloped her once again, and Leah thought, with surprise, how rich and pleasant was the sound of his voice.

Stein sloughed off his coat, laid it on the chair next to them, and began his story.

"During World War II, my grandfather was assigned to a minuscule part of the U. S. military, a section called MFAA, Monuments, Fine Arts and Archives. He was twenty-five, a recent graduate in fine arts from Columbia University, and he had a promising career ahead of him as a sculptor, which he had the good fortune to realize after he came home from the war. While he was studying, he met the sculptor Selma Burke who was in the Harlem Renaissance movement, and she took an interest in his work. He was also introduced to Margot Einstein, who was just getting started as a sculptor, but already famous as Einstein's daughter. What I'm saying is, he was part of, or at least on the periphery of, New York artists, and he loved it."

Stein stared off, remembering something. Leah took the chance to study the clear lines of his jaw and his high, strong forehead, wondering how she could have mistrusted him. His eyes, his face, the turn of his head seemed now to indicate strength and honesty.

"Sorry. Where was I?"

"Your grandfather was studying at Columbia and met several prestigious artists in New York. If you look away every few seconds, and I have to remind you what you were saying, this is going to be a very long story."

"Okay, okay. Anyway, he enlisted and was initially posted to North Africa. From there, he moved north with the troops into Naples and Rome, where some commander found out about his background and, although it seems impossible, it's true: the commander sent him north with the troops under a guy name Keller who was actually one of the Monuments Men. The regular soldiers called them Venus Fixers. They were a special unit. Most of them were older guys. My grandfather was the youngest, the baby of the group I guess.

Anyway, by August 4th of 1944, they were moving into Florence. It was dangerous. The Germans were still in the northern part of the city, but these guys, who had the specific job of locating artworks and saving or repairing them, could make quick forays into the city for a few hours at a time.

Like I said, it was horribly dangerous since the Germans were still in the north part of the city, but my grandfather loved it. He was overjoyed to be out of the regular army and in Florence, saving artwork. The Pitti Palace, the Ufizzi...to be not only seeing and living among magnificent works of art, but helping save them as well."

Stein's eyes glittered, and Leah answered. "I can imagine. Still, during those years it couldn't have been too pleasant."

"No. He said it was chaotic from the German withdrawal and the Americans coming in, and the Italians in confusion. Plus, the work was overwhelming. He said the Italians were amazing. After all, they'd been through, they were ready to help however they could. There was way more to do than the small group of Fixers could handle, and local residents carried most of the weight of the work. The men in his group and the Italians hardly slept.

He said he learned a lot from the Italians and from the other Venus Fixers. They were older and much more skilled than he was, but they took him under their wing.

"And he was a hard worker, so they liked him, right?"

"Exactly. He was young, and he believed in the work and was determined to save whatever he could, however he could. His good experiences with the local people in Florence; the way the Italians loved their works of art and worked hard at protecting them bolstered his spirit. He did what he could, not just the work, but things like always carrying candies and C-rations to share.

He hadn't been there long when a rabbi from Livorno, who was friends with higher-ups in Florence, told his friends there were Jewish treasures in a little town on the border of Lazio—this little town—treasures that the Germans missed. So, my grandfather got orders to find those treasures, and he started off. He was excited, initially."

"The synagogue treasures!" Leah's eyes sparkled.

"I think so. But the story turns a corner. The journey to Scansansiano, which should have been a matter of a few hours, was not what he'd anticipated. He started off in a jeep, with a driver, a special privilege, thinking he would be here from Florence by midafternoon."

A gangly young woman in a police uniform appeared next to Leah.

"Pardon me for interrupting. Signorina MacCleod asked me to tell you, if I saw you, that she is leaving for the day, and there's a paper you need to sign. She would be very happy if you could come sign it now because the Lieutenant needs it before she gets back to the office."

Leah looked at Stein and shrugged her shoulders. The young woman stood waiting. Her clear skin and bright eyes glowed in the morning light, but she destroyed the effect by pulling her hair into a severe bun and wearing her cap so low that her eyes were lost in the shade of the cap's bill.

Leah looked at Stein, palms open. "Sorry, but I'd better do this." She nodded to the policewoman, who smiled.

"Thanks. The Signorina will be glad to get away on time."

Leah dipped her head at Stein. "Didn't this happen the last time? As long as we're taking a break, I'll get the bread too. Can you wait twenty minutes?"

He laughed at the excited look on her face. "I'll run over to see Secondo for a few minutes and then meet you back here."

Leah slipped into her jacket. "By the way, have you told Secondo your story?"

"That's why I can tell you. But you should know that his mother beat me to it."

"His mother?"

"Go sign your papers."

Leah moved toward the door and then turned back, her mouth opened to ask a question. Stein cut her off.

"Go!"

Chapter Fifty-Eight

Leah signed the paper, rushed to the bakery, and stepped inside panting, pleased to be enveloped in the warm smell of fresh baked bread and pastries. Gianni greeted her with his usual bright smile. Brown as berries, his eyes sparkled, but he looked tired, as he always did, from being up most of the night.

His assistants, two young girls from the high school, had just come in. They tied aprons around their slim waists and restrained their long dark hair in the puffy caps they were required to wear.

"Buon giorno, Signora. How are you? Recovered? That bastard Magliotti. I hope your hands are okay."

"Thanks, Gianni. I'm fine, a little tired, but not as tired as you, I think. I owe you thanks for helping me escape the worst. Between me and work at two bakeries, you've lost a lot of sleep."

"I didn't do much. It was Secondo and the American. As for work, I love it. I walk to work in the dark. My footsteps echo off the buildings, and there's no one else around when I come. I feel like I own the whole town, like I could sing at La Scala!"

"I think I'd like walking to work in the dark too. Just peace and the night sky."

"When I come, yes, but not much later, before dawn, there are others. You'd be surprised at the number of people...."

"Oh?"

"Well, not that many, but...."

Before Gianni could finish his sentence, the bell over the doorway tinkled, and another customer came through the doorway. Leah stepped aside while the baker waited on her. Leafy stalks of celery, lacy carrot fronds, and bulges of red onions from the market above town flopped over the lip of her bag. The woman paid and left, fresh bread in hand.

Gianni tilted his head toward the doorway as the woman left, motioning Leah closer.

"What?"

The baker whispered. "Every day, three loaves, and she lives alone. One loaf for herself, one for Secondo, and one day-old for the cats at the little piazza overlooking the valley."

Through the glass doorway, Leah saw the woman packing the bread into her cart. Her tattered clothing hung from her thin shoulders.

"People take care of Secondo."

"More than you know, Signora. It makes a chaotic world better, no?"

He pointed at his bread bins. "Before you decide this morning, have you seen our new multigrain-cornmeal bread?"

Leah laughed. "That's why I'm back; I had a loaf the other day."

He reached for the bread from the slanted bins on the wall, put it in a sack, and handed it to her.

"I'm sorry Nick's not with us anymore, Signora. And I'm sorry you've had such a difficult time this trip."

Susceptible to his kindness, tears welled in her eyes. "Thanks, Gianni. It's been a strange trip; I wanted to ask about who was—"

"And the American?" he interrupted, grinning.

"Well…."

"A knight in shining armor, no?"

"No!"

"Then why does your face go red, Signora?"

Gianni threw back his head and emitted a loud guffaw. "Okay, I'll stop teasing, but you shouldn't let a good man get away, Signora," he winked. "What crime will you solve next?"

How about two good men, Leah thought.

"I didn't solve this one, Gianni; I just got kidnapped. But I do wish I could solve the grave robbery. I can't get over the insult to Anna's body, and I was wondering who was out...."

Another woman bustled through the doorway setting the bell at the top of the door into a furious clangor. She nudged in front of Leah.

"Two loaves of cornmeal bread, please."

"Girls!" Gianni yelled at the assistants, who had disappeared into the back room. They burst through the long plastic strips that covered the open doorway and hastened to help the woman. Gianni nodded to Leah, scooted behind the girls, and disappeared toward his ovens.

Chapter Fifty-Nine

Leah walked slowly back to the bar. Why had the baker teased her about Stein being her knight in shining armor? Did Stein have feelings for her? More importantly, did she have feeling for him and for the Lieutenant too? She cleared her mind. She did not want the confusion of being attracted to two men.

Who had Gianni seen in the very early morning? What could there be to do in Scansansiano so early in the morning unless, like the baker, it was work?

Stein was sitting where she'd left him, reading a book. He looked up as she stepped through the doorway.

"Mmm. I can smell the bread from here. What kind is it?"

It's Gianni's new cornmeal bread; it's delicious." She dangled the sack of bread in front of him.

"I'll get some after."

"I'm teasing. Take half of mine."

Surprised by the offer, Stein watched her tear the loaf in two. "You don't need—"

"What?"

"It's your bread!"

Leah glanced at Daniela, the barmaid, and both women laughed. "Mine. Your's. It's bread."

"But—"

"C'mon Stein, just say 'thank you' and take it. How was Secondo?"

"Why can't anyone call me by my given name? Please, please, please call me David. And Secondo is fine. Sleeping. And thank you for the bread. I'll have some for lunch."

"I hope we're not interrupted again. There seems to be a plague of interruptions in town."

"Meaning?"

"Nothing."

"Okay," he chuckled, "I wish I could always be so well paid. And with such a ready heart."

His look unsettled Leah; her own feelings of warmth toward him surprised her.

He cleared his throat and began again.

"So, my grandfather started off from Florence in an old jeep with a driver, and like I said, they were fine until they got south of Siena. Coming up a hill lined with cypress trees—my grandfather made that detail very clear—the car coughed, burbled a little, and then the engine gave out.

The driver jumped from behind the wheel, cursed a blue streak, and kicked the tire. He had trouble with the car before and was not angry only at having to make the trip, but also because he had told them he needed a different jeep, and they insisted he take the one they were driving.

Anyway, he told my grandfather it would be two or three days before he could get the repairs done, so they might as well set up a makeshift camp in one of the fields.

My grandfather told him to do whatever he needed and then return to Florence, but he was going to set out on foot. In two or three days, he could walk to Scansansiano.

The driver insisted my grandfather stay, but my grandfather waved him off, grabbed his pack, half of the bread and cheese left in their food kit, and started up the hill."

"There was a war going on!"

"It was foolish and dangerous, you're right. He told me he knew it was a stupid thing to do, but he was sick of the driver, who had complained and whined all the way. My grandfather was stubborn as hell, and it was true to character for him to light out. Maybe you two are related!"

"You—"

Stein held up his hand. "I remember many occasions…. Anyway, he walked the rest of the day—"

"Without seeing anyone?"

"He saw men and women working in a vineyard. They stared at him, but he wasn't bothered. They probably didn't want anything to do with him. When he talked about that walk later, he said he remembered the countryside more than anything," Stein hesitated, "during that stretch of the road anyway."

A slight smile crossed his lips.

"What?"

"Nothing. It still amazes me. There must have been troops in every direction. The French and the Americans were coming through in numbers, but except for what I'm about to tell you, all he talked about was how green the countryside was, how the vegetation was thick with grass, bushes, and trees. He particularly remembered a stand of planted poplars, tall and swaying in the wind in perfectly straight rows.

Toward nightfall he spotted a stone hut in a field. It turned out to be a storage building for tools, and it was open. He went in. The hut was empty except for a pile of rags scattered across the floor, and, to his delight, the door had a working bolt on the inside. Since it was getting dark and he was exhausted, he locked the door and settled in.

The last light showed through a series of little holes in the wall. By that light, he ate half the bread and cheese, drank the last of the water from his canteen, and lay down to sleep."

Stein laughed.

"He told me it was the best night's sleep he'd had in months—followed by some of the worst days he'd ever had."

At dawn, he unbolted the door, looked out to see if anyone was around, and when he didn't see or hear anybody, he walked a few yards from the hut where there was a big rock at the edge of the field, with the sun shining on it from a break in the trees.

He'd gotten chilled in the night, so the sun on his face and shoulders was a welcome warmth. I remember his face as he told me. Even much later in his life, after that trip was years in the past, I could see satisfaction emanating from his eyes whenever he recalled that moment on the rock.

But the moment didn't last. I gathered he was just sitting there with his face tilted to the sun and his eyes closed when the guy whacked him."

Leah started.

Stein laughed.

"It surprised him too. The guy slammed him in the head with a thick branch. The blow knocked him off the rock, stunned but conscious. He said he rolled over, and when he looked up, there was this dark-skinned guy in a blue robe with a hood that bunched around his neck. He described it as if he'd walked out of the hut into a Humphrey Bogart movie set in the Sahara. It terrified him, not so much because of the guy's strange dress, but because his black eyes were blank, totally empty.

Once he's gotten my grandfather down, the guy began hitting him, mechanically, rhythmically, 'like a job he had to finish' is the way my grandfather put it."

"But who...?"

The American put up his hand. "It was only a matter of seconds before my grandfather was able to fight back, but it was useless. 'Like hitting at a blanket on a clothesline,' he said. Every swing my grandfather took, his fist met the cloth of the guy's robe, but not the guy himself. My grandfather's punches were no more than a gust of wind.

They slugged at each other and rolled around on the ground for a while, but when the other guy twisted his arm with one final wrench, he heard a snap, and he knew his wrist was broken. He knew the fight was over, and he'd lost; he didn't even resist the last slug in the face. He said he just gritted his teeth for the pain and lay still while the guy riffled his pockets and took the few lire he had."

"But who was the guy?"

Again Stein held his open palm toward her.

"My grandfather wondered why the other man was so mean, so empty. He also wondered why he didn't have a weapon. Thinking about it later, he figured the guy must have had troubles of his own, and maybe he'd been jumped and robbed. Anyway, when he saw my grandfather wasn't going to resist any longer, he grabbed the food sack and canteen and ran off toward the stand of trees at the end of the field. I imagine it was the food he wanted in the first place."

"But who was he?"

"Let me finish!"

"You're perverse!"

"You're impatient."

They both laughed.

"My grandfather lay in the field staring up at the sky. He could feel the blood running down his cheek from a cut by his ear; one eye was swollen shut, his ribs ached, and his wrist was puffed up. Every time he told me the story, he said, 'I hurt like hell, all over, but the arm was worst.'"

While he was lying there, he was thinking about those empty eyes and wondering who the man in the robe could have been. He even thought he might be in the middle of a dream and would wake up—but I think the pain convinced him he wasn't dreaming."

Leah glanced toward the bar. "Listen, since you're going to be mean and make me wait to find out who the guy was, I need something to eat, and I'm going to have a prosecco. Do you want something?"

"Why not? Let me get it."

Leah watched him order two glasses of prosecco and panini and carry them carefully toward the table.

"Ok. Here's your answer. The guy was a *goumier*. They were fighters from a mix of Berber tribes, mostly from the Atlas Mountains, and were mounted and operated under their own tribal leadership but actually served under the French. The French African Army kept them separate from the regular indigenous cavalry and infantry."

"As exotic as their name. What were they doing in Italy?"

"I only know a little about it; the word itself is simple enough. Goum is a unit, like company."

Seeing Leah's smile, he straightened in his chair.

231

"I looked it up."

Leah laughed. "Doesn't sound so frightening."

"Not the word itself, but remember it was war, and hell was empty in those days. From what I've read, the goumier were terrifying. Mostly in the early 1900s, they stayed in Algeria and Morocco, but by 1911, they were permanent fixtures in the French African Army, cavalry, and infantry, working as scouts. When they became part of the regular forces, they gave up tribal dress for the jellaba and turbans, but they kept the sabers and daggers."

"Jellaba, turbans, and daggers: tribal."

Stein put his palms together and shook them up and down in frustration."The tribal dress was more intricate. Now would you let me talk?"

"Sorry. Questions."

Stein shook his head and continued.

"It's hard to imagine that dressed like that, they could do what they did. But my grandfather told me enough, and I read enough, to convince me. In one article, an American officer in North Africa said one of the goumiers attached to his unit went out on a scouting party and spent the whole night right next to a German encampment, so close and quiet a German soldier who came to the edge of camp to relieve himself urinated on the goumier's head without knowing anyone was there."

Leah laughed.

"You laugh, but the American finished by saying the guy had special plans for the German during the attack that night. And he carried them out."

"Oh...."

"Anyway, through the First World War, they stayed stationed in Africa, but then, in the Second World War, since they were auxiliaries of Allied Forces, about 12,000 of them were sent to Italy, and they made a big difference at Monte Cassino. They were top scouts; they were experts in mountain fighting and tracking. My grandfather said nobody could beat them in mountainous regions and rough terrain, and they took no prisoners. That made some people happy, but like I said, the goumiers could be brutal. Ultimately, the military executed many of them for rape and violence against the civilian population.

It's some kind of miracle the guy didn't kill my grandfather. He said of the thousands that came only a few were killed in action.

"The others executed?"

"That's what I figured he was saying. He always told the story in a sort of off-hand manner. Anyway, in early 1944, the troops and some of the goumier came into southern Tuscany, and that's when their story and mine converge."

"Via your grandfather."

"Yes, the beating in the field. It took a while for him to get oriented. Nobody was there to help him, so there was nothing for him to do but wait until he was strong enough to get up.

He stumbled toward the road and started off again, limping and coddling his arm. He said a guy riding a donkey passed him, but when the guy saw his face, he beat the donkey and scuttled away as fast as he could."

"That doesn't sound like the Italians I know."

"I agree, but you can't romanticize either. It was hard times, lots of uncertainty."

Leah nodded.

"My grandfather kept walking. He was in terrible pain, and his arm was swollen tight. Later, he found out he had a Colles' fracture of his wrist, so the end of the radius was broken as well. They were able to fix it eventually, but the wrist was never normal again. I remember when I was little, it scared me.

Anyway, he kept going. He drank water from a cattle trough, slept in the fields at night, and after two more difficult days, he stumbled up the hill, into the piazza, this piazza, where he dunked his head in the water at the fountain and drank from the spout.

Someone came running, shouting to my father that the water wasn't fit for drinking and that he would be sick. The warning came too late. My grandfather crumpled onto a bench at the corner of the fountain, too tired and in too much pain to respond. People had watched him slog up the street, and one of the men watching helped him along. He had rudimentary Italian and was able to explain about his broken arm. Somebody went running off for the doctor, but came back to say the doctor was out of town. Somebody else brought him water, and somebody else bread, and they gathered around and were solicitous, but I think they weren't quite sure what to do with him. An army person—although he wasn't actually strictly army anymore—was an official thing, so they must have been wondering if they should call the police or some other authority.

He told me he was suffering the complete exhaustion of a person who's used all their energy to reach a goal and then, arriving at the goal, gives way. From what he said, people gathered around him hesitantly, but also concerned about what to do.

After he had something to eat and drink, he felt a little better. He explained the full story about what had happened—it must have been a disjointed narrative—but it wasn't until he mentioned the goumier that some of them shuffled closer. They wanted to hear the story all over again. All he wanted to do was treat his wounds and lie down in a bed until he could get his arm taken care of. I think the people, to their credit, were being cautious, maybe not 100 percent certain he was actually American.

At this point, a young woman stepped out of the pharmacy and pushed her way through the crowd. My grandfather said it was like Venus had come to earth and was walking straight toward him. She was wearing a full-skirted flowered dress—he remembered every detail—her long black hair wafted in the breeze, and she had dark shining eyes. He said as she got close, she looked at him with kindness and it made him feel like he was home. Later he learned one of her friends had been raped and killed by a goumier not long before.

Like I said, he spoke rudimentary Italian, but the people here were speaking dialect, and he was exhausted. From what he could gather of all the talk and discussion going on around him, some of the people wanted to take him to the mayor, who eventually heard about him anyway, of course, and some people wanted to help him themselves, but they couldn't decide who."

"What about the police?"

"I don't know. He didn't mention them until later. I'm sure they found out about him, but I never understood why there was no immediate official action. Everybody was bewildered, that may have been part of it. The Germans had retreated, and the Allies had come through in June. My grandfather knew about the mistaken American bombing of Scansansiano in early June, and he said he was amazed people weren't angry at him. He had an American accent, was wearing an American jacket, and he kept telling them he was half Italian.

"He must have seemed an odd guy, when he explained why he'd come."

Remembering his grandfather, Stein laughed.

"The old coot. He was half-German as well, but he left out that part! Anyway, the woman ignored the others and asked him, quietly, why he'd come to Scansansiano since there was nothing there.

He fumbled through an explanation and repeated what he'd said about being in Florence. He told her about the artworks in the synagogue and mentioned the rabbi who had suggested someone come. This made a difference; the crowd got excited, except one guy who called out that the stuff in the synagogue had nothing to do with the town, and they had enough to worry about trying to exist without added problems and strange Americans.

As it happened, the things from the synagogue had been hidden two or three years earlier, and no one knew where they were. The man who did know had left town, and no one knew if or when he might come back. No matter what, my grandfather was injured; the break in his arm was bad, and he was dehydrated, exhausted, and worried about letting his colleagues know what had happened.

"Did he?"

"Yes. Eventually, they placed a call, got in touch with Keller, and they told him to stay until he could travel, but that was later.

The young woman had an angry argument with the man who had yelled. Later my grandfather learned the man was from a fascist family, antisemitic to the core, with no appreciation of any art."

"Was your grandfather Jewish?"

"No, my grandmother and my mother were."

"But your name?"

"I took my mother's. That's another story, but not for now. My grandfather simply loved fine artwork, of any kind, whoever made it. He really was half-Italian, like I said, but he was 100 percent American in his naïveté and determination. The naïveté didn't last long."

Leah snorted. "We're known for naiveté, but people underestimate our determination."

"You're a good example," Stein muttered.

"Of which trait?"

Stein waved his hand through the air. People in the crowd kept talking about who got to take him, but while they were trying to decide, my grandfather was near fainting from hunger and exhaustion. The beautiful young woman sat beside him, and he slumped against her. She saw that it would take hours before anything was done, so she asked if he felt strong enough to move. When he said yes, she put his arm around her shoulder and pulled him to his feet.

Nobody tried to stop her, but they whispered about her, and later they whispered about him staying on to live with her and her mother. It provided new material for gossip, especially later, I imagine. My grandfather said that the police came, but they left without doing anything.

Walking away with that woman was the beginning of one of the happiest times of my grandfather's life. It turned out to be one of the saddest as well, and the sad time lasted until he died."

"Secondo's grandmother."

"Yes."

"What an astounding story. How did Secondo take it?"

"He's delighted. We share a grandfather, so I'm family. That's why I was reticent to say anything. I wanted him to know first."

Stein hesitated.

"Maybe you can trust me a little now?"

"I do trust you a little more since you told me this, and you did save my life. But I still have questions. First, did your grandfather himself tell you about the woman, Secondo's grandmother? Did he already have a wife at home in the U.S.?"

"No, and no. He didn't tell me about his liaison with the woman. I knew she took care of him until his arm healed and he could go back, but he kept their relationship a secret. He didn't have a wife at home, but he did have a girlfriend. He'd promised her he would marry her when he got back, and he kept his promise.

What I found out was that he wrote to Secondo's grandmother for years, and she told him about the daughter they had together, Secondo's mother, and then briefly, about Secondo's birth. Then the letters stopped.

From the journals and letters I found after my grandfather died, Secondo's grandmother died fairly young. I don't know how; when the time's right, I'll ask Secondo. My grandfather never came back to Italy. His wife made him promise. I think he hated himself for promising that, and he felt guilty. I'm hoping I can correct that. I know that it's too late to do anything for Secondo's mother, but I can for Secondo.

You have to imagine what a surprise it was to me when this man, who said his name was Secondo, came up to me the day of Anna's funeral and asked me to come along. I was overwhelmed, but I didn't want to blurt out the whole story because I thought it was too much to dump on him all at once. I wanted to wait and see how we got along, what he thought of me...."

"And you of him...."

"That too. I wanted to move easy."

"I hope so. You said something about his mother telling him something; what did that mean? And if you're going to just appear here out of nowhere, drop the story on him, and leave, it will be awful for him. It must have been awful for his grandmother that your grandfather didn't come back."

"I'm not going to drop the story and then leave! What do you take me for? He's family. I have an idea—and I wonder what you'll think of it."

Chapter Sixty

Grazia and Salvatore sat at their kitchen table. The early afternoon sun slanted through the windows above the sink and cast a golden rhombus across the stone floor, brightening the high-ceilinged kitchen. In front of the couple, steam rose from shallow bowls of deep red *buglione,* and Salvatore leaned over the dish, breathing in the aroma of the thick, deep-red sauce and tender chunks of lamb.

Grazia was a master of the dish. Her combination of simple spices: rosemary, chili peppers, garlic, and salt, were perfectly matched, subtle, and delicate, and the lamb melted at the touch of the large spoon in Salvatore's hand. A broad, fresh loaf of Tuscan bread lay in the center of the table. Grazia had placed the thick end piece next to Salvatore's plate, and now she watched him spoon up the buglione and tear the crusty bread with his teeth. From time to time, she toyed with her own dish, taking a small bite, rolling a piece of bread between her fingers.

Since the scene in the piazza, they had spoken only a few necessary words. She was suffering from the embarrassment of her unrelenting jealousy, her undignified behavior, and the long-lived anger she felt toward Salvatore. Days she could distract herself with work, except in moments like this, directly in front of him, but nights she lay awake, her mind a maelstrom of resentment and rage so powerful it frightened her.

She could barely tolerate herself. Sitting in front of Salvatore, she blushed again at the memory of raising the bucket above his head as he cowered in front of her. She had shamed him in public. That act and the fiasco at Elia's augmented the torment of regret and heartache for the wasted years. Some days, the blood burned in her veins. She was terrified her own fury would overtake her, and when it did, she would burst and vent her stifled emotions in a violence beyond control. She loved Salvatore, but in the same rush of love, there was a strain of hate, the hate of a wounded, cornered animal with no alternative but to attack.

Salvatore scraped his dish.

She stood to bring him more.

He put up his hand.

"The buglione was enough.

"No salad? Fruit and cheese?"

He shook his head.

Turning away, she pursed her lips and exhaled slowly to control herself. This was his method: he never yelled, never hit her, never stomped away. He simply and quietly refused what few gifts she could give him.

Grazia summoned her will, hoping her voice conveyed the desire for peace, the understanding for which she yearned.

"Salvatore...."

Salvatore looked at the woman in front of him, a woman who, from a vibrant teenager, had become a sad, violent creature struggling vainly to win his love. He never cared about hair color, about weight, or about her angers, her violence. He simply did not love her and never had. That was his sin. He married Grazia without loving her. He yearned for Anna, Grazia yearned for him, and they both had become emotional monsters—she a beast of violent acts, he a sadist of silence. Worst of all, he had denied Grazia the children she longed for.

He did not blame her. He deserved whatever humiliation she gave him.

Anna had been his only love. He loved her as a youth; he continued to love her after she married Elia, and he would always love her, even now that she was dead.

He paid for this love with humiliation and guilt. He and Grazia had made a successful farm and dairy together; they had riches and prosperity of a sort, but the two of them stood like dead trees in the middle of a thriving forest. He turned the violence of guilt inward, and she turned the violence of anger outward.

"Don't, Grazia." He raised a palm toward her. "I forgive you. I took your hand in the piazza, remember? I forgave you as soon as we walked away to the car, and I don't want to talk about it anymore."

Grazia gripped the edge of the table, knuckles white with the force of her grasp. She stared down at him.

I could kill him now, this moment. Strangle him. Drown him in the years of words I have.

She leaned across the table and took his dish in one hand, and reached for his wine glass.

"Leave the glass. I'll have more wine."

Stacking her own bowl, utensils, and glass with a loud rattle on top of his dishes, she carried them to the sink, where she wet the sponge, dabbed dish soap on it, and washed the few things they had used. After rinsing them, she set them with a clang in the metal drainer extended over the sink, from which she would take them again in the morning, and the morning after, and the morning after that.

Like a vision, Grazia saw her future: an interminable round of days, with another meal, a sunrise-to-sunset stretch of conflicting emotions, inextricably bound. She despaired of ever knowing peace. The thought of unbruised love had disappeared years before.

Behind her, he drained his glass of wine, rose, slipped on his coat from the hook in the mudroom, and walked out to feed the cattle.

Grazia stared through the window at the land they had worked together: the vineyard, the fields, the fig tree. In that moment, she understood she would leave him, that same day she would leave. She would break the perverse bonds of jealousy and guilt and go to her cousin in Umbria. As much as she loved the farm, the animals, the trees, a world she had helped build with her own labor, she would leave it behind in hopes of peace.

She watched Salvatore cross the yard in front of the barn. In a tangle of desire and anger, which she now understood as anger at herself as well, she watched his easy amble and stooped shoulders. If he had taken her as second best, she had agreed to it. The only way for her to live a decent life now was to stop agreeing. To free him, and herself, she needed to give him his life, uninhibited in his yearning for a dead woman.

He wanted her to go. He wanted freedom from his guilt, but he had no strength to ever say it aloud. He had lived as a coward, in silence, with no strength to leave. His desire for her was born of habit. Salvatore was used to her, accustomed to the daily order of chores and meals. He hated change, and she, excepting occasional outbursts, was a strong farm woman; together, they had a routine. If she didn't act now, they would go on plodding through the days as always, tending the grapes, feeding the cattle, picking the figs, both living a tormented, angry loneliness until they died. She would be the one in front of him, but Anna would be in his mind and heart. Every day she stayed, she agreed to this twisted love.

She finished the last dish and set it on the rack. Having made the decision to leave, a sharp grief sliced her limbs and heart and dissipated. She took the broom from where it stood against the wall, swept the kitchen, and then picked up the phone to call her cousin.

Chapter Sixty-One

From the edge of the piazza, Leah saw the Signora and Idrissa talking together at the fountain. Idrissa wore a wide grin and was nodding his head. Leah saw the Signora pat him gently on the forearm, and as Leah approached, she heard Idrissa say, "Thank you, Signora. Thank you."

He looked up. "Signora Leah!"

"Hello! You two look like you've got something up your sleeve." She had struggled to bring the American idiom into Italian.

Idrissa glanced at the broad sleeve of his brilliant green dashiki and his wrist. Leah and the Signora laughed.

"Sorry, Idi. It's an American saying. It means it looks like the two of you are planning something."

Idrissa glanced at the Signora; she gave a little shake of her head.

"I'm sorry, Signora Leah. I can't tell you."

"Ah, there is something afoot then."

Idrissa looked at his foot, then quickly back at Leah.

"Another saying! You can't make English into Italian, Signora Leah. It doesn't work!"

"You're right. I can't." Leah's eyes crinkled. "I won't ask anymore, and I'll try to remember not to use so much American in my words."

She knitted her brows at the Signora and poked the air with her finger. "Eventually, I *will* find out what you two are doing."

The Signora smiled. "Always the protective Mamma. You'll soon know the whole story. We want you to know."

The Signora tilted her head to Idrissa. "Come see me tomorrow at eleven, and we'll finish up." She winked.

"I'll be there at 11, Signora. Now I'll go to work."

"And I will too. Goodbye, Leah." The Signora walked away with Idrissa.

Leah watched them hurry away and disappear down the street.

"You look lost." Stein suddenly appeared at her shoulder.

"Well, I am a little. I just ran into the Signora and Idrissa having a tete-a-tete. Conspiratorial."

"What a suspicious woman you are! That makes a good detective, which you are not."

"Wait a minute…."

"You're not. You have no talent for logic; you stumble into answers. Still, I admit I noticed the Signora and Idi talking like with their heads together yesterday."

Leah ignored the remark about logic. It was true, but she preferred to think more generously of herself.

Stein glanced around the piazza.

"Don't bother; they've gone off. I wonder what they're cooking up."

"Whatever it is, I'm sure we'll soon know."

"I suppose. What are you up to today?" She smiled at him.

"Secondo and I are going back to the trails." He grinned. "We went yesterday too. He's determined. Except in you, I've never seen determination like it . . ."

"And? Tell me. You're grinning like a Cheshire cat."

"There's more to tell, but I'd rather have Secondo tell you."

"What is this? Secrets from Leah Day? If you're not going to tell me, then let's go after Secondo. I can't stand having things kept from me."

"Now?"

"Why not?"

They found Secondo in the small piazza overlooking the valley. He was lying on a bench, staring at the clouds.

"Secondo, I hear you have news."

His face brightened in a wide smile; he looked at Stein, who nodded.

"Yes!"

"Will you tell me?"

"Didn't David tell you?"

"He told me about your grandfather and mother, but says there's more. He wanted you to tell me the rest."

Secondo tilted his head back and laughed.

"So many stories! The lady at the newsstand tells me stories all the time, and I tell her stories back. She told me she was driving by in her car coming to work at sunrise, and she saw Polish running to the *via cava* above the river; she told me she saw Alessio kissing Giulia...."

Secondo laughed.

"...and she said while she was having coffee, she saw Rinaldo steal money someone left on the bar. Everybody does different things, and she tells me and we laugh like crazy. The only boring one is Polish; he doesn't do anything interesting, he just walks across the road down by the bridge, she said."

Leah gave Stein a puzzled look. "Those are good stories, Secondo, but...."

"I'm not finished!!"

"Sorry."

"So I know Alessio kisses Giulia and I know Rinaldo steals some pennies, but why does Polish always go to the same place? Signor David and I found out! *We* followed the trail! And there's a little side trail I hadn't been down for a long time, so I said we should take it. It went down a gully, into a *cinghiali* trail and . . . How far was it?"

He looked at Stein.

"About 50 meters...."

"...about 50 meters, and then we heard a moaning sound."

Stein broke in, "I thought it was...ah...a couple."

A faint blush spread over his forehead and cheeks.

Secondo blurted, "You didn't think it was a couple! You thought it was sex!"

Stein cleared his throat and glanced toward Leah, "You're right, Secondo. I did think it was sex."

Leah threw her head back and laughed.

"We heard a man talking, but there was no answer. I peeked through some bushes, and there was a cave. Inside I could just see a man holding some sort of vase. It wasn't sex. He was holding it to his chest and talking to it."

Secondo doubled over with laughter. "Talking to a vase!"

"Did you go in?"

Stein answered, "No. It was too strange; I thought if a guy that far around the bend had a gun, Secondo and I could be in danger. I didn't want to chance."

"Who was it?"

"I couldn't tell, but I'm almost sure it was Polish. From the newsstand lady, that seems most likely. You have to admit he's a strange guy."

"But if it was him, Sergio would know something. You could ask him."

"What if Sergio knows and isn't telling?"

Leah thought of the Signora's story about Sergio's family. Valuing the things of the Jews but hating the Jews.

"So, what happened then?"

"We backed away around a curve in the trail and climbed up into some bottlebrush, and waited. We heard the guy leave and thought we'd see him walk by, but he didn't pass us. I'm not sure how he got back. Anyway, we waited another twenty minutes or more and then went into the cave and found the things."

"What things?" Leah knew, but wanted Secondo to be able to announce it.

Second shouted. "The objects from the synagogue! There's a big chest full of things…I can't remember their names."

He turned toward Stein.

"Secondo is right." Stein said, "finials for the Torah, a Torah crown, a Torah case, the upper part of the Aron HaKodesh, the Torah shield, wine cups, Havdalah set. Everything tarnished, but beautiful—and in surprisingly good condition."

"Amazing! After all these years, Secondo. You found them! How happy your grandfather—both your grandfathers—would be." Leah hugged Secondo. "You've done it! You found them. Have you taken them back to the synagogue?"

"We left them in the cave until we can arrange to bring them back; it's a big heavy chest. David called the Lieutenant, and he's sent a man out to meet us on the trail. He'll stay there all night."

She embraced Secondo again. "You've always said you'd do it. Elia would have been so happy. You've worked hard at this Secondo. You too, David. You've completed your grandfather's job."

She turned away to look out over the valley. The ridge on the far side of the river was rimmed with sunlight. A flock of sheep grazed in a green field below. Idyllic. She thought of the Signora's story about the Inuit and the anthropologist in the storm. A newsstand woman and a young man talking had led to the discovery.

"I found something else too, but I don't want to talk about it." Secondo's voice was soft.

Leah laid her hand on Secondo's arm. "Whatever it is, you don't need to talk about it if you don't want to."

"I just mean not yet. I have to think."

He walked abruptly away, calling over his shoulder. "I'm going to get the Lieutenant; you guys wait here."

Surprised by his sense of command, they answered in unison, "Okay."

"What about his mother?"

"That's what he's not ready to talk about. It's painful to him, and we'll need to help, at least to do what we can."

"We?"

Chapter Sixty-Two

Early the next morning, Sergio was out for his usual early morning walk and coffee. After a turn through the old city, he returned to the piazza, where he sat on the bench that encircled the fountain. The fountain bench was his place to eavesdrop on the old crones who kowtowed to their own insomnia by coming early to gossip at the fountain whenever the weather was fine.

When two women sitting around the arc of the bench mentioned the Lieutenant, Sergio scooted as close as he dared without them noticing. He listened a few minutes, stood, and scurried home, his coat close flapping behind him in the chill dawn air.

Approaching the shop, he saw his wife leaning against the doorpost, scowling. Every day she slouched at the doorway, waiting with what he called "a face as ugly as a fencepost" for him to come back from his walk. He felt like smacking her; he often felt like it, and he often carried through, but today he resisted.

"Polish is here—and his friend's with him."

"Wipe that disgusted look off your face. And I told you, don't call him Polish. He doesn't like it. Where is he?"

"Where is he? He's where he always is, in the kitchen stuffing his face."

"So? Let him eat."

"I don't care if he eats, but he slavers all over the tablecloth and takes half the kitchen away with him when he goes. He's a glutton, Sergio. And that greasy creep he hangs out with is here too. They're stuffing their gullets, dirty as pigs. It takes me all afternoon to clean when they've been here."

247

He slapped her hard.

"Shut your whining mouth. He's my brother, and he's welcome."

His slap opened the cut in her mouth that hadn't yet healed from the last slap he gave her. She spat blood in the street.

"Spit and polish," she mumbled.

"What? What did you say?"

"I said my gosh," she stepped quickly past him back into the shop toward the living quarters, standing to the side when Polish appeared through the beads.

"Ahhh, is my little sister-in-law unhappy? What's that red on your cheek?"

"Shut up, Pol...Gino, just shut up," she glanced back at Sergio to see if he had heard her.

Gino puckered his lips at her, making smacking sounds, then lumbered through the shop to where Sergio stood, looking out the window.

"Hey, Sergio, what's up?"

Gino slapped him on the back.

Sergio leaned to whisper in Gino's ear. "Nothing. But I think you need to check the merchandise today."

Gino stiffened. "I just checked."

"Take the Api, and go now."

Sergio could see his wife across the room, watching them, rolling her eyes.

"Do as I say, Gino. Now!" He raised his voice, so his wife could hear. "I need it back by this evening though. I've got a delivery."

"Liar," his wife mouthed.

Sergio raised an open palm toward her.

Gino made a face and whispered. "Can't it wait? Yesterday..."

"Yesterday was yesterday. This morning is this morning, and this evening is this evening. Beggars can't be choosers, go—now!—and have the Api back." He lowered his voice again. "I heard something about the Lieutenant finding something off the trail, and I want to find out what it is."

Gino's face crumpled in fear.

"Terzo, come!" Gino yelled to his friend waiting in the shop. "Come, now!"

"Don't be long, Gino!"

"But—"

"Go! I'm going to eat, and then I'll come.

"What're you talking about?" His wife had heard. "We're supposed to go shopping."

Sergio looked at his wife with disgust. "Forget shopping. And didn't you hear me? I said I want to eat something before I go."

"Alright, already. If Polish didn't eat it all," she whispered.

"What did you say?" He raised his hand.

"Nothing." She turned and walked into the kitchen.

Chapter Sixty-Three

Below the cave that morning, Enrico, the young policeman who had been assigned night watch, sat on a rock that poked through the brush beside the game trail. Looking for something to eat for breakfast, he drew out the things his mother had prepared and found bread smothered with Nutella. Shoulders hunched against the early morning cold, elbows propped on his knees, he tore off great bites of the sweet hazelnut spread and the tough, bland bread and chewed with soft moans, like a baby savoring its milk.

When Enrico's mother discovered he was to spend the night in the woods, she went to her closet to find a large bag and then to Enrico's room, where she packed a long sleeve undershirt and a sweater. In the kitchen, she set the bag on the table and prepared food.

True to every detail that might delight her son, she prepared a large round thermos full of pasta with meat sauce for his supper, a small bottle of wine, a tall thermos of coffee for the morning, with cream and sugar as he liked it, bread and Nutella, and, in the sides of the bag, an apple, more bread, cheese.

When it was time for him to go, she straightened the collar of his jacket.

"Are you going to be warm enough? Is it enough food? It's cold out there, Enrico, and be careful; there are the *cinghiali*. Do you have your gun?"

"I'll be alright, Mamma. You gave me enough food for three people; I've got a sleeping bag; I've got a gun."

"I think it's crazy, them sending you out alone."

"I'm a policeman. It's my job, so no fussing." He tapped her nose with his finger.

"There are jobs, and there are jobs. Why couldn't you have chosen to work with the cabinetmaker? Something safe. He wanted you, and you're good at it."

"Mamma! The cabinetmaker's in jail! He's a thief and a murderer!"

The irony of her suggestion evaded her. "Someone else then. The library…"

"I've gotta go." He pulled away from her, then turned back and kissed her on the cheek. "You're a good mom, but you worry too much; I'll be okay."

He was not okay.

The night turned particularly cold, and Enrico found no level ground on which to sleep. He woke before dawn, leaned against a rock, and while he sat eating his bread with Nutella and drinking his coffee, considered what his mother had said about a different job.

Mulling over the possibilities of working in a bar, where he would always have hot coffee, he didn't hear the two men approaching quietly up the game trail.

Gino saw the young policeman as they came around the hillside. He turned to Terzo, put his finger to his lips, then scanned the ground around him. When he spotted a thick, short branch fallen from a holm oak, he picked it up and, motioning to his accomplice to stay, moved quietly forward.

Enrico turned just as Gino struck. The cudgel connected at his right temple. Enrico pitched forward across the narrow path, his coffee spewing from the cup in a wide arc. The bread rolled off into the prickly humus beside the trail.

"Oh, shit! Did you kill him?" Terzo's voice cracked with fear.

"How the hell do I know? Come on." Gino growled, wiping his sleeve across his face.

"But…."

Gino raised the cudgel high over his head to threaten Terzo.

"There's no 'but' about it. Get up here and help me, and for God's sake, stop whining."

In the cave, the two men secured the chest by carefully tilting it up from one end and slipping a rope underneath and over the top.

"You grab that handle; I'll take the other one."

"How'er we going to get the damn thing down the hill? And what is it anyway?"

"How the hell do you think we're gonna get it down? We're going to slide it. And it's no business of yours what it is."

"I don't like it. They're going to catch us. And now the policeman. Why didn't you tell me?"

"Stop sniveling!" Gino could see Terzo was on the verge of flight. He forced a smile. "It's a surprise, dumbbell. I thought you'd like to know there really are treasures in the world."

"A surprise for me?" Terzo grinned, his eyes wide.

Gino, saliva running out his mouth in a stream, looked at him and shook his head. "Yes, yes, for you, for god's sake. Now take the handle!"

Terzo bent his knees, seized the handle with a firm grip, and lifted. The leather snapped with a loud pop, and the trunk landed on his foot.

"Fuck! Ohhhhhh! Fuck! It broke my foot!"

Pushing at the trunk, he plopped onto the dirt, carefully slipped off his shoe, and, grasping his foot in both hands and whimpering in pain, inspected his foot.

"Get up, you idiot! Pick it up. We haven't got all day."

"I told you the handle's broken. I can't lift it from the bottom; it'll break my back, and it's already broken my foot."

"Fuck it! If we don't get out of here soon, we'll both be in jail. Then how will your damn foot like it!"

Wincing, Terzo slowly pulled on his sock and shoe, pushed himself to a stand and hobbled in a little circle before he bent to grasp the chest by the bottom corners. On the count of three, they both lifted.

"Okay. Now, slowly, slowly. Back out; I've got this end."

"I got it."

They shuffled to the edge of the cave and eased their way down, sweat pouring off their foreheads.

"I don't know how much longer I can hold on."

"You've gotta hold on, stupid. We've gotta go down; there's an old trail nobody uses; once we get there, we're safe. We just gotta be careful 'til we get to the—"

Before Gino could finish the sentence, Terzo's feet appeared in the air beside the trunk, and Gino saw him crash hard to the ground on his back. The chest surged forward and slammed into Terzo. The poorly tied rope slipped off, and the lid of the trunk burst open. Silver wine cups, candle sticks, a large washing pitcher, a delicately worked crown, and Torah dressings tumbled in bright flashes into the bush.

"I told you!" Terzo yelled.

"My things!" Gino dropped to his knees and, crawling on all fours, frantically gathered pieces of silver in his arms.

"Mine!" His eyes glistened; he hugged the objects to his chest, and his lips curled back like an angry dog's.

"Gino, leave it for god's sake! Let's get out of here before they come."

Terzo struggled quickly to his feet and watched in horror as Gino stroked the silver objects. Terrified by the change in Gino, his distorted face and wild menacing eyes, Terzo slowly moved backward down the hill.

"It's mine!"

"I'm not going to jail for you, you crazy bastard."

He turned away and bounded down the hillside.

"Mine!" The word wafted through the trees into the air.

Chapter Sixty-Four

Leah, Secondo, Stein, the Lieutenant, and the Lieutenant's sergeant hiked in single file up the *via cave* with Secondo in the lead. They moved at a quick pace without speaking, heads bent to watch their footing on the rough-hewn steps cut into the tufa.

More accustomed than any of them to the trails, Secondo surged ahead to the place the trail broke from between the steep tufa walls, leveled off, and widened into a dirt path shaded by holm oaks. He stopped to wait for the others.

Above, they could hear a farmer on his Api on the way to the field to check his sheep, and in the distance behind them, toward the highway, the faint sound of cars rumbling across the bridge floated through the air.

The Lieutenant caught up and stood beside Secondo, who stared through the treetops at the sky.

"Much further now?" The Lieutenant asked. "I can't remember."

"Just a little way. At the end, we'll have to veer off. I piled rocks where to turn."

Leah pulled a bottle of water from her pack and passed it around. Grateful, the others finished it.

"Come on." Secondo had started off again at a fast pace and was thirty meters ahead.

One hundred meters behind, Sergio stopped to take his water bottle from his pack. He could hear snippets of their conversation.

The Lieutenant, Leah, Stein, and Secondo found Gino groveling in the brush, clasping the objects to him, encrusted in silver like a giant fish with barnacles. Spittle seeped from the side of his mouth, and he murmured, "mine, mine."

Seeing the spittle seep from Gino's mouth, Leah remembered the hint Magliotti had given: "Soldiers and their uniforms." Spit and polish. His salivating, his sick love for handling his things.

Still unconscious, Enrico lay beside the stone where he had been mulling over the possibilities of some other kind of work.

Unaware of the Lieutenant and the others, Gino stroked the rounded belly of a pitcher, touched and petted it. Compelled by possession, lost in a world of greed and sickness, he muttered, "mine, mine."

Leah stepped forward to go to Enrico, but Secondo, Stein, and the Lieutenant all reached to stop her. The Lieutenant signaled her to stay back.

"Let me handcuff Gino first," he whispered. He motioned to the others, and they moved slowly toward Gino. The Lieutenant spoke.

"It's okay, Gino. Of course they're yours. We're going to help you collect them and put them back in the chest."

"Mine!" He jerked away, clenching a wine cup to his neck. "I don't like cloth. I gave the cloth to Magliotti; he likes it. Sergio and I like silver and sometimes gold. We like silver, and I visit, and sometimes we have to let it go, and I am sad, but there wasn't any in the grave. Sergio was so angry!"

He grinned at them, cackled, and suddenly turned serious.

"These are mine! Mine! I love them, and you can't have them!" He made a disgruntled face, a child with his toys.

"Yours. Of course, they're yours. But they'll be safer in the chest, no? You want them safe, don't you?"

The Lieutenant snapped the cuffs on Gino, who seemed unaware of what was happening. Stein and Leah knelt beside Enrico, who was just waking.

"I'm sorry we didn't get here sooner, Enrico. We'll get you to the hospital," Stein helped him stand; Leah pressed a clean handkerchief to his head.

"It's okay. Just don't tell my mom what really happened. They got me by surprise. Tell her I fell or something. Something courageous if you can think of it."

There was the snap of a stick above them on the trail. The Lieutenant whirled around to see Sergio rise from a squatting position and run toward town. The Lieutenant burst up the hill after him. Twenty minutes later, panting and sweating, he returned, Sergio in tow.

"Sergio," Gino whined, "they tried to take my stuff, but then they said I can have them back in a little while. I didn't tell them about the grave robbery." He paused, "Or did I?"

He laughed wildly. "The grave robbery that wasn't a robbery because there was nothing to rob, was there Sergio!" He cackled.

"Shut your mouth, Gino, just shut up."

Chapter Sixty-Five

The following day, Leah, accompanied by the Signora, Stein, and Secondo, met with the Lieutenant in his office. Gino was locked in a room in the psychiatric ward of the hospital, waiting for evaluation. Sergio was in a cell.

"Both of them confessed to the grave robbery, if you can call Gino's a confession. Anyway, it was clear from his ranting he did it." The Lieutenant shook his head with a look that conveyed a profound sadness.

"We knew as much when we saw him on the trail, didn't we, Lieutenant?" said Stein

"I've never seen anything like it; I didn't even know there was such a sickness. He was here all the time, getting worse and worse. That sick desire, objectophilia, was, in this case, love for the things of the people he hated."

Leah shook her head. "Common enough during the war, Lieutenant, not in Gino's sense maybe, but that desire for things of people you hate. Think of Hitler's plans to have a Jewish museum after he'd killed all the Jews."

"What about Enrico?" Stein asked.

"The nurse told me they're keeping him another day or two; they're concerned about concussion," Leah said. "His mother's with him, and she's brought him chicken soup and, as she put it, 'all the things he likes.'"

They all laughed.

"We'll have to see if she lets him keep his job or turns him into a bartender."

Secondo, who had been sitting quietly, jumped up. "A party!"

The others stared at him. "A party?" The Lieutenant asked.

"A party at the Signora's."

Stein flushed. Leah punched him lightly on the arm. "You knew about this."

"Yes, I did."

"What's it all about? Tell me."

Stein glanced at Secondo. Secondo nodded.

"Ok, I have the go-ahead: It's about a trip to New York for Secondo to meet more of his extended family and about a new business relationship between Idrissa and the Signora involving a buying trip to Venice."

Chapter Sixty-Six

At six o'clock the next evening, Stein, the Lieutenant, the Signora, Secondo, Idrissa, and Gianni were gathered in the Signora's living room, serving themselves from a table laden with savory tarts, olive paste crostini with fresh tomatoes, bruschetta, the local red and white wine, and the Signora's Venetian prosecco. While they waited on Leah, they tried to piece together the last of the puzzle.

Idrissa was perplexed. "How did the treasure get to the cave?"

The Lieutenant set his glass on the table. "Everybody's wondering that. I think Stein knows best, but I can tell you what happened here. During the war, the Jews of Scansansiano realized the Nazis were looting Jewish art and religious objects from all over Europe and Russia. Hitler was a failed artist, but still considered himself a connoisseur, I suppose, and he had great plans for a '*fuhrermuseum*' in his hometown of Linz, in Austria. It's unlikely any of the Scansansiano things, I mean the Jewish objects from here, would have been included, but the Germans were taking what they could get and storing it away. So, the Jews hid their things.

First, they gave the things to a man named Primo, who had land outside of town. He hid the things in one of the caves on his land, but the Germans had started spreading out over the farmland to caves, so he decided to find a place in the hills, off the little-used vie cave.

I've never figured out how Gino found out about the cave on the trail, but he did. Maybe gossip he heard through family. I don't know, and he's too far gone to make any sense when I ask him."

Stein made a face. "How'd you figure all this out?"

259

"It wasn't easy. Primo got killed in the American bombing. He had told a friend approximately where it was, but the friend left during the war to be with family in Milano, and has only recently come back."

The Signora interrupted, "Who is it?"

"You know him, Signora. Signor Rossi."

"The very old man with the cane who sits at the front of the library all day?"

"Yes."

The Signora grunted. "Why didn't he tell?" Her face flushed. She remembered she hadn't told her suspicions about Sergio.

"Never mind, Signora. Rossi's old. He'd forgotten all about it, and with most of the Jews gone, no one was asking, so it didn't occur to him, and it must never have occurred to Elia to ask because Elia couldn't have known about the connection between Rossi and Primo."

Idrissa leaned toward the Lieutenant. "But how did you think to ask?"

"It was circumstance. I went to the library to pick up a book; he was there, as usual, but this time there were some friends with him. I try to keep up with the people in town, so I suggested we go out, sit in the sunshine at the bar, and have a glass of wine.

It occurred to me that he—and the others, too—were all old and must have been here during the war, so I simply asked them if they knew anything about the objects from the synagogue. My question jogged their memories. They all started talking, and the more they talked, the more they remembered, and before long, we made the connections, the trail, Gino, all of it."

Secondo beamed.

"The Inuit," the Signora muttered.

"What?" Stein asked.

"Oh, nothing," the Signora smiled.

Stein gave her a puzzled look, but put it out of his mind when he sensed movement outside the window. He rose and stepped to the filmy curtains.

Leah was standing at the door, but had turned her back to it and was gazing out over the valley. Stein watched.

Oblivious of the others, Leah stopped outside the door of the Signora's house, looking at the distant hills, remembering a particular hike with Secondo. As they walked, Secondo chastised her in a moment when she indulged her grief over losing Nick.

"You're not the only one carrying a bag of stones on your shoulders," he said. "Everyone else, including all your friends, have burdens to carry too. You don't have to give up, Nick. There's plenty of room for grief and old love in anybody's heart. Nobody will take any of it away, but you have to keep enough room for the other stuff too. Like us—and new stuff."

She thought about what he meant. There had been another murder, fear, pain, and upset in the community and in each of her friends' lives. Yet it was all paralleled by the great joy and gift of friends.

Stein opened the door and slipped his arm over Leah's shoulder.

Her voice faltered. "I was just—"

"I know. I know. Nick. The Lieutenant…. Let it all rest for now. It's cold. Come inside; we're all waiting for you."

"How did you know?"

"The Signora told me about Nick. I'm sorry, Leah. And as for the Lieutenant, I have eyes." He glanced toward the window and pointed. "But, look. This is now. No one knows the future, but here are your friends, people who love you and who'll keep up with you as you blunder into your future, what it is, whatever choices you make."

Leah laughed. "Is that what you think I'll do: blunder into my future."

"Won't you? Is there another word for the way you go about things?"

"You're 100 percent right about me."

Through the sheer white curtains at the window, as if through mist in a dream, Leah looked at her friends: the Signora, Secondo, the Lieutenant, Idrissa, Gianni. They stood together at the table, talking, laughing, then suddenly, as if they sensed her, they turned toward the window and raised their glasses in unison.

Stein squeezed her arm gently. "Your friends."

"And now yours too," she said, smiling up at him.

With one last glance at the distant hills, Leah took Stein's arm, and the two stepped through the doorway to join the others.

Acknowledgements

Many people have a hand in making a book. I cannot thank all of them here, but I would like to express my thanks to at least some.

My husband and children deserve profound thanks for supporting me in every way. I thank my husband for the many hours of conversation about my writing, when he put off his own work to listen, critique, and augment my ideas with his scholarly knowledge and incisive mind. He also read various drafts of the book, aiding me at every turn by his editorial expertise. My sons, Dov z'l, Lev, and Gidon, deserve deep thanks for the myriad ways they encourage and support. All four of these men, by their courage, indomitable spirit, and love of life have given me more than storyteller can tell or pen can write.

For many years my Italian friends have renewed and sustained me by offering their knowledge and expertise, by inviting me to a place at their tables, by taking me into their homes, and into their friendship and vibrant community. I'm honored to have known those gone and am privileged to continue to know those still walking in the piazza. The characters in my books are imaginary people in an imaginary place, but I hope something of the sense of community I experience in Italy comes through in my writing. The following people have helped me understand what community is and I thank them:Pino Zennaro, Lorenzo Zennaro, Gianni D'Este Widmann, Umberto Sartori, Angela Pampanini, Roberto Nizzi, Martina Nizza, Elena Servi, Luigi Cerroni, Enzo Giuliani, Maria Rosa Pucci; and I acknowledge in memory, Annalisa Longo, Bruno Nizzi, Elise Brugi, and Filomena Travagli.

I want also to thank my U.S. and Israel communities: Roz Stein, master educator and sister-in-law; Pamela Lazarus, who opened the door to in-the-field experiences I could not have had without her help; Mary and Steve

262

Sharp, the best of neighbors and friends. All of these generous people read and helped improve my manuscripts.

Finally, I want to thank my editor, Harriette Sackler, Agatha Award-Nominated Short Story Writer and co-publisher of Level Best Books. She is a woman of insight and great patience who has helped make me a better storyteller. Her colleagues at Level Best Books, Verena Rose and Shawn Reilly Simmons, have also helped improve my work by their sharp eyes and forbearance when I needed time.

About the Author

Libi Siporin [*aka* Ona Siporin] has lived between the U.S. and Italy for many years. Her Leah Contarini Mysteries take place in the life of an imagined Tuscan village. As Simon Brett has said, Siporin believes "what happens before a murder is at least as relevant as what happens after it." Siporin is the author of fiction, essays, poems, radio commentary, and magazine articles. She has won various honors and fellowships. *Bitter Maremma*, the first of the Leah Contarini Mysteries was published in 2021. *My Secrets Cry Aloud*, second of the series, will be out fall of 2022.

SOCIAL MEDIA HANDLES:
  Facebook: @libisiporin

AUTHOR WEBSITE:
  www.onasiporin-writer.com

Also by Libi Siporin

Bitter Maremma, A Leah Contarini Mystery

Uncommon Common Women: Ordinary Lives of the West, by Ona Siporin, history and fiction

Stories to Gather All Those Lost, by Ona Siporin, published radio commentary

Poems for a Primitive Mythology and *Girl on a White Gate,* by Ona Siporin poetry

www.ingramcontent.com/pod-product-compliance
Lightning Source LLC
Chambersburg PA
CBHW050153120726
47903CB00002B/601